I0762736

The Amish Quiltmaker's Unlikely Match

THE AMISH QUILTMAKER

The Amish Quiltmaker's Unlikely Match

Jennifer Beckstrand

THORNDIKE PRESS
A part of Gale, a Cengage Company

Thorndike Press, a part of Gale, a Cengage Company.

Thorndike Press® Large Print Amish Fiction.
The text of this Large Print edition is unabridged.
Other aspects of the book may vary from the original edition.
Set in 16 pt. Plantin.

LIBRARY OF CONGRESS CIP DATA ON FILE.
CATALOGUING IN PUBLICATION FOR THIS BOOK
IS AVAILABLE FROM THE LIBRARY OF CONGRESS.

ISBN-13: 979-8-88579-832-7 (hardcover alk. paper)

Published in 2024 by arrangement with Zebra Books, an imprint of Kensington Publishing Corp.

Print Number: 2 Print Year: 2024
Printed in Mexico

The Amish Quiltmaker's Unlikely Match

Chapter 1

"Help, help! Don't eat me! Don't eat me!"

Mary Yoder snapped her gaze out the window, and her heart did a somersault and two backflips. An elderly Englisch woman in a bright magenta parka and lemon-yellow pants ran toward the house with all four goats and the dog chasing after her. *Ach, vell,* she wasn't exactly running. She looked too old to be able to muster any speed, but she was certainly shuffling her feet very rapidly in an attempt to escape the animals. "Dat!" Mary yelled. "There's trouble out front."

Mary didn't wait to see if Dat had heard her. She sprinted outside, ran past the brightly colored Englisch woman, and waylaid the goats and the dog before they could catch up to the poor old lady. Mary shot out her hand and grabbed Pepper by the collar, then knelt down in the late October snow and corralled all four goats in her outspread arms. "Smiley, Blue, you should be ashamed of yourselves," Mary cooed, "chasing a nice old lady like that. She's a perfect stranger and never did you no harm."

Pepper barked, but the goats just stared at Mary with innocent looks on their faces, as if they hadn't been doing anything but following Pepper's orders.

"They tried to eat me," the Englisch woman said, who had managed to make it to the porch unmolested.

Mary turned to the old woman. Her frown looked as if it had been pounded into her face with a chisel, but her blue eyes were lively and intelligent, like someone much younger lived in her aged body. "They really are harmless," Mary said. "And quite friendly. I'm sorry they frightened you."

"I wasn't frightened for myself. I was frightened for my wardrobe." The old woman brushed her hands down the front of her blindingly bright pants. "These are brand new joggers. I had to special order them in yellow."

"I'm *froh* they didn't scare you."

The woman grunted. "I don't scare easy, but I do get mighty irritated at times."

Mary patted Fluffy's soft white head. "Goats like to explore things with their lips, sort of how babies put everything in their mouths at first. Your pants are safe from the goats." But Mary couldn't guarantee those yellow pants would be safe from bumblebees, wasps, or hummingbirds.

The woman frowned like a trout, but her eyes twinkled with amusement. "I guess a little goat saliva never hurt anybody."

Mary giggled in relief. The woman wasn't ferociously angry or wildly frightened. It wasn't likely she'd die from a heart attack on the front porch.

Dat appeared from the side yard carrying a galvanized bucket. He glanced at the woman on the porch. "I heard a ruckus and thought you might need help." He held out his hand for the dog. Mary released Pepper, and Pepper sprinted to Dat's side. Dat was Pepper's favorite person, and Pepper was Dat's favorite person. The horse, Patty, was Dat's second favorite person, and the goats were favorite persons three, four, five, and six. Dat liked animals much more than he liked people, and he loved Pepper most of all.

"All is well, Dat. Pepper was just making mischief, and the goats never seem to have anything better to do."

He nodded. "Pepper never saw a person he didn't want to bark at." He patted

Pepper's head. "I know you're making quilts today, and I have to mend some fences. I'll stay out of your way." Dat stared a little too long at the woman on the porch, probably wondering at her outfit choices, then gave her a friendly wave of his hand. "Have a nice day."

Mary shooed the goats away. As expected, they followed Dat around the side of the house, trotting energetically as if there'd never been any trouble to begin with. Never a dull moment with four pygmy goats and an incorrigible dog living on your farm. Mary smiled at the woman. "Would you like to come in and have a drink?"

The woman nodded, shifting her huge purse from one shoulder to the other. "Just as soon as Esther catches up."

Mary bloomed into a smile as she saw Esther Kiem climb out of the van parked in front of the house. Esther cradled her new baby in one arm while her other hand held tightly to her daughter Winnie's wrist. "Esther!" Mary ran to her friend and grabbed the baby from her arms, burying her face in the folds of the *buplie*'s sweet-smelling neck. "*Ach,* Esther, he's just adorable. Look at those cheeks."

Esther laughed. "Only four weeks old and already a double chin."

Mary smiled to herself. Esther had a habit of tucking strange things behind her ear for safekeeping, and today, just under her *kapp,* a baby binky hung from the top of her ear like a bucket hanging from a hook. Mary pointed to the binky. "That's something I haven't seen before."

Esther curled one side of her mouth and fingered the binky at her ear. "*Ach,* I keep misplacing Levi Junior's binkies. This way, I always know where at least one is."

Even though Esther was six years older than Mary and married with a family of her own, she was one of Mary's closest friends and one of the finest quilters in Colorado. Her quilting skill was the reason Mary had invited her over today. Winnie, Esther's three-year-old daughter, skipped to the porch and wrapped her arms around the old woman's yellow leg.

Esther pointed at the woman. "Mary, this is Cathy Larsen. She drives a lot of Byler Amish around town, and she's also a master quilter. That's why I asked her to come today."

Cathy patted Winnie's head. "I wasn't thinking straight, or I would have got back in the car instead of letting those goats chase me around your yard. I think I pulled a hamstring."

Mary drew her brows together. "*Ach,* I'm sorry. Come in the house and rest."

Cathy waved away that suggestion. "I can rest when I'm dead. I came to talk quilting."

Mary liked that idea. She opened the door and herded everyone into the great room. "Please sit. I'll fetch the others."

Mary quickly ran upstairs and stuck her head in Beth's room. Beth, as usual, was lounging on her bed reading a book. "Beth, Esther is here to talk about our quilt."

Beth didn't even look up. "Okay, I'm coming." Beth was the youngest of the Yoder *schwesteren* and the prettiest. At least Mary thought so. All three of her sisters were much prettier than Mary was, even though Great-grandmother Beulah kept insisting that Mary was the prettiest of them all and that she would have no trouble finding a husband. But such talk only made Mary anxious and unhappy. She panicked at the thought of even talking to a boy, and the pressure to be entertaining and charming enough to snag a husband made her heart race and her chest tighten. At twenty-eight years old, Mary hoped she was finally too old to attract attention from any boys in the district. She'd much rather spend her time caring for Dat; Dat's dog, Pepper; their old horse, Patty; and the four goats that roamed their farm like stray cats.

Mary would gladly let her sisters attract all the attention and all the suitors. There was too much for Mary to do on the farm to spend any time caring about boys and romance and marriage.

Mary skipped downstairs to the kitchen where Joanna was just popping a pan into the oven. "I'll be right in," Joanna said, closing the oven door, then setting the timer. "I thought our guests might enjoy a piece of coffee cake while we chat."

Mary nodded. "That's very thoughtful of you."

"Everyone is happier with a full stomach." She glanced at the clock. "How long do you think this will take? I don't want to be difficult, but I need to make a batch of bread for our trip tomorrow."

"It depends on how long it takes you to pick which quilt block you want to make."

Joanna's eyes danced. "I can be very quick when I have to be. It's you I worry about. You've never made a decision that you didn't overthink."

"I know, but I think I've already picked the one I want."

Joanna's eyes flashed with a tease. "You *think* you've already picked one?"

Mary giggled. "I *think* I have."

Joanna put her arm around Mary. "Have you *thought* about coming with us tomorrow? We hate to go without you."

Mary's three *schwesteren* were going to Iowa tomorrow for Cousin Lily's wedding. Mary and Dat were staying home. Dat was staying home because he didn't want to leave the animals and he didn't want to face Aunt Gloria, and Mary was staying home because she didn't want to see Cousin Peter. She sighed. "I've already *over-thought* this one. I'm staying."

Joanna was just younger than Mary, twenty-six, and as fresh as a daisy, as Mammi Beulah always described her. Joanna smiled constantly and was always planning a practical joke to play on someone. She had beautiful chestnut-brown hair that was unmanageably curly, and there was always a spiral lock or two peeking out from under her *kapp.* Joanna had already been proposed to four times. Her beauty and her cooking skills attracted the boys like honey attracted bees. But Joanna was also very particular — about her cooking and her suitors — and she had confided to Mary that she didn't think she'd ever find a man who lived up to her standards. She'd much rather stay single than settle for just anyone.

Joanna poured some milk into a saucepan and set it on the stove. "I'll make up a quick batch of hot chocolate. Nothing warms the heart like chocolate."

Mary donned her coat and went out the back door in search of her oldest *schwester,* Ada, whom she found in the barn mucking out. Ada wore a thick wool kerchief on her head in place of her *kapp,* her black work coat, and a pair of brown woolen mittens. Two of the goats, Blue and Apple, were playing in the barn and keeping Ada company.

Ada tapped the manure fork on the floor to remove the straw. "Are they here?"

Mary curled her fingers over the stall door. "*Jah.* Can you come?"

"Almost done." Ada stabbed at a clump of straw. "Did you invite them in and hang up their coats?"

"*Jah* and *nae.* I haven't hung up their coats yet."

"We should have Joanna whip up a batch of cookies, and have you warned Beth not to complain in front of our guests?"

"Beth is Beth. I'm not responsible for her behavior, and Joanna already has a coffee cake in the oven." Mary quickly turned and walked away before Ada could give her any more instructions. Ada liked being in charge, even though the other *schwesteren* were perfectly capable of being in charge of themselves. Mary sighed. She loved Ada with her whole heart, and more than anything, Ada wanted to feel needed. If bossing her sisters around brought Ada that much joy, then Mary saw no harm in letting Ada be the boss.

Mary went back into the great room where Beth and Joanna were chatting with Esther and Cathy Larsen. Without any help from Mary, both visitors had managed to get their own coats hung on the hook by the door. Mary sat next to Esther and pulled Esther's daughter, Winnie, onto her lap.

Cathy reached into her massive purse and pulled out three books. "I brought my favorite quilt pattern books for you to look through. What kind of quilt do you want to make?"

Joanna held the ticking kitchen timer in her hand. She was very serious about her baked goods and refused to let a cake bake for one minute longer than was appropriate. "We want to make a sampler quilt for Great-grandmother Beulah to celebrate her one-hundredth birthday." She pointed to Mary. "It was Mary's idea. We're each going to pick a particular quilt block for the quilt."

Cathy got a funny look on her face. "I don't mean to offend you, but you didn't think this through very well. It's a nice idea, but there are only four of you. That's a terribly small quilt."

"We want to make a quilt with four sections. Nine of each block sewn together. Like four smaller quilts put together in one quilt top."

Cathy frowned and nodded. "That has potential."

Mary couldn't decide if Cathy thought it was a *gute* idea or if she was just being polite. "Is . . . is that . . . will it look nice?"

Esther patted Mary's knee. "It will be darling. We could also try putting the individual blocks in a pattern over the entire quilt. What do you think about that, Cathy?"

"That's a bad idea," Cathy said, and Mary nearly laughed out loud. Cathy was obviously not inclined to be diplomatic.

Esther didn't seem offended in the least. "We can experiment with patterns after the blocks are finished."

Cathy pursed her lips. "I suppose." She opened one of the quilt pattern books and slid on her glasses, which dangled from a chain of chunky beads around her neck. "This book has five hundred of the most popular quilt blocks. Unless you're picky, you should be able to find a block you like."

Ada marched into the great room and plopped down on the sofa right next to Cathy. "I'm sorry I'm late. I had to finish mucking out. What did I miss?"

"Ada, this is Cathy Larsen," Mary said. "She's going to help us with the quilt we're making for Mammi Beulah."

Ada nodded at Cathy. "Nice to meet you. Thank you for helping us with our quilt."

Cathy peered over her glasses. "You're welcome, and I'm dependable as long as I don't get the flu or a bladder infection. I'm completely useless with a bladder infection."

Mary wasn't quite sure what a bladder infection had to do with quilting, but she was too polite to ask. "Have you tried baking soda?"

Cathy cocked an eyebrow. "For the flu?"

Esther handed Beth one of the pattern books. "Why don't you start looking through this and see if there's a pattern that catches your eye."

Beth nodded and leafed through the book with little interest. She was not excited about Mary's quilt idea because she'd never had the patience for quilting or handwork.

Ada looked over Cathy's shoulder while Cathy pointed out her favorite quilt blocks. Mary picked up the third book and offered it to Joanna. Joanna shook her head. "I already know what block I want to make for Grossmammi Beulah. I love to bake desserts, so I thought the Sugar Bowl quilt block would be fun."

Esther nodded enthusiastically. "That is a darling block, perfect for you."

Cathy thumbed through her book, found the page, and held the book up for everyone to see. The Sugar Bowl block was a series of triangles arranged to look like a basket with a handle. Cute and sort of tricky. "Sugar Bowl has lots of small pieces and corners to match," Cathy said. "Are you sure you're up to it? I won't stand for unmatched corners."

Joanna scrunched her lips to one side of her face. "I've always been careful with my corners."

Cathy narrowed her eyes. "I believe you, but be sure not to get overconfident. Overconfidence is a quilter's downfall." She scratched her head. "Actually, now that I think about it, arthritis is a quilter's downfall." She shook her finger in Joanna's direction. "Don't ever get arthritis. You'll immediately regret it."

Joanna's timer dinged, and Joanna jumped up to get her coffee cake from the oven. "I'll be right back."

Beth landed on a page toward the back of her book. "I want to do this one. Grandmother's Flower Garden, since this quilt is for Grossmammi Beulah."

Esther glanced doubtfully at Mary. Then Mary and Ada exchanged looks.

Ada shook her head. "That is one of the hardest quilt blocks to make, Beth. You should choose something easier like a nine-patch."

Beth lifted her chin. "You don't think I can do it."

Ada sighed. "I never said that."

"You don't think I'm good at anything."

Ada sighed louder. "I never said that either. You don't like to quilt, Beth. Why would you choose a hard block to sew?"

Beth turned her face away. "Because it's cute, and I want to do it, and you'll see I'm not as incapable as you think I am."

"I never said that," Ada murmured through gritted teeth.

Cathy eyed Beth for a few seconds. "That's a lot of corners. I have no patience for unmatched corners."

Beth folded her arms around her waist. "I'll do a good job."

Cathy huffed out a breath. "I like your determination, even if it's completely misguided. If you're willing to try Grandma's

Flower Garden, I'm willing to help, as long as my gout doesn't act up. Gout is a quilter's downfall."

Beth seemed pleased. She closed the pattern book and handed it to Mary. "Choose one, Mary."

Joanna came back with a tray of mugs and handed them out. "Hot chocolate for a cold day. I put a little extra milk in Winnie's so it wouldn't be so hot."

"Denki," Esther said, motioning for Winnie to sit next to her on the hearth. "Use both hands, Winnie, so you don't spill."

Joanna left again and came back with a tray of coffee cake cut into squares.

"This smells heavenly," Esther said.

Joanna smiled. "It's one of my favorite recipes. You can never have too many chocolate chips."

Cathy set her mug and her piece of cake on the table and continued thumbing through her book. Ada stopped her on one of the pages. "Wait. I like this one. It almost looks like it's moving."

Uncertainty traveled across Cathy's face. "It has a lot of corners."

Esther laughed. "Cathy, they all have lots of corners. They're going to do fine."

Cathy's frown was so deep it practically scraped against her chin. "I suppose."

"I like it," Ada said. "It doesn't look too hard."

Cathy pressed her lips together. "It's not the corners necessarily that concern me." She tapped her finger on the page. "Do you see the name of this one?"

Ada's gaze traveled down the page. "Bachelor's Puzzle."

Cathy leaned back, her eyebrows traveling up her forehead. "You know what they say about that."

Ada paused and looked to Joanna and Mary for help. "Um, no. What do they say?"

Cathy lowered her voice as if sharing a shocking secret. "There's a little magic in every stitch you sew into a quilt block."

Beth took a sip of hot chocolate. "The Amish don't believe in magic."

"Then call it superstition, and don't tell me you Amish aren't superstitious. I've heard plenty of talk about charming warts and burning eggshells." Cathy eyed Ada. "Every quilt you make has a little bit of magic in it. Don't be surprised if you start meeting all sorts of bachelors once you finish your blocks."

Ada sputtered with laughter. "I'm not superstitious, Cathy. It's only a name. Nothing magic about it. It certainly doesn't have anything to do with real life."

Cathy shrugged. "Keep telling yourself that if it makes you feel better."

Mary didn't believe in such hogwash, but just the same, she was reluctant to mention the name of the quilt block she wanted to make.

Unfortunately, Cathy was too curious. "Have you chosen your quilt block, Mary? I'll try not to get upset about the number of corners it has."

Mary swallowed hard and nodded. "I want to do Drunkard's Path. It's tricky, but I think Mammi Beulah will love the pattern."

Cathy's eyes widened, and she looked as if Mary had just announced she was joining the circus. "That will never do. Corners are hard, but curves give me a headache. Nobody ever gets them right."

Esther turned to Drunkard's Path in her quilting book. "Mary is a wonderful-*gute* quilter. I don't wonder but she'll do very well with the curves." She showed everyone a picture of a quilt made up of Drunkard's Path quilt blocks. "Look how delightful this looks."

Cathy didn't look the least bit convinced or impressed.

"I like a challenge," Mary said. "And you don't need to worry. I've done curves before. I once made a Flowering Snowball quilt for the church auction."

Cathy pushed her glasses up her nose. "Of course I'm worried. Did you hear anything I just told Ada? Mark my words, if you go through with this crazy plan, I'll start getting migraines and you'll start hanging out at bars."

Cathy seemed so concerned and so earnest, Mary nearly burst into laughter. She valiantly curbed her amusement. "Please don't worry about any such thing. As a general rule, the Amish don't drink, and I don't plan on starting, no matter how frustrating my curves are."

Cathy raised her hands in surrender. "I've said my peace, and it's obvious I can't convince you otherwise. I suppose I should be grateful you didn't choose Wild Goose Chase or Bear's Paw or Rocky Road to California. Those would definitely get you into all sorts of trouble." Her expression softened into something a little less hard than granite. "If you all can manage to make your corners match, it's going to be a fine quilt." She snapped the quilt book shut. "Just remember what I told you. Every quilt has little magic stitched into it. You'll see it if you're watching for it."

Chapter 2

Mary shot up from her pillow, her heart hammering against her chest as if it was trying to get out. Downstairs in Dat's room, Pepper howled like a coyote. Had he had a bad dream? Or had something else awakened Pepper too?

Mary leaped out of bed and tore down the stairs to Dat's room where a single lantern was burning. Dat was hurriedly pulling on his trousers as Pepper jumped up and down in front of Dat's window, barking and carrying on like Judgment Day had come. "What is it, Dat?"

Dat jerked his head toward the window. "Look."

Mary pulled the curtain aside and gasped. A car was wedged against the corner of the barn tilted at a lopsided angle with one front tire completely off the ground and smoke seeping from under its hood. The car shuddered violently, as if taking its last breaths before giving up the ghost. Mary stiffened in terror when she saw bright orange flames crawling up the barn wall. *"Ach, du lieva!"*

Dat grabbed the lantern and stomped out the door. "Get the fire extinguisher. I'll get the chickens out of the coop and the animals out of the barn."

Mary hesitated only a second. Should she change out of her nightgown? Run upstairs and put on her shoes? *Nae.* There wasn't time. Her *schwesteren* were in Iowa, Dat had no one but her, and that fire could level their barn in a matter of minutes. She quickly slipped a pair of Dat's work boots onto her feet and raced down the hall as fast as she could in footwear five sizes too big. She yanked open the pantry door and grabbed the two fire extinguishers from the shelf. They were heavy-duty ones, and she could barely carry both of them together, but something told her she'd need two, for sure and certain.

Dat had left the back door open. She kicked the screen door, and one of her boots fell off. No time to retrieve it. With one shoe on and one shoe off, she hobbled as fast as she could toward the fire.

Mary caught her breath as she got closer to the car. Someone was still in there! Should she save whomever it was or put out the fire first? *Ach,* she wasn't smart enough by half to make that decision, but she was already holding a fire extinguisher. Wouldn't it be better for everyone if the fire was out?

Ignoring the motionless figure in the driver's seat, Mary dropped one extinguisher on the ground and pulled the pin on the other. With hands shaking violently, she aimed the chemical stream at the base of the fire, then slowly worked her way up the wall of the barn. The flames sputtered. The smoke thickened.

Pepper, their four goats, and Patty the horse raced past her, along with their five chickens and Dat. Once the animals were safely away, Dat circled back, closed the barn door, and picked up the other extinguisher. "*Gute* thinking, Ladybug, bringing out both extinguishers at once." He pulled the pin and sprayed the wall, though most of the fire was already out. He peered at Mary and exhaled a long breath. "*Gute* work. I'm going to spray the inside wall too, just in case."

The car was still fighting for its life, sputtering and groaning and clicking like one of Joanna's kitchen timers. Mary pointed to the man inside the car. "What about him?"

Dat's frown was fierce and tight. "We've got to help him, for sure and certain, but spray everything one more time just to make sure the fire doesn't start up again. We can't help him if he's surrounded by flames." Dat tromped back into the barn, and Mary could hear the hiss of his extinguisher as he sprayed down the wall.

She gave the barn wall another coating of white foam. When the fire extinguisher was completely empty, she dropped it and rushed toward the passenger side of the car. She pulled the door handle, and her heart sank. Locked. She cupped her hands around her eyes and peered in the window. It was dark, so she couldn't see much, but she could make out the motionless figure of a man slumped over the steering wheel. Her stomach lurched. Was he dead?

Pepper barked and barked but kept his distance. Dat must have ordered him to stay back. When Dat was firm, Pepper always obeyed.

Dat came out of the barn, breathing heavily and dragging the stand-up propane lantern behind him and holding his small lantern aloft. "Is it locked?"

She nodded.

"Is he alive?" he said.

"I can't tell."

Dat handed Mary the lantern and picked up her spent fire extinguisher. "Stand back,

Ladybug." He brought the extinguisher down hard on the window, and it shattered into a thousand pieces.

Mary reached in the window and pulled up the lever to unlock the door.

"Wait," Dat said. He ran into the barn and came back with one of Patty's saddle blankets. He opened the car door, spread the blanket over the shattered glass on the passenger seat, and motioned for Mary to climb in. "Can you help him?"

Mary was the one her family called on when someone got hurt and needed doctoring, probably because she wasn't bothered by the sight of blood and because she had a fascination with medicine and survival books. She had read *Ditch Medicine, The Survival Medicine Handbook,* and *First on Scene Medicine* cover to cover, plus *The A-to-Z Guide to Home Remedies.* Helping people with their injuries was something she was *gute* at. Her family depended on her. She never wanted to let them down.

Mary handed Dat the lantern and slid into the passenger seat. A sharp pain immediately traveled up her leg. She bit her lip and held her breath. She must have stepped on a piece of glass with her bare foot. *Ach, vell,* she couldn't do anything about it now. She wasn't going to lose a toe or anything, so might as well ignore it.

The interior had a new car smell, but it also smelled like burnt rubber, sweat, and alcohol. Mary crinkled her nose. Had the driver been drinking? What else could explain his crashing into the barn?

Dat held up his lantern, and Mary gently placed her hand on the man's shoulder. She nearly jumped out of her skin when he suddenly groaned and turned his face toward her. She pressed her hand to her heart. He'd scared the daylights out of her, but at least he wasn't dead. He was young, surely not much older than Mary, and fair-haired, like Mary's mother had been. There was a three-inch gash just above his eyebrow where he had probably met with the steering wheel in the crash. A trail of blood ran down the side of his face, and his complexion was deathly pale. He seemed to look right through her with his blue, glassy gaze.

"Are you okay?" Mary said, unable to keep her voice from shaking.

He slowly lifted his head and pressed his fingers to the gash above his eyebrow. "Apparently not." He leaned back against the seat and grimaced in pain. "I'm sorry, ma'am. You don't deserve my sarcasm."

Mary didn't even know what sarcasm was. "Where does it hurt? How can I help?"

He couldn't seem to keep his eyes open. "My head feels like a freight train ran over it, and my ears are ringing."

"Don't make any sudden movements," Mary said. "You might have a concussion or a neck injury."

"My money's on a concussion." He gritted his teeth and huffed out a breath. "I'm such an idiot." He shook his head as if trying to clear his muddy thoughts, even though she'd just cautioned him against any sudden movements. He was already proving to be a terrible patient. He leaned forward and peered out the front windshield. "Is that a barn?"

"Yes."

He closed his eyes and, to her surprise, chuckled softly. "And the *Tribune* says I can't hit the side of a barn."

Mary tried to be patient. The man was injured and drunk. "Can you walk? Does anything else hurt besides your head?"

"I'm sorry about your barn, ma'am." There was real regret in his voice. "I didn't mean to . . . I'm an idiot."

"We can worry about the barn later. We put out the fire, and the animals are safe. But we need to get you out of this car and to a hospital."

"There was a fire?" He buried his face in

his hands and groaned. "I'm so sorry." He studied the blood on his hands, as if trying to decide whether it was his. "Was anybody hurt?"

"Nobody but you." How surprising that he cared more about the harm he might have caused than he cared about himself. "What's your name?"

He drew his brows together in confusion. "Don't you know?"

That was an odd question. He most definitely had a concussion. She spoke slowly and clearly. "Do you remember your name?"

His lips curled upward ever so slightly. "Clay. My name's Clay."

"Okay, Clay. I'm going to send my dad down the road to our neighbor's house to call an ambulance."

Clay snapped his head up and winced in pain. "No, ma'am. Please don't call an ambulance. They'll send me to jail for a DUI, and it'll be all over the papers. Please no ambulance."

Mary glanced at Dat, still holding the lantern. His eyebrows inched closer together.

"You're hurt," Mary said. "We need to get you to a hospital."

The stranger shook his head, though Mary could see it caused him great pain. "It's just a concussion, and I *cannot* go to jail."

Mary sized up the very drunk, very injured man sitting next to her. She certainly couldn't drag him to the hospital. He was too big. Not fat or portly, but solid, like a tree, with sculpted, muscular arms and shoulders as broad as the Mississippi River. She glanced at Dat again. She wouldn't even be able to pull Clay out of the car, not even with Dat's help. She made a silent concession. "Okay, I won't call an ambulance, but we've at least got to get you out of this car and into the house. You must get out of the cold before hypothermia sets in."

He lowered his head, pressed his palm against his good eyebrow, and paused. "Did you know you only have one boot?"

Clay definitely had a concussion. "I lost the other one when I kicked the screen door open," Mary said.

"I bet your other foot is cold."

Mary took a deep breath and remembered she was trying to reason with a drunk. "That's why we need to get inside before we both get frostbite."

Clay finally seemed to come to his senses. "Okay. Let's go inside. But no hospitals." He pulled the latch to open his door, but it wouldn't budge.

Mary shook her head. "You can't get out

that way. Your car is wedged against the side of the barn."

Clay gave her a tilted grin, revealing a mouthful of straight, white, brilliant teeth. "Well, don't I feel sheepish?" He laughed, winced in pain, then sucked in a breath. "That's just a little farm humor to make you forget I just wrecked your farm."

Mary smiled in spite of herself. She was being charmed by a drunk guy with a concussion. Her standards must be slipping. "You didn't wreck our farm, but you most certainly wrecked your car. I don't think they'll be able to fix it."

His jaw dropped in mock surprise. "Oh, ye of little faith. This baby will be back on the road within a month. She's not hurt too bad, or the engine wouldn't still be running."

It was true. The persistent engine was still coughing and gasping, even after a collision with the side of a barn. "I think you'd better turn it off," Mary said. "We can't leave it running all night."

Squinting at the dashboard as if he was trying to bring it into focus, Clay pushed the button that turned the car off. "There. I put it out of its misery." He patted the steering wheel. "Don't worry, sweetheart. I'll be back for you in the morning." He leaned toward Mary, and for one insane moment, she thought he was going to kiss her. Her heart did a complete somersault. Then she realized she needed to get out so Clay could also climb out the passenger side. She jumped out of the car so fast she nearly fell flat on her face. Fortunately, Dat caught her arm and kept her upright.

Clay's long legs couldn't escape from under the dashboard, so he sort of crawled out of the driver's side on his hands and knees. Dat took one arm and Mary took the other, and they helped extricate him from the car. Clay's feet touched the ground, and he stood up, but he was so unstable that he nearly toppled over. Mary threw her arms around his waist and held on tight. *Ach,* he was as solid as a rock, and he smelled like the woods on a warm autumn day. She felt her face get warm, but it was sort of buried in his shirt, so neither Dat nor Clay could witness her embarrassment. As soon as Clay stopped swaying, she let go of his waist, but both she and Dat held tight to each of his arms, just in case.

Clay squeezed his eyes shut and took a deep breath. "I'm just a little dizzy. I'll be okay." Suddenly, he yanked himself from Mary's grasp, fell to his knees, and vomited into the sagebrush.

Mary took his hand. "Clay, we have to get you into the house. You need to lie down."

He coughed and spat out the remnants of his stomach. "Wouldn't you rather I stay out here until I'm done being sick?"

"No. You need a warm bed." He also needed a hospital, but Mary wasn't going to bring up that fight unless absolutely necessary. Her foot was freezing, and she was lightheaded with exhaustion.

"Okay, okay," Clay said.

Dat and Mary helped Clay from the ground and held tightly to his arms as they ambled toward the house. Pepper and the four goats followed close behind because none of them ever wanted to miss out on any excitement. Beth said Pepper and the goats had FOMO, which was an Englisch word that meant "fear of missing out." Mary never had FOMO. She liked being left out of all excitement, all mischief, and all adventure. Too bad trouble had just fallen into her lap. Lord willing, it wouldn't stay long.

Clay glanced down and noticed the goats. "They're cute. Do you eat them?"

Mary pressed her lips together to keep the laughter from bursting out. It was wrong to laugh at a drunk man with a concussion. But she was sorely tempted.

Clay stumbled only once going up the porch steps, but his earlier regret returned with full force. "Your foot is bleeding," he said. "Did I do that? I'm real sorry. I'm sorry about your barn. I'm sorry about everything. Did the animals get out okay?"

Mary nearly fell over as an unexpected, horrifying realization hit her. The quilt block she'd chosen for Mammi Beulah's quilt was Drunkard's Path.

Had Cathy Larsen been right all along?

Chapter 3

Mary had never understood what it meant to be "bone-tired" until this very minute. Her fatigue was so heavy, she couldn't see straight as she walked up the stairs to check on her patient. She'd been at his side almost all night and had left the bedroom just a few minutes ago to check in with Dat and make Clay some tea to clear his head.

One of her survival medicine books said that you should wake up a concussion victim once every hour on the first night after a head injury or he was liable to slip into a coma. After she and Dat had helped Clay up the stairs and into Beth's bed, Clay had drifted in and out of sleep while Mary had cleaned and dressed the gash on his head, slipped off his shoes and socks, and heaven help her, removed his filthy, blood-encrusted shirt and undershirt before tucking him under the covers and keeping vigil through the night.

She had tried to tamp down her discomfort at being in the same room with a shirtless man and attempted to think of him only as her patient and a drunk who had crashed into their barn. By sheer force of will, she had avoided looking at his broad chest and washboard stomach — another thing she hadn't known actually existed until now. She was especially enamored with his hands. Clay's fingers were long and slender, and the bulging blood vessels that crisscrossed the backs of his hands bore witness that he was used to hard work. Mary had a lot of respect for that, even if he was a drunk.

Mary had been so worried that Clay would die, she had woken him up every hour and taken him through a short concussion protocol. He hadn't been especially happy about being awakened over and over again during the night, but he had been so incoherent, he probably wouldn't remember anything this morning.

The sun was just peeking over the mountains when Mary tromped up the stairs and into Beth's room with a glass full of home-remedy tea. She stopped in her tracks. Clay was gone. Her stomach lodged in her throat.

Ach, vell, at least he hadn't slipped into a coma or died in the fifteen minutes she'd been gone, because the bed was empty.

She tiptoed down the hall to the bathroom. The door was slightly ajar, and she hesitated. Maybe she should go back to Beth's room and wait. Her concern for her patient got the better of her, and she knocked.

A low moan came from the other side. "Come in."

Mary pushed the door open. Clay knelt on the bathroom floor with his arm draped around the toilet seat and his face pointed into the toilet bowl as if he were attempting to see his reflection in the water. The pink and purple quilt from Beth's bed was draped around his shoulders.

He slowly lifted his head and looked at Mary, his face as white as a sheet, sweat beading on his upper lip. "You're Amish."

"You didn't notice that last night?"

"You weren't wearing that hat thing," he murmured, "just an extremely virtuous nightgown and one boot."

Mary felt the heat travel up her neck. She really should have changed into a proper dress before running outside to put out the fire, but she never would have guessed he'd have such a good memory of the previous night. "It's a prayer covering."

"I'm real sorry about your barn, ma'am." He cradled his head in his hand and gazed into the toilet bowl, every move deliberately slow and labored. "This toilet is very clean."

"Ada cleans the bathrooms twice a week."

"At this moment, I really appreciate it."

Mary frowned at the pitiful sight of Clay hugging the toilet for dear life. "How do you feel?"

He cocked his uninjured eyebrow and winced in pain. "How do I look like I feel?"

"Like you'd be better off dead."

He pointed at her and winked. "You got it." He rested his head on his forearm. "Could you bring a sledgehammer and put me out of my misery?"

Surely he was trying to be funny, though she didn't see anything funny about his miserable situation. He'd brought this on himself, but she still felt wonderful sorry for him. She lifted the glass so he could get a better look at what she'd made. "Drink this. It will make you feel better."

His whole body shuddered. "No thank you, ma'am. It looks like liquid manure."

"It does?" Mary lifted the glass to her nose. It didn't smell very good, but it didn't look like manure. It actually looked more like brownish urine.

Oh.

No wonder he'd shuddered. She pressed her lips together. "*Ach, vell,* it has never failed to settle an upset stomach."

"Is that what it's called? *Ach Vell*?"

Mary cracked a smile. "No. *Ach, vell* just means 'Oh, well' in *Deitsch.*"

"I don't care how many foreign words you use on me, ma'am, I'm not drinking it."

"It's just ginger tea with a few other spices thrown in. For sure and certain, it will help."

He pressed his hand to his eyes and grimaced. "*Ach, vell,* then. Give it to me. Nothing could be worse than how I'm feeling right now."

She handed him the glass. He sniffed it and retched. "Will you step out of the bathroom, ma'am? You don't want to see this."

Nodding, she backed away and closed the door after her. She moved farther down the hall as the noises from the bathroom started and then got louder. Clay had been right. She didn't want to see what was going on behind that door.

She went into Beth's bedroom, straightened the sheets, and fluffed the pillow. Lord willing, Clay wouldn't throw up on the quilt. Beth would be irritated if her bedspread got dirty.

After about ten minutes of obvious unpleasantness, she heard the bathroom door open. She stuck her head out of Beth's room. Clay was standing at the end of the hall, looking a little tipsy but much less pale. She hurried down the hall, shoved aside her misgivings, and put a firm arm around Clay's waist. Her efforts to keep him upright were really quite silly. If he fell over, she'd go down with him. It would be like trying to catch an oak tree. With her free hand, she tightened the quilt more securely around his shoulders and nudged him toward Beth's room.

"That wasn't very nice," he said.

She glanced at him in surprise. "What?"

His eyes danced mischievously. "That glass of brown urine."

She smiled because he didn't seem to be angry. "It worked, didn't it? You look much better."

"That's because I threw up everything I've eaten in the last month plus two teeth."

She laughed. "You did not." Clay was unexpectedly charming for a man with a hangover and a concussion.

They managed to get back to the room without falling over, and Clay climbed into the bed. Mary took the quilt from his shoulders and pulled the covers over him. She sat on the chair she'd brought up from the kitchen last night. Clay propped his elbow on the pillow and touched the gauze bandage on his forehead. "You?"

"Yes."

"Thank you."

For some reason, his piercing gaze made her feel shy and self-conscious. "I cleaned and dressed it as best as I could. The bleeding stopped, but you need stitches."

He looked at her through hooded eyes. "I'd like to avoid the hospital, if at all possible."

"You don't like hospitals?"

"Something like that."

Mary shrugged. "Nobody likes hospitals, but you need to see a doctor. A concussion is a serious injury. I don't wonder but your head is throbbing."

He sat up and leaned his head back against the wall. "It feels like it's going to explode, but I don't know if the pain is from a concussion or alcohol. I remember most of what happened last night. Aren't you supposed to have gaps in your memory when you get a concussion?"

Mary tried to recall what her book said. "I don't know."

"It might just be a hangover." He gave her a tepid smile. "You probably didn't notice, but I was drunk last night."

"Oh, I noticed. My *dat* noticed. Our dog and the goats noticed."

He massaged his jaw and rolled his eyes. "I was hoping to pull one over on the goats at least." He dropped his hand to his lap and studied her face. "You said 'your dad.' Was that the guy with an iron grip on my arm last night?"

Mary nodded. "We were afraid you weren't going to make it to the house."

"I'm sorry."

Mary looked down at her hands to avoid his intensely brilliant gaze. "Water under the bridge."

He grunted. "Not really, but don't worry about the damage. I promise I'll pay for everything."

"That would make my *dat* happy, for sure and certain."

With his eyes glued to her face, he lifted his hand and ran those very attractive fingers through his hair. "Do you mind if I ask you a personal question? I mean, I'm a perfect stranger, but you've already seen me throw up, bleed all over myself, and stagger up your stairs. Now I'm half naked in your bed . . ."

"Beth's bed." Mary's face was on fire. She had thought Clay was polite, but polite men did not say "naked" in front of women.

"Who is Beth?"

"My sister."

"Where's Beth sleeping?" he said.

Was that the personal question? That wasn't so bad. "She and Ada and Joanna are in Iowa for a wedding. My *dat* and I stayed home to care for the animals." And because of Aendi Gloria and Peter.

"So, you're not married?"

Mary's heart skipped a beat. Why did he want to know that? "Um, no. I'm an old maid."

His eyebrows crashed into each other. "An old maid? How old are you? You can't be more than twenty-five."

"I'm twenty-eight. For an Amish girl, that's an old maid."

His piercing gaze never faltered as a smile grew slowly on his lips. "That's a perfect age."

Was that the personal question? Mary relaxed a bit. She didn't care that he knew how old she was. She'd only be uncomfortable if he asked about Cousin Peter or said "naked" again, and he didn't even know Peter existed.

"You don't have a wedding ring, so I assumed you weren't married until I remembered that the Amish don't wear wedding rings. So then I had to ask. I think you're cute, but I didn't want to let my mind wander in that direction if you're married, if you know what I mean."

Okay. She'd only be uncomfortable if he asked about Peter, said "naked," or told her she was cute. It was completely uncalled for and terribly embarrassing.

His smile faded. "Sorry. I didn't mean to upset you."

Mary cleared her throat. "You didn't upset me. I just . . . I've never been . . . why do you think I'm cute?" *Ach!* The words had escaped her mouth before she could pull them back. Clay would think she was fishing for compliments.

Perhaps sensing her discomfort, he looked down at Beth's quilt, as if memorizing the pattern. "Well, any girl who can heft a fire extinguisher, tromp around in the snow with one bare foot, and make brown urine ginger tea is worth noticing. I just . . . think you're . . . cute. There's no other word for it."

"Oh. Okay." Should she return the compliment, tell him that she thought he was good-looking? It seemed both childish and reckless to do that. No matter how handsome Clay was, she must keep her thoughts to herself, if only to avoid paralyzing embarrassment.

"So why hasn't some lucky Amish guy swept you off your feet yet? I can imagine there are like ten or eleven just wishing they had the courage to ask you out. Do the Amish date?"

How was it possible that Clay could come so close to Peter without even suspecting it? "Believe me," she said, "there are no interested Amish boys." Peter had seen to that. "I'm too old."

He laced his fingers behind his head. "I have a very hard time believing that."

Mary didn't know what to say. Her face was surely as red as a beet.

Thankfully, Clay changed the subject. Maybe he could see she was embarrassed. "So Ada, Joanna, and Beth are your sisters. Ada is a good toilet cleaner, and I'm sitting in Beth's bed. Will Beth be mad that I'm in her bed?"

"For sure and certain, but what she doesn't know can't irritate her."

He laughed. "Beth must be the youngest. They tend to get their feathers ruffled."

Mary couldn't contain a smile. "That is definitely Beth."

"What about your mom? Is she in Iowa too?"

Mary brushed some imaginary lint from her dress. "Mamm is gone. Cancer, three years ago."

He reached out and squeezed the hand

she'd been resting on the bed. "Oh, I'm so sorry. I can't even guess how that must feel."

"It hurts, but we accept God's will and move on with our lives."

He frowned. "What if we don't like God's will? What if we don't think God is doing a very good job?"

Mary furrowed her brow. "You shouldn't say such things about God. He'll smite you to the ground."

He shook his head. "God knows how I feel whether I say it out loud or not." Mary pulled her hand away, and his expression softened. "I'm sorry about your mom, and I'm sorry I tempted God's wrath while in your house. I don't want to be responsible for setting both your barn and your house on fire." He tilted his head to catch her eye. "Am I forgiven?" He pumped his eyebrows up and down and coaxed a reluctant smile out of her.

"I'm Amish. I hear about forgiveness in church every other week."

His mouth fell open. "You only go to church every other week? No fair."

Mary giggled. "Don't act so indignant. How often do you go to church?"

His eyes flashed with amusement. "I'm afraid to go into a church because, like you said, God might smite me."

Mary didn't know why the disappointment suddenly bubbled up inside her. Clay was a drunk. Of course he didn't go to church. Of course he was out of favor with God. She shouldn't expect anything better from someone like him. Her heart sank as her own hypocrisy caught up with her. The Lord said, "Judge not that ye be not judged." She shouldn't find fault with anyone, not when she had so many faults of her own. And there was something else. She'd known Clay for all of half an hour, but he didn't seem like an evil man — drinker or not.

She didn't know what to say, but she should at least encourage him on the path of righteousness. "Everybody needs church. You should go."

"Even if I get smitten?"

She rolled her eyes and curled her lips. "Even then." A wave of fatigue overtook her, and she couldn't stifle a yawn.

He cocked his head to the side and narrowed his eyes. "Did you get any sleep last night?"

"A little."

His eyes got narrower. "How much is *a little*?"

"I don't know."

He leaned toward her, concern commandeering his features. "Ten minutes? Five hours?"

She folded her arms. Why did she feel defensive all of a sudden? She'd done what she had to do for the health of her patient. "I was afraid you were going to stop breathing or fall into a coma, and since you refused to go to a hospital . . ."

He leaned back on his pillow. "Fair enough. That was real kind of you. I remember you waking me up several times, but all I remember is you asking me how many fingers you were holding up and what my name was. It seemed like a dream."

"I really didn't want you to die."

"Well, thank you. I appreciate you saying that, because a lot of people think I'd be better off dead. Just ask Twitter."

A heavy weight pressed down on Mary's chest. "Who's Twitter? And shame on him for saying that about anybody! How could anyone wish another person dead?"

He scrubbed his hand down the side of his face. "Some of us are pretty much a waste of skin. *I'm* pretty much a waste of skin."

"That's not true," Mary said, her chest tightening with distress. "Don't say that about yourself."

Clay's frown etched itself deep into his face. "I'm sorry, ma'am. I keep upsetting you, and I don't mean to. I guess I'm just numb to the harsh words people throw around so easily these days."

Mary wiped her eyes. Why was she so upset all of a sudden? "You didn't . . . *ach, vell,* I suppose you did upset me, but I'm not mad at you. People are just mean sometimes, and it's so unnecessary. We all need to be kinder to each other."

"I suppose we do."

She patted his hand, wishing she had the nerve to hold on tight and show him how sincere she was. "I'm very, very glad you're not dead, and if Twitter disagrees, he can just come talk to me about it."

His lips twitched with the hint of a smile. "I'll tell him that." He ran his fingers through his hair. "I've been very insensitive. You're exhausted, and I haven't even asked how your foot is feeling."

"My foot?"

"It was bleeding last night."

After she'd cleaned and bandaged Clay's head, she'd sneaked to her room and changed from her nightgown to her purple dress, and grabbed some warm slippers for her feet. Then, she'd washed her feet in the sink and put a bandage on the cut on her pinkie toe she'd gotten from the shattered glass on the floor of Clay's car. "It hurts, but it's just a small cut. I'll be fine."

"Are you sure?"

"I'm sure, though I do regret not going back for Dat's boot when it fell off my foot."

He grinned. "It looked kind of cute."

At least he didn't say that *she* looked cute. That would have been too much embarrassment to bear, especially with the way he was looking at her.

Pepper announced his approach by wildly barking all the way up the stairs. He tore into Beth's room and jumped up on the bed and planted his front paws on Clay's bare shoulders.

"Pepper!" Mary shouted. "Get down. Get off the bed."

Clay's surprise was evident in his wide eyes, but he didn't seem alarmed by a forty-pound dog on his bed. Instead, he grinned and cupped his hands around Pepper's black and white face and cooed as if Pepper was the cutest dog Clay had ever seen. "Oh, look at you! What a beauty you are. What a good boy."

Even though Clay was a stranger, Pepper ate up the affection and wagged his entire body as Clay ran his hands down Pepper's coat and scratched his head and behind his ears. Pepper licked Clay's face again and again, and Clay didn't seem to mind. Beth, Joanna, and Ada all hated being licked. Mary thought it was a sweet sign of a dog's true devotion. Clay obviously liked dogs. That thought melted Mary's heart. It no longer mattered that Clay was a drunk. No one was half bad who liked dogs.

Pepper was so ecstatic, he jumped up and down and ran three full circles on top of Beth's quilt while Clay grinned and tried to catch Pepper in his arms. "What a beautiful dog," Clay said. "I love border collies. I had a mutt growing up that was part border collie."

Mary laughed. "I should have let Pepper sleep here last night. You've perked up a hundred percent since he came in."

Pepper came to rest at Clay's side, and Clay smoothed his hand down Pepper's back. "Dogs are good medicine for sure. They don't care how many mistakes you've made or how unpopular you are. They love you just the same."

A pair of feet stomped loudly up the stairs, and Dat appeared at the threshold of Beth's bedroom looking very much the stern Amish *fater.* His chestnut-brown beard had not a trace of gray in it, and his dark, heavy eyebrows hung over his blue eyes like storm clouds. Dat was almost always unusually good-natured, but he wasn't smiling now, and Mary could tell he was determined to give Clay a *gute* scolding before serving him a generous helping of forgiveness and Christian charity. Dat was kind and reasonable, but he could also be righteously indignant when he thought himself justified.

Pepper jumped off the bed and away from his new best friend and trotted to Dat's side. Pepper and Dat were bosom companions, and no one took the place of Dat in Pepper's heart. "Young man," Dat said, motioning to the window where light was peeking from between the curtains. "Will you join me at the window?"

Clay slowly slipped out of bed and stood next to Dat. If Clay knew he was going to get a lecture, he didn't seem defensive, anxious, or particularly uncomfortable, as if determined to bear and accept anything Dat wanted to say to him. Dat opened the curtains, and Clay squinted into the bright light.

Mary didn't know if she should intervene for Clay's sake. He had already apologized to her five times, and his regret was real. Dat didn't need to make him feel worse than he already did. But Clay seemed like the kind of man who didn't shy away from unpleasantness or discomfort simply to make things easy on himself. Mary would stay out of it.

From Beth's window, there was a perfect view of the backyard, the barn, and Clay's mangled car, sitting exactly where it had been last night, one front tire completely off the ground, the driver's side bumper curled snuggly around the outside corner support beam.

Dat pointed out the window. "We live right on Highway 15, and we are fully aware that cars go fast down this stretch of the road and there are no streetlights. But how did you manage to drive off the highway, through our fence, over our sagebrush, and into our barn without stopping to think that maybe you shouldn't? Were you aiming for us, or was it just an unhappy accident?"

Clay cupped his fingers around his neck and tilted it one side as if trying to work a year's worth of kinks out of it. "I'm real sorry about your barn, Mr. . . ."

"My name's Try," Dat said, "as in, 'Try your best to explain yourself.' "

"Is that short for something?" Clay was very *gute* at changing the subject. Mary had already noticed that.

Dat huffed out a breath. He'd explained his name hundreds of times over the years.

"I'm the third Mervin Yoder in my family. My grandfather was Mervin Yoder and so was my *dat.* They named me Mervin and called me Mervin Number Three. That was a little too long, so they shortened it to *Drei,* which is *Deitsch* for three. 'Try' is the Englisch way of pronouncing it, and that's what everybody calls me now." He probably wished his parents had just named him John or something else that he didn't have to explain every time.

Clay raised his eyebrows. "Clever. There's a guy on the team who is Ricardo Guzman the Fourth. Everybody calls him Four." He glanced at Dat, who didn't seem inclined to be patient, and cleared his throat. "Okay, I'll try, try again, *Try.*"

Dat's expression did not change one bit. "I've never heard that one before."

Clay grinned. "Okay, I'm sorry. I couldn't resist."

Mary checked a laugh. Clay had a completely disarming sense of humor.

"I'm real sorry about your barn. There is no excuse. You might not believe me, but I didn't realize I was that drunk. Siri told me to turn left, and I took the turn too sharp. I didn't see the fence until I plowed into it, and I stepped on the gas instead of the brakes and crashed into your barn. At least that's what I think happened. It's kind of fuzzy after Siri told me to turn left."

"Our barn could have burned down."

Clay nodded. "I know. It was reckless and foolish."

Dat pointed to Mary. "If it hadn't been for my daughter, you might have been trapped in that car and burned to death."

Clay gave Mary a smile that could have melted an icicle in January. "I hope you know how grateful I am to you and your daughter for saving my life. I don't deserve your help or your kindness, but you offered it just the same."

Dat held up his hand. "Our Lord and Savior commanded us to show kindness and mercy to everyone, no matter how undeserving. None of us is deserving of God's grace. That's why it's called grace."

Clay pressed his lips together, as if he didn't believe a word. "Well, whatever the reason, I'm very grateful for your help. I'm especially grateful you didn't call the police, even though I deserved to be hauled away."

"We all deserve punishment. Grace covers us."

Clay nodded, though he didn't look convinced. "And don't worry about the damages. I promise I'll pay for everything and extra for your trouble."

Dat squared his shoulders. "Money is not your way out of this mess. If you're truly sorry and really want to help, you need to commit to doing the repairs yourself."

For the first time since she met him, Clay was speechless. He opened his mouth and closed it again like a fish out of water struggling for breath. "You want me to fix your barn and fence and sagebrush?"

"That's right."

Clay scratched his head. "You don't want my money?"

"You won't learn anything by just writing a check."

Clay thought about it for a few seconds. "It would be so much easier if I just paid for it."

"Yes, it would," Dat said.

Clay seemed truly puzzled. Mary was a little surprised too. Wouldn't it be better for everyone if Clay just gave Dat the money? "It might take me several weeks."

Dat didn't seem to care. "Maybe."

Clay eyed Dat with a mixture of respect and suspicion on his face. "I do have a few months off, but it's going to be pretty cold work."

Dat was unsympathetic. "You can wear a coat."

Clay stared out the window, silent for a

full minute. He glanced at Mary, and to her surprise, burst into a grin. It was like the sun coming out from behind the clouds. "I'll start tomorrow."

Dat seemed a little surprised too, but he didn't say anything about it. "Not until you can stand without danger of falling over."

Clay acted like a child in a candy store with ten dollars to spend. "Okay. Okay. I'll take it easy the first few days." He offered his hand to Dat, who shook it with some hesitation. Dat was probably wondering the same thing Mary was. Why was Clay so eager? He most certainly wasn't the typical Englischer. "But where can I stay while I finish the work? I'm pretty sure Beth will want her bed back."

Dat looked out the window at the damage Clay had caused. "You can't stay here. I have four unmarried daughters, and I don't trust you."

Clay didn't seem to take offense. "I suppose I could set up a tent."

Mary had to protest. "It's almost November. Too cold to stay in a tent. Maybe it would be better to just take a check, Dat."

Clay shook his head. "Absolutely not. I won't learn my lesson if I just write you a check."

Mary was more and more confused. Clay

was a strange sort of man, for sure and certain. "It wonders me . . ." She stopped as a wonderful-*gute* idea came to her. "I think I know where you can stay, but give me a few days to work it out."

"You have until Friday," Dat said. "That's when Beth and the others come home."

Clay slapped Dat on the back enthusiastically. Dat gave Clay the stink eye, and Clay pulled his hand away before it got bit off. "I hope I can earn your forgiveness for being so reckless," he said.

Dat took a tiny step away from Clay. "We have already forgiven you."

"Thanks. That means a lot to me."

Dat wasn't finished. He always liked to tack on a moral lesson at the end of one of his lectures. "Do you know how irresponsible it is to drink and drive?"

"I do," Clay said. "It's very selfish, and I let myself get out of control. It won't happen again."

"Good. Your life is too valuable to treat it so carelessly."

Clay pressed his lips into a hard line. "It's not as valuable as it used to be."

Dat narrowed his eyes. "Every life is priceless. Don't forget it." When Clay didn't say anything, Dat nodded his head as if the conversation was over. "I'll bring you one of my shirts to wear while your other shirt is drying. I washed it this morning and hung it on the line."

"That's real nice of you," Clay said.

"There will be no more bare chests in front of my daughter."

Mary thought she might sink into the floor with embarrassment, mostly because Clay was looking at her, his eyes dancing with unchecked amusement, and partly because she was completely ashamed of herself for sneaking more than one peek at Clay's chest this morning. *Ach!* This was worse than Clay saying "naked" right out loud.

Clay swiped his hand across his mouth, probably to wipe away that widening smile. "I need to go out to my car and find my cellphone and wallet so I can call someone for a tow."

Dat pulled two things from his pocket. One was a slim silver wallet that he tossed to Clay. The other was a cellphone, its screen shattered beyond recognition. "I don't think you'll get this to work."

Clay groaned and took the phone from Dat. "Wow," he said, pressing the button below the screen. "I've never seen a screen crack into this many pieces before. It must have met with my hard head in the crash."

Mary gazed at the phone. "Maybe I accidentally sat on it."

One side of his mouth curled upward. "No, this is definitely how I got my concussion."

"Maybe I can take you into town later today to buy a new one," Dat said.

Clay pressed a few more buttons on his dead phone, then stuffed it into his pants pocket. "It doesn't matter. Nobody cares where I am anyway."

"Okay," Dat said. "I'm available to help if you need me." Dat strolled out of the room. "Get some rest, and do what my daughter tells you. She's a good nurse."

Clay smiled at Mary. "Yes, she is. The best."

"I'm not really a nurse," Mary said, when Dat disappeared down the stairs.

"You're better than a nurse. You're an angel."

Mary was surely breaking some sort of record for how many times she had blushed in one day. "That's silly. Would an angel make you throw up?"

"It was absolutely necessary." He laughed, then sucked in a breath and pressed his hand to his forehead. "I think I'd better get back in bed. I'm not a hundred percent yet."

Mary pulled back the covers for him, and he climbed in. "Get some sleep. I'll bring up a peanut butter sandwich and leave it on the dresser. You can try to eat it when you wake up."

"You should sleep too. You were up all night making sure I didn't die."

"Maybe," Mary said, "after I make you a sandwich and feed the chickens."

His eyes drooped as if they'd suddenly decided they'd worked hard enough for one day. "You never told me your name."

"Don't you know?" Mary said, her lips twitching upward as she repeated what Clay had said to her last night when she'd asked his name.

Clay's eyes filled with mischief. "Do you remember your name?"

Mary laughed at the look on his face. "I'm Mary."

He smiled as if she'd told him how to cure cancer. "Mary. Just what I would have expected."

Mary didn't know what to think of the way he looked at her. "You seem very happy to be fixing our barn and fence. Don't you have anything better to do?"

He sank back into the pillow. "As a matter of fact, I don't have anything better to do. What could be better than getting to see you every day?"

"Very funny."

He closed his eyes. "I'm not joking."

Chapter 4

"This is a very bad idea," Clay said, as he slid into the second row of Cathy Larsen's passenger van.

Mary wasn't sure if she should sit next to Clay or climb into the front seat next to Cathy, but she decided to sit in back with Clay, just in case he tried to escape before they made it to the hospital. "If you don't get stitches, you'll either get an infection or have a horrible scar on your face. We've got to go to the hospital."

Cathy pulled onto the road and glanced in her rearview mirror. "Is there a problem?"

Mary eyed her patient, more handsome than any man had a right to be. She'd changed his gauze pad this morning, but his wound was still a gaping mess, and stitches were absolutely necessary. He wore the shirt and pants he'd been wearing the night of the crash and a black baseball cap pulled as low as it would go over his face without knocking the gauze dressing from his forehead. "Clay is afraid of hospitals," Mary said.

Clay scrubbed his hand down the side of his face. "I'm not afraid of hospitals."

Cathy glanced behind her and almost drove the car into the ditch. "It's nothing to be ashamed of. You're smart to be afraid. My great-aunt Clara went in for melanoma surgery and came out without her gall bladder. Those doctors just want your money."

Clay had slept most of the day yesterday, the day after the accident, and he'd looked much better this morning, but Mary was worried about that cut, and she had finally insisted on taking Clay to the emergency room, no matter how loudly he protested. Mary was puzzled by his hospital phobia. She hadn't known Clay very long, but he didn't seem like the type to be afraid of anything. He mostly seemed to view the world with casual amusement without getting flustered by much of anything.

Ach, vell. Everybody had a weakness. Hospitals must have been Clay's.

Cathy glanced in her rearview mirror again. "Have we met?"

Clay folded his arms and scooted lower in his seat. "I don't think so."

"Whatever you do, don't let them take you

into surgery. You'll never come out the same."

Mary didn't want to seem forward, but she did want to offer Clay some comfort. "It will be okay. I'll be right here with you. There's nothing to be afraid of."

A slow smile grew on Clay's face. "You are the sweetest girl I've ever met, and I'm not just saying that." He leaned back against the seat and chuckled. "I know you don't believe me, but I'm not afraid of hospitals. And truly, I'm not opposed to getting stitches. I would prefer that women don't draw back in horror when they see my face. I'm just . . . I'm not a very popular guy right now, and the whole state of Colorado hates me."

Cathy frowned into her rearview mirror. "Mary, you should have them check for brain injuries. Paranoia is a symptom, you know."

Mary furrowed her brow. "You might be right."

Clay rolled his eyes. "I'd appreciate it if you didn't talk about me like I'm not here."

Cathy pursed her lips. "But maybe you're not all here. That's the point."

Clay huffed out a breath and looked out the window. "I shouldn't give you a hard time. I really don't want a hideous scar. I was just hoping to lay low for a few days until the worst blows over."

Mary eyed him doubtfully. "You want to wait until the whole state stops hating you?"

He chuckled softly. "Ain't gonna happen. But maybe their rage won't be so hot after a few weeks. After Christmas maybe. Or maybe after Easter. Easter always puts people in a good mood." He sat up straighter. "It doesn't matter what people say. I'm Clay Markham. I'll take it like a man."

Mary had no idea what Clay could have done that would make millions of people mad at him. She was almost afraid to ask. Almost. "What did you do?"

Cathy looked over her shoulder. "He's got a head injury, Mary. It's not more complicated than that."

Clay laughed again. "That's a good enough explanation for now."

Maybe it was the head injury. Maybe it was his fear of hospitals. Maybe everybody in Colorado really did hate him. In truth, Mary barely knew anything about Clay, but she hated seeing him so uncomfortable. "If everyone in Colorado hates you, then we'll just try not to attract attention."

He scrunched his lips to one side of his face. "I don't think that's possible. You're too pretty. Everyone will notice you the minute you walk in."

Mary was getting really irritated at her tendency to blush whenever she was with Clay. "That's not true. I'm as plain as a sparrow."

"You can be modest if you want," Clay said, "but it's just a fact that you are astonishingly pretty."

Mary pressed her cool hand to her hot cheek. Clay needed to stop looking at her like that or her face would burst into flames. She glanced at him out of the corner of her eye. The one who would attract attention was Clay. He was tall and handsome and rippling with muscles. It would be easier to overlook Pike's Peak.

Cathy pulled in front of the emergency entrance at the hospital. "Good luck. I'm going to Walmart. Call me when you're finished."

Clay unbuckled his seatbelt. "We can always hope it's a slow day at the hospital, and the whole staff are Diamondbacks fans."

The emergency room doors parted, and Mary and Clay walked up to the plexiglass window where a man in black scrubs sat staring at his computer. There were five people in the waiting room. An older man sat next to an older woman wearing a mask, and what looked like a father and two teenage sons lounged in front of the TV watching a baseball game.

Clay nudged his baseball cap farther down his forehead. Mary patted his arm. "It's going to be okay. Nothing to be afraid of."

He growled softly under his breath. "I'm not afraid." His gaze migrated to the game on the TV. "Oh boy. It's my lucky day."

The man behind the plexiglass looked up. "May I help you?" He glanced down at his computer and then snapped his head up and peered at Clay, his eyes growing as round as saucers. "Oh, it's you," he said.

Clay gave the man a weak smile and pointed to the bandage on his forehead. "I need stitches."

The man at the desk shot from his chair and slowly backed away, nudging his rolling chair backward with him as he went. "Just one minute, Mr. Markham. I'm really . . . I'm a big fan."

Clay flashed that grin that was quickly becoming one of Mary's favorite sights. "Thanks. I didn't think I had any fans left after that last game."

The man shook his head hard enough to fan up a breeze. "That's not true. Everybody can have a bad stretch. You're the reason we got there in the first place. And if the trade rumors are true, I'll boycott the Peaks for the rest of my life." He turned and walked out of the plexiglass office as if he was late for something very important.

Mary stared at Clay in astonishment. "Who are you?"

Clay adjusted the cap on his head. "I'm kind of famous, or infamous, depending on who you ask."

"Why are you famous?"

Clay inclined his head toward the television in the waiting room. "That's a rebroadcast of the last game of our playoff series."

Mary looked at the TV. "That baseball game?"

"Yeah. That's the top of the second inning, when people still liked me."

The man in the black scrubs came back into the plexiglass room holding a white piece of paper with a black-and-white photo printed on it. "Okay, Mr. Markham. I just need you to fill out this form and give me your insurance information, and we'll get you right back." He handed Clay a clipboard and slid the white piece of paper on top of the other forms.

Mary's eyes nearly popped out of her head. It was a black-and-white close-up photo of Clay's face.

The man behind the plexiglass pulled his lips across his teeth. "I hope you don't mind, Mr. Markham. I just quickly printed out a photo of you. Could I have your autograph?"

"My pleasure," Clay said. He pulled a pen from the jar of pens on the counter and signed the photo in the bottom right-hand corner.

He handed the photo back to the man, who took it and reverently pressed it to his chest. "Thanks, man. I'll remember this forever."

Clay leaned closer to the circular opening in the plexiglass. "Do you think you could get me back as soon as possible? I'm injured, and I'd kind of like to avoid attention."

The man nodded. "Yeah, for sure. I'll go back and tell them to call you in."

Clay led Mary to the farthest corner of the waiting room. They sat down, and he adjusted his cap a third time and glanced around the waiting room, his eyes once again landing on the television. He hunkered down in his chair and started filling out the forms. He'd pulled his baseball cap so far down over his eyes that Mary wasn't altogether sure he could see the forms he was trying to fill out.

She pointed to the plexiglass office, which was, once again, empty. "I thought you said everyone in Colorado hates you."

He shrugged. "Everybody but him."

"And me," Mary said.

Clay stopped writing, and his expression got sort of mushy. "That's the nicest thing anyone has ever said to me."

"Really? The nicest thing? I have a very hard time believing that."

He cleared his throat. "Well, it means more coming from you because I wrecked your barn, and you have to buy new fire extinguishers, and your foot got wounded, all because of me. I've caused you all sorts of trouble, so for you to say that you don't hate me is truly the most wonderful thing I've ever heard."

Mary wasn't sure what to say to that, so she decided to change the subject the way Clay always did. "So tell me why you're famous."

A nurse with bright orange hair stuck her head into the waiting room. "Clay Markham?" she said, her eyes shining with excitement. Plexiglass Man must have told her that a famous person was in their waiting room. Mary felt kind of indignant that she still wasn't in on the secret.

At the sound of Clay's name, the man

watching the TV with the two teenagers turned around, found Clay in the corner, and gave him a glare that would have made Pepper tuck his tail between his legs and run away. "Clay Markham," the man hissed. "How dare you show your face here."

Mary caught her breath. She'd never heard a person talk like that.

Clay stood up and raised his hands. "I'm just here to see the doctor. I don't mean any harm to anyone."

"Sure you don't."

Mary was paralyzed with alarm and disbelief. Frowning, Clay reached out, took her hand, and pulled her to her feet. "Come on," he murmured. "Let's get out of here." With his arm firmly around her waist, he led her quickly past the snarling man and through the open door to the treatment rooms.

The man yelled and jabbed his finger in Clay's direction. "You're a bum and a cheater, and I hope they run you out of town. I hope they run you out of the league." As the door closed behind them, they could still hear him yelling. "We've been waiting an hour, and he comes and strolls right in ahead of us. What kind of a place are you running?"

Mary's heart was beating so fast her chest

ached. The nurse led them to a little alcove with a bed, two chairs, a sink, and some medical equipment. She pulled a long curtain around a track in the ceiling, enclosing Mary and Clay in their own little private space. The nurse smiled apologetically. "I'm really sorry about that. People tend to be at their worst in the emergency room." She pulled the curtain aside. "My name's Brittney. I'll be back to get your forms in a few minutes, but if you need anything at all, just let me know."

Mary plopped into one of the chairs. Clay gazed at her, concern saturating his features. He pulled a paper cup from a dispenser by the sink, filled it with water, and handed it to Mary. "Drink this. You're as pale as a sheet."

Mary did as she was told. "No wonder you're afraid of hospitals. I thought that man was going to punch you."

Clay sat next to Mary and took her hand. She felt the warmth of his touch all the way up her arm. "I'm really sorry that you had to see that. That guy was a real jerk."

"It was foolish of him to come at you like that. You're a foot taller."

Clay's lips twitched upward. "It's not worth getting lathered up about. One misplaced fist, and you're looking at a ten-million-dollar lawsuit."

Mary took a deep breath and another sip of water. "So are you going to tell me why you're famous, or I am going to have to force it out of you with another batch of ginger urine tea?"

His grimace made Mary laugh in spite of herself. "Please, anything but that tea." He took Mary's cup and filled it with water again. "I play ball for the Colorado Peaks. They're a baseball team."

"I know." Mary was embarrassed to admit that the *only* thing she knew about the Colorado Peaks was that they were a baseball team. "So you're famous because you play baseball?"

"Yeah."

Mary was impressed, even though she didn't know much about baseball, the Peaks, or Clay Markham. "So why does everybody in Colorado hate you?"

Clay propped his arms on his knees and looked at the floor. "I'm one of the starting pitchers. That means I throw the ball to batters, and they try to hit it."

Mary was pleased to know that she wasn't completely ignorant. She'd played enough softball at recess in grade school to know what a pitcher did.

"The pitcher gets a lot of pressure to be

perfect. If you screw up, the fans can be brutal." Clay laced his fingers together. "Last week, I started in a very important game, that one they were showing on the TV when we came in. If we had won, we would have gone to the World Series. Do you know what that is?"

"No," Mary said, sad that she'd come to the end of her baseball knowledge.

"The World Series decides the world champions in baseball. Anyway, I pitched the first two innings, and the other team got two home runs off of me. Our offense never could get it going. We lost 2 to 0." He winced. "The fans booed me off the field."

Mary's heart hurt. "That's terrible."

He shrugged. "I get paid to pitch a good game. I deserved to be booed. I let my fans and my teammates down. I let myself down, and my dad. But I want you to know, nobody felt worse about the game than I did. It's a real struggle for me not to sink into despair after a game like that."

"I'm sorry."

"But I've learned that I can't dwell on it, or I don't play well the next game. You have to just keep picking yourself up and dusting yourself off. If you let it get you down, your career won't last very long." He hung his head, as if he hadn't been able to take his own advice after the last game. "Anyway, a day after the game, a rumor floated around Twitter that I had thrown the game for a friend."

"What does that mean, that you threw the game?"

"A friend of mine bet ten thousand dollars that the Peaks would lose, and the story got spread that I lost the game on purpose so my friend would win his bet. It's the stupidest rumor ever because ten thousand dollars is pocket change. I never would have thrown the game for any price, but it really hurts that people think I'd throw it for ten thousand dollars. There's an investigation going on, but there's no truth to it. It looks like that guy in the waiting room is one of those who believes I threw the game."

"That's terrible," Mary said. "Spreading a rumor is like releasing a bag of feathers into the wind. You can't get all the feathers back in the bag no matter how hard you try."

"People are pretty disappointed. The Peaks have never won a World Series." Clay gave her a halfhearted smile. "But I'll be back next year better than ever. I'm going to see a specialist next month."

"A specialist?"

He cleared his throat and glanced into the open slit between the curtain and the wall.

"I just mean that I'm not washed-up like the papers say I am. I'm only thirty-four. Nolan Ryan was forty-six when he retired. I've still got a lot of good years left."

"I'm sure you do." Clay was the perfect specimen of health. He could probably pitch until he was sixty.

Brittney, the orange-haired nurse, sort of inched her way past the curtain with two other young nurses in tow. The youngest looking nurse couldn't have been more than seventeen or eighteen. "Mr. Markham," Brittney said, looking back at her two companions and giggling like a teenager. "I'm really apologetic, and this is really unprofessional, but Hazel and Jackie were wondering if they could get your autograph."

Without waiting for the answer, the girl with her hair in a ponytail pulled a pen and a notepad from behind her back and handed them to Clay. "Could you make it out to Jackie?"

Clay was as unfailingly charming as ever. His smile could definitely turn any girl's knees into jelly. He took Jackie's pen and notebook. "Should I make it out to Nurse Jackie or just Jackie?"

"Just Jackie. My brothers are going to be so jealous. My little brother Randy pitches for the high school team, and you're his favorite player."

Clay was all smiles. "Thank you for telling me. That really means a lot after last game."

"Oh, nobody cares about that," Jackie said. "One time, Randy hit four batters in a row and walked in a run. They would have pulled him, but there are only two pitchers on the team, and the other one sprained his ankle the inning before."

Clay signed his name to the notebook. "Tell Randy I've had my share of wild pitches. One time, I was throwing pitches against my barn, and I actually killed one of our chickens with the ball. My mom wasn't too happy, but we got to eat chicken and dumplings for dinner that night."

Brittney gasped. "Oh no! That poor chicken."

"I felt pretty bad about it, but chickens aren't known for their smarts."

The three girls hung on every word that came out of Clay's mouth and followed his every gesture with their eyes. Mary understood the fascination with Clay. He was dazzling, like a flame to a trio of moths.

Clay turned the page on Jackie's notebook and wrote a note and an autograph for Randy.

Jackie beamed like a pair of headlights.

"Oh, thank you, Mr. Markham. Randy will love me forever. Maybe I'll give this to him for Christmas."

The other girl handed Clay a piece of copy paper. "Could you make it out to Hazel Williams?"

Clay showed those beautiful teeth, and Hazel swooned. "Are you a nurse too, Hazel?"

"No. I'm a CNA. I'm still in high school. My dad's a huge Peaks fan. Sometimes Mom wants to take our TV and throw it in the garbage. She was glad when the Peaks lost the last one. She said, 'At least I'll get my husband back.' "

Clay chuckled. "I'm glad someone was happy we lost."

He finished signing all the autographs while he and the girls talked about baseball. Jackie knew much more about the Peaks and baseball in general than Hazel or Brittney, and she and Clay had a nice conversation about batting averages and ERAs. Mary had no idea what either of them were talking about, but Clay acted like he'd died and gone to heaven. Jackie pulled a cell phone from her pocket, and the three girls took turns posing with Clay for photos.

Hazel turned to Mary. "I'm super sorry for bothering you guys. Are you Clay's girlfriend?"

Mary coughed as if the word "girlfriend" had lodged in her throat. "Um, no. I just came to help Clay. He cut his head, and I'm worried about him."

Hazel frowned. "I'm worried about him too. Do you think he'll have a scar?"

"Probably." Mary pursed her lips to stifle a smile. Clay had said something about not wanting women to draw back in horror when they saw his face. Hazel was obviously concerned, though Mary couldn't see anything — not even a scar — diminishing Clay's appeal.

Brittney pulled the curtain aside. "You guys, we've got to go before we get fired."

Jackie covered her mouth with her hand. "I'm so sorry, Mr. Markham. We probably broke all sorts of rules, but I would never forgive myself if I hadn't come to say hi."

Clay tilted his head so he could see around the other side of the curtain. "I didn't see any rule breaking." He put his index finger to his lips as if hushing a conversation. "I won't tell if you don't."

All three girls giggled hysterically and tiptoed out of the little alcove.

A ribbon of warmth trickled down Mary's spine. Clay was handsome, polite, *and* a wonderful nice guy. "That was very kind of you, especially since your head has got to be hurting. Those girls will never forget that."

"I love the fans, even when they don't love me." He motioned in the direction the girls had gone. "I was like that as a kid, full of excitement for the game and the players. I love when I can share that joy with other people."

Clay's goodness took Mary's breath away. "I don't know what I'd do with all that attention. Probably crawl into a ball and pray everyone would go away."

A man in red and yellow scrubs and yellow Crocs pulled the curtain aside and walked into their little space, followed by Brittney, who was holding a clipboard. The doctor reached out his hand to Clay, who stood and shook it. "I'm Dr. Jensen. It's very nice to meet you." He grinned at Mary and shook her hand next. "I'm Dr. Jensen. Are you Mr. Markham's escort this afternoon?" Dr. Jensen had a firm handshake and pictures of little yellow sponges with eyes and pants on his scrubs.

"I'm Mary."

The doctor noticed Mary staring at his scrubs. He laughed. "Do you like them? Sponge Bob seems to put my younger patients at ease." His gaze flicked between

Clay and Mary. "And most of my older patients too."

"They definitely draw attention," Mary said.

Dr. Jensen pulled a rolling stool next to them and sat facing Clay. "Are you allergic to any medications?"

"Not that I know of," Clay said.

Dr. Jensen slipped on a pair of latex gloves. "I'm assuming you're here because of this very impressive bandage on your head."

Clay peeled the tape and gauze away from his cut. Mary winced. The wound looked worse than ever. It oozed with blood, and the skin surrounding it was purple and blue.

"What happened?" the doctor asked.

"I plowed my car into Mary's barn, and my face met the steering wheel. Mary thinks I have a concussion."

The doctor drew his brows together. "Were you drinking?"

Clay pressed his lips together. "Yes." He glanced at Brittney. "That's private information," he said, tempering his words with a smile.

The doctor nodded. "There are HIPAA laws. Your privacy is safe with us."

"He crashed into my barn," Mary said.

Clay reached out as if to touch her, then

pulled back. “She rescued me.”

“I didn’t rescue you. I just helped you out of the car.”

Dr. Jensen studied them with an amused look on his face. “That would explain why an Amish girl is hanging out with Clay Markham. Did you lose consciousness?”

“Yes.”

Dr. Jensen pulled a small pen light from his chest pocket and shined it in Clay’s eyes. “Headaches?”

“Yes.”

The doctor slipped the light back into his pocket. “Well, Mary, you are an excellent diagnostician. Clay definitely has a concussion.” Brittney wrote something down on the clipboard. The doctor turned his attention to Clay’s forehead. “Not to bring up a painful memory, but if there was ever a good time for you to have a concussion, it’s right now. Your games are over, and you shouldn’t have much going on for the next few months.”

Clay gave the doctor a self-deprecating smile. “My own fault.”

Dr. Jensen shook his head. “Baseball is a team sport. Murphy struck out three times, and your outfield was on their heels all night.” He gently pressed his fingers around Clay’s cut. If Clay felt any discomfort, it didn't show on his face. "This is a straightforward injury. Six stitches should take care of it. You okay with that?"

Mary had to ask. "Will he have a bad scar?"

"Oh, I shouldn't think so. It's in a place where the skin comes together nicely."

Clay winked at Mary. "That's good. I don't want Mary to turn away in horror every time she sees me."

"I would never do that."

"Because you think I'm good-looking no matter what?"

Mary felt herself blush, a very common occurrence when she was with Clay. "I . . . I didn't say that."

Clay's smile drooped. "I'm sorry. I didn't mean to embarrass you."

Mary glanced at the doctor. "You didn't. It's just that I'm not used to being teased, and I get self-conscious when people look at me, and I'm uncomfortable being the center of attention." A laugh escaped her lips. "I suppose I am embarrassed, but I'll live through it."

Clay grinned. "That's a very mature attitude. I don't want to argue with you, but you must be uncomfortable all the time. No doubt you're the center of attention everywhere you go."

Mary looked at him sideways. "Of course I'm not."

"I'm not buying it." Clay smugly folded his arms across his chest and flashed his white teeth. A look of pain traveled across his face for maybe a second and then was gone. Mary wasn't altogether sure she'd seen it.

The doctor peeled off his gloves. "Be sure to consult with the team doctor. He knows more about the concussion protocol than I do."

"Okay."

Dr. Jensen rolled his stool slightly backward. "How long has your shoulder been hurting?"

Clay stiffened like an icicle in January. "My shoulder? What's wrong with my shoulder?"

The doctor seemed to sense Clay's sudden coolness. "The last few times I've seen you on the mound, you hold your arm like it hurts you. I notice those kinds of things because I'm an orthopedist."

Clay's gaze flicked in Brittney's direction. He lounged back in his chair as if he didn't have a care in the world. "That's just another rumor. The shoulder's fine. I've never been healthier." His posture was casual enough, but Mary could tell that he was uncomfortable and unhappy with the question.

"Do I need to leave the room while you give him stitches?" she asked, just to get everyone's mind off Clay's shoulder.

Dr. Jensen cocked an eyebrow. "Are you squeamish?"

"Not at all. I've delivered a baby before."

Clay, Brittney, and Dr. Jensen gaped at her as if she had just said "naked" right in front of them. "You've delivered a baby?" Dr. Jensen said, his words slow and disbelieving.

She shouldn't have said anything. In an attempt to divert attention away from Clay's shoulder, she had attracted all the attention to herself. "*Ach, vell,* me and my sister. It's a long story, but I have a strong stomach."

Clay stared at her, surprise, admiration, and gratitude in his eyes.

Dr. Jensen didn't push her for more details, showing him to be a kinder, more sensitive person than most Englischers. "Oh, okay," he said. "Then there's no reason for you to leave the room. I'm going to clean carefully around the spot where I'm going to inject Mr. Markham with Lidocaine, then when he's numb, Brittney will clean the wound thoroughly. When it's clean, I'll put in the stitches." He rolled farther back and patted the examination table. "Climb up here and lie down, Mr. Markham."

Clay did as he was told, but he didn't fit on the table so well. He was too broad and too tall. The doctor pulled out the little table extender at the bottom, but Clay's legs still hung over the edge. Mary stood beside him, and one side of his mouth curled upward when he looked at her. "Will you remind me of this moment the next time I want to take a drink of anything harder than a Sprite?"

"Or just remember how my ginger tea made you feel."

He grimaced. "I can still smell it. I promise never to drink again."

Chapter 5

The papers and the forms and the handouts were endless, but finally, everything was filled out and signed, and they told Clay and Mary they could go. They'd been in the emergency room for over two hours. Lord willing, Cathy hadn't been wandering aimlessly around Walmart waiting for Mary to call.

Brittney gave them four handouts for their reading enjoyment. Two handouts were about head injuries, one was about caring for Clay's wound so it wouldn't get infected, and the other was about medications Clay could take if he wasn't feeling well. Clay looked through the approved medications list. He grinned at Mary. "Nothing here about ginger urine tea. They've really got to update their information."

Clay had been very brave, just as Mary knew he would be. He'd also seemed more concerned for Mary's comfort than he was about himself. He had made jokes and teased Brittney while she cleaned his forehead. He and the doctor had a lively discussion about something called the designated hitter and the shortage of ash trees to make baseball bats. In the middle of the conversation, Clay would squeeze Mary's hand or wink at her, helping her feel part of things even if she wasn't part of the conversation. Dr. Jensen was very careful with the stitches and ended up putting eight in for *gute* measure. He saw Mary's obvious interest and carefully explained everything he did to Clay's forehead.

Mary couldn't fully relax until Brittney had finished putting a secure gauze dressing on Clay's forehead, and Clay had given her a dazzling, reassuring smile. At that moment, she had needed that smile like she needed air. Was that a normal emotion? Was it really possible to get firmly attached to someone you'd only just met? Or was her fascination more about Clay's good looks than his kindness and character?

Clay put on his jacket and helped Mary with her coat. They strolled down the hall, but before they could open the doors to the waiting room, Jackie ran after them and positioned herself between them and the doors. "I promise I didn't tell anybody," she said, breathlessly. "But there is at least one reporter and like fifty people out there waiting for you."

Mary's heart skipped a beat. "In . . . in the waiting room?"

"No, security came and told everybody they had to wait outside."

Clay looked behind them. "Is there a back way out?"

"Yes, but it just leads to the back parking lot, which leads to the front. You can't escape that way unless you scale a seven-foot fence." Jackie wrung her hands. "I swear I didn't tell anybody but my brother."

Clay didn't seem irritated with Jackie. Instead, he looked at Mary, his eyes full of sympathy. "If you want to escape now, I won't be offended. I'll figure out another way to get back to your house. I bet Jackie would give me a ride."

Jackie's eyes flashed with excitement. "Oh, for sure. Anywhere you want to go. I won't even tell my brother."

Clay fingered the stubble on his jaw. "Even if Jackie doesn't tell anybody, someone is bound to follow me. Then everyone would know where you live, and you might get unwanted visitors."

Mary's chest tightened. "You . . . you think they'll follow you?"

He frowned. "I didn't think this through very well. Even if I ride with you and Cathy, someone is bound to follow Cathy's van to your house. You'll get unwanted visitors, and they'll see my mangled car sitting in your yard. I don't want that kind of press, and I'm guessing you and your family don't want the attention."

Yesterday, Dat had hitched up Patty and pulled Clay's car a few feet away from the barn. It sat in the yard, and the crumpled bumper couldn't be seen by passing cars. But people looking closely would readily see the damage.

Mary felt dizzy with panic. "We don't. The goats will be upset and I . . ."

He wrapped his long fingers around her hand. "I'm sorry, Mary. I don't know what I was thinking."

Mary tried to take deep, calming breaths, but Clay seemed genuinely worried, and his expression did nothing to make her feel better. Her heart pounded so hard she could feel it in her throat.

"I think you'd better go, Mary. If you leave now, no one will know that you and I came in together. You'll be able to walk through the crowd without anyone guessing you know me."

Mary swallowed hard. "Okay. That's a

good idea." She'd walk out the doors, pretend she didn't know anything about a famous baseball player, and climb into Cathy's van. Her heart sank before she even touched the door. She turned to Clay. "What about you?"

He gave her a beautiful, fake smile. "I'll be okay. I'll find a hotel in town. Surely there's one within walking distance." He pulled his useless phone from his pocket. "No one will be the wiser that you and I are even acquainted."

Mary took a shaky breath, ashamed that she had almost abandoned her patient. She may have been shy and quiet and completely uncomfortable with the attention, but she wasn't a coward, and Clay needed her. He was alone and injured and phoneless. Englischers couldn't survive without their phones. She thought she might faint with terror, but she took a step back and lifted her chin. "I can't leave you."

His smile was real this time. "Mary, that is really, really nice of you, but you know I'm right. This whole mess is my fault. I've brought all this inconvenience and discomfort on you, and you don't deserve any of it. I'll be okay."

"The Good Samaritan didn't abandon the man who fell among thieves. I won't abandon you."

He took her hand again. Every cell in her body came alive. "Even the Good Samaritan had to get on with his life. He bound up the guy's wounds, set the guy on his own donkey, and left him at an inn."

For a man who didn't go to church, Clay sure knew a lot about the Bible. "Quote scripture if you want, but I'm staying with you."

Clay's eyes were like two pools of deep, warm water. "Oh, Mary, you've been more help than I deserve, and you don't deserve this turmoil in your life." Regret traveled fleetingly across his face. "I'll write your dad a check for all the damages. It will be easier for everyone."

It didn't matter what Clay said. He wasn't going to win this argument. She'd stay with him, for all the reasons she'd told him and for some she could hardly admit to herself. She wasn't ready to be free of Clay Markham. He wasn't like any man, Englisch or Amish, she'd ever met, and it stunned her how much she liked him. She wanted to be with him, to bask in the warmth of his smiles, and savor the embrace of his kind heart. *Ach,* she was turning into a crazy woman, but crazy or not, she couldn't deny that she was drawn to this almost-complete stranger.

"You said it yourself; everyone is mad at you. I won't leave you here to fend for yourself. I've got to protect you."

His mouth twitched upward. "You're going to protect me?"

She didn't even blink. "Yes."

He chuckled. "I'm guessing I've lifted a few more weights than you have over the years."

She folded her arms. "It doesn't matter. You've got a concussion. You'll be useless in a fight." Her heart fluttered like a thousand butterflies. She would also be useless in a fight. Lord willing, there wouldn't be any kind of a fight.

His smile nearly blinded her. "There's no one else I'd rather have watching my back." He pointed to the doors. "Is Cathy here yet?"

"I hope so. I called her fifteen minutes ago, and she was sitting in her car listening to something very loud on the radio."

He ran his hand down the side of his face. "Is she a fast driver?"

Mary shook her head. "I don't know. Esther says she's a terrible driver, but that might mean she goes too slow or too fast or doesn't stay in the lines."

Jackie was more distressed than either

Mary or Clay. "You don't want to try to outrun your fans. Remember what happened to Princess Diana?"

Mary drew her brows together. "Who is Princess Diana?"

Jackie opened one of the doors just a crack and peeked outside. She growled in frustration. "My brother has his face plastered against the window. When I get off, I'm going to kill him."

Clay gazed at Mary. "You're as white as a sheet. I'm so sorry." He cupped his hands around her shoulders. "The only thing we can do is split up. You go with Cathy, and I'll find another way to your house."

"I already told you, I'm not going to leave you to fend for yourself, and in truth, I don't want to make my way through the crowds all by myself."

"You're right. I don't want you going out there all by yourself either. We'll just have to make a run for it and hope Cathy is right outside."

Mary grabbed onto his wrist. "You can't run. If you run, you look like you've got something to hide."

"I do have something to hide, like my wrecked car and your half-charred barn. I'm telling you, Mary, you've got to leave me here."

Clay was obviously more concerned for her than he was for himself. She'd just seen how much he loved interacting with his fans. "You're more afraid for me than you are for yourself, aren't you?"

"You're not used to this craziness. I don't mind it. I like thinking that my life means something, that what I do is important to somebody. That *I'm* important to somebody."

"If I weren't here, you'd go out there and talk to them."

He eyed her doubtfully. "Yeah. I mean, my head hurts, but I'm not opposed to signing a few autographs, talking to the local paper."

"It's not even a paper," Jackie said. "It's more like a newsletter."

Mary ignored her galloping heart. "Okay, then. Let's go out, and you can say hello instead of trying to run away."

Clay massaged the back of his neck. "But they're bound to follow us to your house."

"And you don't want them to see your car."

"They're going to find out about the car sooner or later. I've got to call my insurance company, and they'll eventually send a tow." He squared his shoulders and adjusted the hat on his head. "I'll take the fallout like a man, but I'd feel real bad if people disturbed your family."

Mary almost lost her resolve. Concern lined Clay's face. If he knew enough to be concerned, she probably should abandon him. But that simply wasn't who she was. She thought of the Good Samaritan. "We'll cross that bridge when we come to it."

He sighed and grinned. "You're a very brave woman, Mary Yoder."

"Not that brave. I feel like I'm going to have a heart attack."

"You pulled me from the wreckage of my car, you put out a barn fire, you've delivered a baby. That takes courage, especially for a girl who doesn't like attention." He gave her a reassuring look and zipped up his jacket. "Okay, then. Let's get out there and meet some fans."

"Good luck." Jackie pushed one door open, and Clay pushed the other. There were only three people in the waiting room, and they were all staring dumbly at the hullaballoo outside. There were at least four dozen people out there, probably half of them teenagers. Jackie's brother had been busy.

The crowd gave a cheer as Clay and Mary walked into the waiting room. The cheer was muffled by the glass, but Mary still felt the enthusiasm. *Ach, du lieva.* She had gotten herself into this, had chosen her fate willingly. How would she live through it?

Clay took her hand and pressed it to his heart. "Remember that you've delivered a baby. This will be a piece of cake."

Delivering a baby seemed easy right about now.

Clay seemed to know instinctively that she wouldn't want to be seen holding an Englischer's hand. He quickly let go but kept her in his orbit as they walked out the automatic doors and into the crowd.

"Clay, can I have your autograph?"

"Clay, what happened to your head?"

"Who is the Amish girl? Is she your girlfriend?"

Mary kept her head down and her hands clasped in front of her, not saying a word, even when someone talked directly to her. Her heart pounded wildly, and her face was so hot, steam must surely be rising from her cheeks. She glanced up long enough to see Cathy's van parked not twenty feet away, and she was tempted to break away from Clay and retreat to the safety of the van. But she refused to give in to her fear. Clay needed her, and she would lend him her support by sticking close.

She dared a glance at Clay, who was getting a "selfie" with one of the teenagers. She was only kidding herself if she thought Clay needed her support. He was doing fine on his own. Her heart sank even further. The truth was, at this moment, she needed him to need her.

Clay was cheerfully answering questions, and surprisingly, he was unfailingly honest in his answers. He didn't say anything about driving drunk, but he told the story of how he'd crashed into the barn, gotten a concussion, and slept two nights at an Amish farm. He said nothing to draw attention to Mary, even though there was no getting around the curious eyes of just about everyone in the crowd. The Amish were used to being stared at wherever they went, and Mary had learned to either pretend no one was looking at her or avoid going out at all. She had everything on her farm that she needed to be happy.

One of the teenage boys in the crowd stuck a phone in Mary's face. "Can I take a picture?"

Mary's mouth dried out like the desert. "Um, no. That's not allowed."

The boy groaned. "Aw, come on. I want a picture of Clay's new girlfriend."

She didn't know where he'd come from, but Clay was immediately at her side with a hand in front of the boy's camera. "She isn't my girlfriend," he said, still wearing that friendly, best-buddy smile. "And the Amish don't allow photographs. Thanks for being respectful."

The boy lowered his phone, his excitement fizzling with Clay's gentle rebuke. "I'm sorry. I didn't know."

Clay draped his arm around the boy's shoulder. "But you can totally take a picture with me. What's your name?"

"Henry Zimmerman."

Clay took Henry's phone and held it away from them to get a photograph. "Do you like baseball, Henry Zimmerman?"

"Are you kidding? It's my favorite sport. I'm the first baseman on the high school team."

"Then you must know Randy, Jackie's brother."

Henry nodded. "He's a bad pitcher but a really nice guy."

Mary smiled at Clay, and he smiled at her, and all was right with the world.

Mary didn't keep close track, but he must have signed fifty autographs and taken pictures with at least that many people. After half an hour, he began to droop just a little, and Mary wanted to escape just so she could take him home and let him take a nap.

A woman, young and pretty with a very short skirt and very high heels, walked up to Clay as the crowd began to disperse. Her smile was so wide it looked like she'd fastened it into place with clothespins, and her eyes danced like stars. She held her phone in front of her and shoved it in Clay's direction. "Hi, Clay. I couldn't believe it when I got the call that you were in town. I'm Haley Thorpe from the *County Bugle,* and I'm wondering if I could ask you a few questions."

Clay gave the *Bugle* woman one of his most beautiful smiles. "Sure. What do you want to know? Are you a baseball fan?"

The *Bugle* woman looked a little sheepish. "Um, no, but I've seen you in a magazine as one of the sexiest men alive."

Clay laughed. "Oh, well, don't believe everything you read."

There was no reason for it, but Mary felt about as small as a ladybug, which ironically, was her *dat*'s nickname for her. She'd never be able to compete with a woman like that, with her long golden hair and her long, beautiful legs. Mary frowned and bit down her tongue. Why in the world was she thinking about competing with anyone for Clay?

He wasn't her boyfriend or her friend or even much of an acquaintance. She was acting like Pepper when another dog dared pass by their farm. Pepper barked and carried on as if he owned the whole street.

The *Bugle* woman must have been recording Clay's voice on her phone, because she lifted it close to his mouth when he talked. He told her about the accident, leaving out the drunk-driving part. "The doctor says I just need a little rest, and I'll be fine."

Haley Thorpe nodded. "Your fans will be glad to hear that, but what I really want to know is why did you and Gwen Rinaldi break up, and did you break up with her or did Gwen break up with you?"

Mary's heart felt as heavy as a stone. Clay had a girlfriend, or *used to* have a girlfriend? Why hadn't he told Mary about this Gwen person?

Mary closed her eyes and took a deep breath. Now she was just being ridiculous. She had known Clay for less than forty-eight hours. She didn't even know if he had siblings or parents or a favorite ice cream. *Ach, vell,* of course he had parents. Everybody had parents, but asking Clay about an old girlfriend was way down on the list of get-to-know-you questions. Still, as silly as it was, Mary was jealous of a woman she'd never met because of a man she barely knew. She felt a bit nauseated.

Clay backed away from his smile. "I've said everything I'm going to say about that. It's not my story to tell, and I know you'll respect my privacy and Miss Rinaldi's privacy. We're not dating anymore, and I wish her all the best."

Haley wasn't as compliant as Henry Zimmerman. "Gwen doesn't wish you all the best. She says you led her on and dumped her for no reason. She says you're a jerk."

Clay didn't seem upset about her horrible accusations, but his smile dwindled to nothing. Mary didn't want Haley to notice her, but she moved closer to Clay to lend him some support, which he probably didn't need. "I don't have anything else to say about Gwen. I really do wish her well." He rested his hand lightly between Mary's shoulder blades and nudged her away from the reporter. "My head feels like it weighs a thousand pounds. I'm ready to go home. How about you?"

Mary had been ready before they'd even ventured outside. "Yes. Cathy is right over there."

Clay's smile was brilliant but also a little forced as he looked at the seven or eight people still standing around the emergency room door. "Thank you all for coming, but I have a concussion, and the doctor says I need to take it easy. I've got to say goodbye."

"Does Gwen know you're dating an Amish girl?" It was Haley again, and Clay didn't even acknowledge her or the question as he turned around, cupped his hand around Mary's elbow, and led her to the van.

They climbed inside, shut the door, and leaned back against the vinyl seats. *Ach,* it felt so *gute* just to sit in the silence with no curious eyes tracking her every move.

Clay buckled his seatbelt. "Sorry to keep you waiting, Cathy."

Cathy pulled out of the parking lot. "I'm eighty-four I don't have anywhere better to be. It's either here or watching *Dallas* reruns. And yes, I already know who shot J.R. Besides, it was very entertaining watching you work a crowd. Are you a famous politician or something? A famous criminal?"

"No, Cathy. He's a baseball player. He pitches for the Colorado Peaks."

Cathy slammed on the brakes, pulled to the side of the road, and turned her whole body to get a *gute* look at Clay. "I can't believe I didn't recognize you before. It's probably because I wanted to forget the entire horrible experience." She narrowed her eyes. "You should be ashamed of yourself, giving Toli the high inside fastball. He'll hit that every time."

Clay glanced at Mary and gave her an I-told-you-so look. "See? The whole state is mad at me."

Cathy pulled back onto the road. "Of course the whole state is mad at you. You've got to get your act together before spring training, or nobody is going to think you're worth three million a year. The Peaks should trade you and get rid of the dead weight."

Clay's countenance fell, and he wilted before Mary's eyes, as if all the happiness in his life drained away like water from a sieve. He turned his face to the window and propped his elbow on the armrest. "Yeah. That's about the size of it."

Mary's heart hurt so badly she could barely breathe. She didn't have the courage to chastise Cathy, but she also couldn't let Cathy's words go unchallenged. She laid her hand on Clay's arm. He shifted in his seat. "You are *not* dead weight, and you are priceless to God. Never let anyone tell you otherwise. Your real fans love you no matter what."

He wouldn't look at her. "Maybe for a while. But if you don't win games, their love dies pretty quick."

"Well, it doesn't matter to me if you win games."

She didn't know exactly what she'd said, but when he turned to look at her, light and life were back in his eyes. His expression was almost buoyant. "Because you'll love me no matter what?"

She giggled, though on the inside she was mortified. Had she just told him she loved him? *Nae,* he had somehow twisted her words to make it seem that way. "You are an incorrigible tease, Clay Markham, and all I do is blush when I'm with you."

He grinned, then stared at her until she got embarrassed and looked down at her hands. "I like making you blush. It's almost too easy."

Too easy indeed! All sorts of thoughts tumbled around in Mary's head. Cathy said Clay made three million dollars. Had she heard wrong? That seemed an indecent amount of money. She was curious about the money but even more curious about the mysterious Gwen Rinaldi. Who was she? Did Clay still love her? Did she break Clay's heart? He certainly hadn't wanted to talk about it with Haley Thorpe. Mary wouldn't dare mention it, but she was intensely interested.

She leaned back in her seat. Clay's ex-girlfriend was none of her business and never would be. Clay was virtually a stranger and an Englischer, and Mary didn't see that changing ever. The thought made her sort of sad.

Cathy huffed out a breath. "Don't feel bad, Clay. I always say what I think, and I hurt a lot of feelings. I mean, how much stock can you take in an eighty-four-year-old woman's opinion about baseball."

Clay shrugged. "Anyone who knows how much I make a year knows enough about baseball to have a valid opinion."

"I'm really a football fan. Baseball is more of a side hobby." Cathy peered into her rearview mirror and frowned. "Someone is following us."

Mary looked behind them. "We expected that."

Cathy turned on her blinker and made an unexpected left turn. The tires squealed in protest. "Let's go see Esther and shake these guys."

Clay grabbed onto the back of Cathy's seat. "Don't speed. We're not going to lose them, and we don't want to end up in a ditch."

The van slowed almost immediately. "You're right," Cathy said. "What can they do but park in front of Esther's house and stare?"

How convenient that Mary had already talked to Esther about the Clay problem. Esther had agreed to help Mary with a solution.

Cathy pulled to a stop in front of Esther's house. Esther's husband, Levi, had hung a piece of wood on a pole advertising Esther's quilt shop: QUILTS FOR SALE, OPEN THURSDAY, FRIDAY AND SATURDAY, 10-6, OR BY APPOINTMENT. CLOSED SUNDAY. They all jumped out of the van and walked quickly to the house before whoever was following them could catch up. Cathy knocked on the door, then boldly opened it and herded Mary and Clay into the front room.

Mary nibbled on her bottom lip. "Is it okay if we just walk in?"

Cathy went to the big picture window in the front room, parted the curtain, and peeked out of the opening. "It is if we don't want to end up on the evening news."

A beautiful red and white quilt sat on quilt frames in the front room, taking up so much space there wasn't any room to sit on the couch unless they crawled under the quilt and came up on the other side. Until recently, Esther had hung all her quilts for sale in this room, but Levi had built an addition to the house and now Esther had a nice, spacious area for her quilts with its own entrance so customers didn't have to come into their private space.

The house smelled heavenly, like chicken dumplings and buttered noodles. They'd been at the hospital so long, it was almost dinnertime. Mary's stomach grumbled. She hadn't eaten anything but two hospital crackers for supper.

Cathy sat down at the quilt, picked up a needle, and started quilting. That was probably why Esther always had a quilt up on frames. Anyone who came to visit could take a few stitches while they were here.

"Esther?" Mary squeaked apologetically, already very sorry for just walking into Esther's home.

The door left of the entryway opened, and Esther emerged with Levi Junior in her arms, Winnie holding tight to her skirts, and a piece of chalk behind her ear. Her gaze immediately flew to Clay, which was only to be expected. Clay took over every room he was in with his size, his good looks, and the force of his personality. Esther pursed her lips. "Is this him?"

Mary caught her bottom lip between her teeth. If Esther didn't agree to her plan, she didn't know what she'd do. "You got my note."

Esther nodded, never taking her eyes from Clay's face. "I got your note."

"So, you've already heard about me," Clay said cheerfully, even though he obviously knew exactly what Esther had heard about him, and it wasn't a *gute* report. He stuck out his hand.

Esther narrowed her eyes and took Clay's offered hand, but she seemed reluctant about it.

Clay reached out and ran the back of his finger down Levi Junior's cheek. "Cute baby. What's his name?"

Esther softened around the edges a bit. "This is Levi Junior." She pulled Winnie from behind her. "This is Winnie."

Clay knelt down and shook Winnie's hand. "Nice to meet you, Winnie. How old are you?"

"She doesn't speak much English," Esther said. "*Deitsch* is what we speak at home. She's three."

"What a sweetie," Clay said. "I love kids. They don't care how much money you have or how important you are. They just give you their whole hearts."

Esther tilted her head to one side. "Do you have kids?"

"No. Five nieces and no nephews. I've been to a lot of tea parties."

Esther pursed her lips. "Mary says you need a place to stay while you fix her barn."

Clay glanced at Mary, good humor on his face. "I'm not opposed to a tent."

Esther smirked. "It's too cold this time of year, and everybody deserves a good toilet."

Clay grinned. "I'm very fond of a good toilet."

"Mary has asked me to take you in because her *dat* won't let you stay there with four unmarried daughters. I don't blame him, but I don't know why I should let you stay here except Mary is a good friend and people who take in strangers will be on the right hand of God at the last day."

Cathy tugged a strand of thread from the quilt. "Why don't you just stay in a hotel in Alamosa?"

Clay's brows inched together. "It's not a bad idea, but I don't want to have to fight the crowds every morning just to get to Mary's place, and what if the roads are bad?"

Esther looked at Mary. "Crowds?"

"We took Clay to the hospital for stitches, and by the time we came out, there were fifty people outside waiting for him."

Esther's eyebrows inched up her forehead. "Why?"

Esther wasn't going to like the answer, but Mary wouldn't feel *gute* unless she was completely honest. "Clay is a famous baseball player. He pitches for the Colorado Peaks, and most of Colorado is mad at him."

Cathy raised her hand. "Me included."

Esther fingered the chalk tucked behind her ear. "Are you rich?"

Clay stretched his lips across his teeth. "I suppose?"

"Then why don't you just pay Try for the damages and be done with it?"

It was a sensible idea, but Mary was more opposed to it than ever. She wanted to see a little more of Clay Markham. Just a few more days with him, and she could die happy. "Dat doesn't want Clay's money," Mary said, a little too loudly. "He says Clay will never learn a lesson if he doesn't fix the damage himself."

Esther's eyebrows kept traveling upward. "Your *dat* said that?"

Mary nodded vigorously. "*Jah.* That's what he said. We wouldn't want to go against Dat."

"I don't know how I feel about a famous person staying here. You might be nothing but trouble."

Clay gave Esther his ridiculously dazzling smile. "I do dishes."

Mary suddenly felt desperate to convince Esther. "No one will know he's here, Esther. You're too far out of town. And he does dishes."

Esther sighed in surrender. "I suppose I can let you sleep here until you finish fixing the barn."

Clay's smile got even wider. "I would really appreciate it."

"What's the damage like? How long is it going to take?"

"It shouldn't take more than a few days," Mary said.

Clay shook his head. "I'm pretty slow. I'd give it to the first part of January."

Mary's heart did a little jig. Clay might be here for Christmas! She didn't know how she knew, but she just knew it would be *wunderbarr.*

Esther peered at Clay as if seeing him for the first time. "Hmm."

Clay's smile stuttered. "Does that mean I meet with your approval?"

Esther paused and kept her gaze glued to Clay's face. Then she seemed to snap out of whatever thoughts she was thinking. "I have a few conditions. First, if you live in this house, you have to go to church with us."

Clay leaned over and whispered to Mary loud enough so Esther could hear. "Didn't you warn her about the lightning?"

Mary jabbed her elbow into his ribs. "Clay thinks God will smite him if he steps inside a church."

Esther wasn't impressed. "It's lucky for him that we don't worship in a church. You won't be electrocuted at our services, but I'll warn you now. They're three hours long. Now would be a good time to work on your posture. The second condition is that I don't want any complaints about the food. I'm not a good cook, but it's better than starving."

Clay nodded, an earnest look on his face. "Ma'am, I grew up on a farm, and my mother, bless her heart, served us cow tongue and cow stomach, and if we complained, our dad would smack us on the head with the handle of a butter knife. There isn't anything I'm not willing to eat."

Esther winced. "I'm not quite that touchy about my cooking."

"I do dishes," Clay said, "but I can cook too if you need me to."

Esther pressed her lips together. "Do you make cow's tongue?"

"No. I can't stand it." Clay shuddered,

probably remembering all those home-cooked meals.

"He'll mostly be eating at our house," Mary said. "Joanna is a wonderful-*gute* cook."

Esther's gaze flicked between Clay and Mary. "You're not so bad yourself, Mary. I've never tasted anything better than your cinnamon bread pudding."

"Whoa," Clay said. "I've got to try that."

Esther handed Cathy the baby and found a book for Winnie to look at. "Let me show you where you'll be sleeping. It's the perfect place. Private, with a nice big bed and your own bathroom, and customers will only bother you Thursday, Friday, and Saturday."

Clay cleared his throat. "Customers?"

Esther motioned for them to follow, and she led them through the kitchen, down the hall, and through a door that looked brand new.

Mary clapped her hands. "Oh, Esther, it's your new quilt shop."

Esther smiled for the first time since they'd come into the house. "Levi finished it last week, and we moved all the quilts in on Saturday."

Dozens of quilts hung on hangers hooked over a pole along one wall, and three more spectacular quilts were pinned to the opposite wall. A bed covered with several layers of quilts sat in the middle of the room. "We spread the quilts on the bed if people want to see them close up."

Clay patted the corner of the bed. "Is this where I'll be sleeping?"

"Yes. You'll have to make it perfectly every morning and clean up after yourself. I can't have a mess for the customers to see."

"Of course," Clay said. "I make my own bed every morning."

Esther smoothed her hand down the quilt on top of the bed. "I should hope so."

Esther didn't realize how extraordinary it was that Clay made his own bed. If Mary had three million dollars, she'd hire someone to do it for her.

"I'll bring you a blanket to put on the bed at night. You can't sleep with any of the quilts on the bed because they're for sale." Esther pointed to the skylight. "It's nice and light during the day. At night, you'll need to light a lantern. And no need for a wood-burning stove. The solar panels heat water that goes through pipes under the floor and heat the room. That's Levi's doing. He's a genius with contraptions."

"Clever," Clay said. "It's perfect. I'm really grateful for your hospitality. I'll be the best guest you've ever had."

Esther snorted and made Mary jump. "That won't be too hard. The only other guest I've ever had is my sister, and she abandoned her baby, stole my money, and tried to take my boyfriend. I trust you'll behave better."

Clay's mouth fell open. "Much better."

Esther grinned. "It all turned out for the better. Ivy is living in a little house not ten minutes from here, and she supports herself by making jewelry and selling it online. She let me adopt Winnie, and we're closer than ever."

"I'm glad to hear it," Clay said. "I hope you'll never have cause to regret letting me stay here."

Esther huffed out a breath. "I don't mean to be rude, but I regret it already. Lord willing, you'll finish that barn quickly."

Mary wouldn't hope for any such thing. Lord willing, Gotte would pay more attention to Mary's prayers than Esther's.

Someone knocked on the door to the quilt shop. Esther rolled her eyes. "Doesn't anybody read the sign? We're closed on Wednesdays." She trudged to the door and unlocked it.

A middle-aged woman strolled into the room, followed by a younger man who had to be her son. They both had the same dark brown eyes and square jaws. An even younger version of the man, eleven or twelve years at oldest, sort of slinked into the room as if he was too embarrassed to walk in properly.

The woman, who was wearing a bright purple scarf and matching beanie, zeroed in on Clay. "We are sorry to bother you all, but not incredibly sorry or we wouldn't have knocked." At least she was honest. "We heard you were at the hospital, but by the time we got there, you were just getting into a van, and we had to see you. So Jason followed the van here." She pointed to the man and then to the boy. "This is my son Jason and my grandson Darnell."

Darnell gazed up at Clay with awe on his face, then bowed as if he were meeting a prince. That's when Mary noticed. Darnell's left arm and hand were missing just below his elbow.

Clay chuckled. "No need for bowing. It's nice to meet you." He reached out and shook Darnell's hand. "Are you a baseball fan, Darnell?"

How could Clay act so casual, as if Darnell were a regular kid with two good hands? It seemed to be one of the things Clay did best, make everyone feel easy and comfortable, as if they were just as important as he was and he was truly happy to know them.

Darnell studied his feet. "Yeah. I used to play."

Clay squatted so his head was lower than Darnell's. "It looks like you had something bad happen to your arm."

Mary stiffened. Clay was brave to ask such a question. Would Darnell's dad think it was rude?

"Yeah. I got bone cancer, and they had to amputate."

Clay winced. "I bet that was really terrible."

Darnell glanced at his dad. "I guess it's better than dying."

Clay eyed Darnell intently. "I promise you, it's better than dying. You've got a lot of great things to accomplish before you die."

"I know," Darnell murmured. "I can still be a doctor or a teacher."

Darnell's grandma sidled behind him and put her hands on his shoulders. "Darnell plays soccer, and he made the Olympic development team last spring."

"No kidding? That's great."

Darnell's dad nudged him on the side of his head. "Ask him what you came to ask so we can go and let these nice people get on with their lives."

Darnell stuffed his hand in his coat pocket and yanked out a baseball. "Can I have your autograph?"

Clay stood. "Sure. Do you have a Sharpie? Those work real good on baseballs."

Darnell's grandma pulled a marker from her purse and handed it to Clay.

Clay took Darnell's baseball and signed it. Then he and Jason and Darnell started talking about baseball and soccer and the Olympics. Mary did her best to follow the conversation. Baseball was the most important thing in Clay's life. She loved how his eyes lit up whenever he talked about it. She determined then and there to buy a book about baseball and learn everything, so she would be able to talk to Clay about it. That would make him so happy.

While Clay talked with Jason and Darnell, the grandmother sidled next to Esther. "I know you're not officially open, but do you think I could buy a quilt? That blue one hanging on the wall would be beautiful in my guest room."

Mary's eyes traveled to the blue quilt pinned to the wall, and she stifled a gasp. The price tag said "$1000."

Esther might have been slightly irritated before, but now she was all smiles. "Of course. You're welcome to buy any quilt in the shop."

Darnell's grandmother pointed to the blue one. "Well, I for sure want that one."

"I'll take it down," Mary said.

Esther nodded. "*Denki,* Mary."

Esther and the grandmother strolled around the room looking at quilts while Mary retrieved the stepladder and unpinned the quilt from the wall. It wasn't easy because there were no less than a hundred pins securing the heavy fabric to the wall, and Mary couldn't reach the highest pins, even on the stepladder.

She didn't notice that the men had stopped talking until Clay was next to her at the foot of the stepladder. "Can I help?" he said.

It was probably the only time Mary would ever look down at Clay. "Yes, but you have a concussion. I don't want you to get dizzy and fall over."

He smiled. "Really, Mary, I'll be fine." He took her hand and helped her down, then climbed up and took out the last few pins at the top of the quilt. Mary was ready, and she caught the quilt as it tumbled into her arms.

"No fair," Mary teased. "You didn't even have to stand on the top step of the ladder."

"It makes me much more intimidating on

the pitcher's mound."

Darnell's grandmother ended up buying four quilts: the thousand-dollar quilt from Esther's wall, a lap quilt, and two baby quilts. Both of her daughters were expecting babies. Esther boxed up each quilt and tied the boxes with country red ribbons. When Darnell's family left the shop, Esther had made almost $1500.

Esther locked the door behind them and twirled around to look at Clay. "I like you already, Clay Markham. You're welcome to stay as long as you want."

And with that, Mary's greatest worry was put to rest. Now she just needed to figure out how to make the work go slower so Clay would be here come Christmas.

Chapter 6

Joanna stood at the sink washing dishes, gazing out the window that afforded a perfect view of the barn and pasture. She turned and smirked at Mary. "Clay and Dat are arguing again."

Mary returned Joanna's smirk with one of her own. Clay's arguments with Dat usually consisted of Dat standing his ground and Clay trying to talk Dat into something he didn't want. "Dat is the most stubborn man in Colorado."

Joanna laughed. "And Clay has fooled himself into thinking he can get Dat to change his mind about anything."

Last week, Clay had tried to talk Dat into new siding for the house. Dat thought it was a waste of money and time. Clay thought it would make the property look "so much nicer" and also be less upkeep in the long run. Dat had won that argument because it was his house, and Clay needed to "stick to his knitting."

Clay had been completely baffled by that proverb.

Joanna and Mary were alone in the kitchen. Ada and Beth had taken the buggy to the Bent and Dent grocery store to buy supplies for Thanksgiving next week.

To say that Joanna, Ada, and Beth were shocked when they came home from Iowa was an understatement. A six-foot-three, muscular, handsome athlete hanging around the farm was a rare and unprecedented event. Beth had been beyond offended that Clay had slept in her bed, and Ada had been quite dismayed at the condition of the toilet. With her wry sense of humor, Joanna had never been one to overreact, and she found a lot in the situation to laugh about. When Mary and Dat had told her *schwesteren* the whole story, Ada had strongly suggested that Dat take Clay's money instead of making Clay do the work himself. "An Englisch man loitering on our farm will bring ruin to all of us," she'd said.

"Vell," Dat had said, "he won't be loitering. He'll be working and, Lord willing, learning a hard lesson."

Dat was firm when he thought himself to be right, and he wouldn't even consider taking Clay's money. He had said he'd rather forget about any repayment than just let Clay write a check. Ada finally gave in. She didn't feel *gute* about letting Clay off without consequences, even if that meant he would be on the farm for several weeks. Ada had a strong sense of justice, and thought it was only fair that, one way or another, Clay pay for the damage he'd done.

Soon the family had gotten into a rhythm with Clay around. He had grown up on a farm, so they had a lot in common. He ate all three meals with them every day, and he often got them laughing with stories of his life; from losing over a hundred baseballs in the cornfields to getting sprayed by a skunk to seeing a baseball fan take off all his clothes and run onto the field naked during a game.

Mary loved Clay's stories. Ada tolerated them. Joanna and Beth seemed to see him as the big brother they'd never had. Clay was the oldest in his family, with two younger *schwesteren* and a baby *bruder.* His *schwester* Amy had four daughters, Ashlyn had a new baby girl, and Clay's brother, Kirk, was almost finished with medical school.

Clay had come to *gmay,* or church, with them for the first time last week, and he'd created quite a stir in the district. Of course,

Clay created a stir wherever he went, so the stares and whispers didn't seem to bother him. The reception wasn't as warm as he was probably used to because everyone in the district was suspicious as to why a tall, friendly Englischer wanted to invade their church services. Services were held at Jethro Coblenz's house, and Clay sat at the back of the great room behind all the members. Mary had glanced back a time or two during the meeting, but she couldn't really look at Clay without attracting attention herself, so she hadn't really been sure what he'd thought of the services.

After *gmay* was over, Mary had rushed to his side because she was a little worried about how he'd like the service, but he was grinning like a cat. "God didn't smite me today," he'd said. "It was probably because I was sitting too close to the rest of you. He wanted to avoid collateral damage." Mary didn't know what collateral damage was, but for sure and certain, God would never smite Clay, especially in church. Clay was a *gute* man, even if he was a drunk and an Englischer. Mary frowned to herself. Was Clay a drinker? She hadn't smelled a whiff of alcohol on him since the night of the accident. If he drank, Mary didn't know about it.

Clay had helped set up benches and tables for fellowship supper and struck up a friendship with two or three of the boys in the district when they sat down to eat. *Die buwe* loved talking about baseball and sports, and Clay was a walking sports encyclopedia. Overall, it was a *gute* day at church for all of them.

Mary joined Joanna at the sink and peered out the window. Clay and Dat were both dressed for the cold, Dat with his black coat, work boots, black wool hat, and sturdy leather gloves. Clay wore a navy-blue parka that he claimed was good to fifty degrees below zero, black gloves, and a purple beanie with the Colorado Peaks logo stitched across the front. He somehow managed to make winterwear look attractive.

The doctor had taken out the stitches two days ago, but Clay still wore a bandage over his wound for extra protection. There was going to be a scar, but Mary thought it only made his face more interesting.

Clay was holding a clipboard and pointing to it with a pen that was wedged tightly in his gloved fingers. Dat frowned and shook his head, as if he'd decided not to agree with anything on that clipboard.

Mary giggled. "I guess I should go out and break it up."

"*Ach,* don't," Joanna said. "It's very entertaining watching them butt heads."

Mary nudged Joanna with her elbow. "It is not. Dat wins every time because Clay is too kind to push hard."

Joanna glanced sideways at Mary. "*Jah.* Clay is perfect in every way."

Mary nudged Joanna a little harder. "I didn't say that."

Joanna handed Mary a newly washed saucepan to dry. "You didn't have to. You were thinking it."

Mary caught her bottom lip between her teeth. She had been thinking it, but she didn't want Joanna to gloat about being right. "Clay isn't perfect. He has many faults."

Joanna wiped her hands on a dishtowel, folded her arms, and pinned Mary with an amused gaze. "Like what?"

Mary wanted to kick herself. Joanna was already gloating, and Mary couldn't think of one thing she didn't like about Clay. "Well, I don't know him that well yet."

Joanna leaned against the countertop. "I'll tell you one flaw. He's not Amish."

Mary's heart felt as heavy as a buggy full of anvils. She slumped as the weight of the world pressed down on her. "It doesn't matter. He's not going to be here much longer."

Joanna's expression fell. "*Ach,* I'm sorry." She pulled Mary in for a hug and spoke softly into her ear. "I was trying to tease you, but I've made you unhappy instead."

"Can we not talk about it? It might be weeks and weeks, and I'd rather enjoy the time I have left rather than dread what's to come."

Joanna nudged Mary to arm's length and brushed a wrinkle out of Mary's apron. "Of course. Let's only talk about happy things, like how Clay has only been around for two weeks, and the goats have adopted him as their mother."

The picture of four goats pestering Clay everywhere he went coaxed a smile from Mary. "How about the fact that Clay eats more than all four *schwesteren* combined."

Joanna groaned. "That's not so happy. My grocery bill has doubled."

"He knows how to milk goats." Mary said.

"He mopped my floor last week. I don't mind having him around."

"I don't either." Mary plopped into a kitchen chair. Clay wouldn't be around forever, and the thought stole her breath.

Joanna gave her a pitiful look and turned back to the window. "You really should go out there before Dat pops a blood vessel in his neck."

"I really should." Mary jumped from her chair and donned her boots, coat, mittens, and black bonnet. "If I'm not back in ten minutes, come save me." Mary skipped down the back porch steps and marched to where Dat and Clay were still debating.

Dat stood with his feet apart, his arms crossed over his chest, like an immovable telephone pole. "Chain-link is cheap, it's easy to put up, it doesn't rust, and you never have to paint it. And the goats don't chew through it."

"I know, Try," Clay said, "but chain-link is ugly. Just think how nice a custom vinyl fence would look all around your property."

Dat shook his head. "Folks will say I'm trying to be fancy. I'll not be accused of pride in my own district."

"The Millers have vinyl fencing," Clay said, pointing in the general direction of the Millers' house.

Dat had an answer for everything. "Comparison is of the devil. We shouldn't care about keeping up with our neighbors as much as taking care of our neighbors."

"What's wrong with doing both?"

Mary hooked her arm around her *dat*'s elbow. "Would anyone like to come in for some hot chocolate?"

Dat shoved his hands in his pockets. "This

farm has been protected by chain-link for almost twenty years. There's nothing wrong with chain-link." With that, he trudged across the snow, up the porch steps, and into the house.

Clay grinned at Mary. "I think I might be able to talk him into vinyl yet."

Mary laughed. "Not a chance."

He sighed. "It was worth a try."

Mary raised her eyebrows. "Was it?"

Clay swiped his hand across his mouth. "Maybe not." Beth's goat, Fluffy, galloped up and nibbled on the bottom of Clay's coat. Clay bent down and patted Fluffy on the head. "You like my vinyl idea, don't you, Fluffy?"

Fluffy bleated her approval and trotted into the barn.

Mary and Clay met eyes and laughed. "If only Fluffy was the final decision maker," Clay said.

"Fluffy would probably choose wrought iron." Mary and Clay strolled toward the house, and Clay took Mary's hand as if it were the most natural thing in the world. "What time do you leave tomorrow?" Mary asked, her hand warming to his touch, even past two layers of gloves.

"Early. My plane flies out of Colorado Springs at noon." A few days after the accident, Cathy had taken Clay to Walmart to get a new phone. Once he had a phone, he'd called a tow truck to haul his car away. The insurance company had totaled it, which Clay had explained meant they weren't going to pay to have it fixed. He'd gone to Colorado Springs the next day and bought something much less fancy. He had told Mary that since he was going to be spending so much time at Mary's house, he'd gotten a reliable vehicle that wouldn't draw attention to itself, the Yoders, or their farm.

Mary smiled to herself. Her *schwesteren,* Dat, and all the neighbors were still teasing Clay about that truck.

"Thanksgiving isn't going to be near as fun without you." Had she ever been happy before Clay came along?

His lips curled upward. "You think so? I feel the same way. My sister's house is fun, and I have a great time entertaining my nieces, but it's even colder in Indiana, and I kinda wanted to see what an Amish Thanksgiving is like. I'm sure the food is to die for, but I'd be perfectly content with a bowl of your famous buttered noodles."

"*Ach,* anyone can make buttered noodles. It's Joanna's pies you're going to miss."

"My sister Amy makes a mean stuffing. That will have to be enough, I guess." He tugged Mary away from the house. "I bought you a going-away present."

Mary's face got warm. She wasn't the one going away. Should she have gotten Clay something? "You didn't need to do that."

"I didn't need to. I wanted to. It's in my truck."

Mary followed Clay around to the back of the barn where Dat insisted Clay park his truck so it wouldn't attract attention. It was the ugliest truck Mary had ever seen, with a two-tone paint job of baby blue and cream where there was paint at all. The rest of the truck was covered in pockmarks of rust. It was a thirty-year-old truck, but it looked much older, as if Clay had driven it out of a junkyard.

Clay opened the cab door and grabbed a present wrapped in bright yellow paper from the front seat. Grinning, he handed it to Mary. "I hope you like it."

Mary felt more and more guilty that she didn't have a present for Clay. She peeled back the paper to reveal the box inside. Would Clay be disappointed that she didn't know what it was?

Thankfully, Clay saved her the embarrassment of asking. "It's a fecal testing kit."

She still didn't know what it was. "A what?"

His face fell. "They told me it's what all the goat people want for Christmas. You use it to test for parasites in animal fecal matter, specifically goats."

"You mean goat poop?"

He closed one eye and pointed at her. "Correct. I feel like it's been a theme of our friendship."

"Goat poop?"

He laughed. "Well, first there was the ginger urine tea, then the throwing up, then blood and guts in the emergency room. It's been one long string of disgusting things since we first met."

"I wouldn't call the ginger tea disgusting."

He pursed his lips. "Um, no, of course not. Not disgusting at all." He pointed to some words on the box. "All the instructions are in there. Parasites are super bad for goats, and if you find parasites in the goat poop, you can get them medication so they won't get sick."

Mary clutched the kit to her chest. "That's a surprisingly thoughtful gift."

"I wanted to get you a diamond necklace, but I didn't figure you'd wear it."

"For sure and certain."

Since Clay had grown up on a farm, he obviously knew a practical, useful gift when he saw one. "I'm glad you like it."

"Is your whole family going to be there? For Thanksgiving."

Clay kicked at the snow at his feet. "Yeah. Everybody always comes. Mom and Dad are still on the family farm. Amy lives about ten minutes from my parents. Ashlyn is an hour south in Greenwood with her husband and baby girl. Kirk drives home every year for Thanksgiving and Christmas from Chicago. I always make it for Thanksgiving." He looked down at his hands. "Sometimes it's just too hard to go for Christmas."

Mary sensed a deep ache sitting at the bottom of Clay's throat. He had opened the door. Maybe he wanted her to walk through it. "Why . . . why is it hard?"

He glanced up and tried to smile, but she'd never seen any expression so unhappy. "Oh, it's nothing. Dads can be hard sometimes." He fell silent for a few moments, then snapped his head up and clapped his hands together as if swatting away distressing thoughts. "Like *your* dad, who won't let me put up anything but chain-link," he said, with forced cheerfulness.

She wanted to wrap him in her arms and lend him some warmth, but instead she leaned back against the truck. "Do you want to talk about it?"

"My dad was pretty hard on me as a kid,

and I don't know if I'm angry or still longing for his approval."

"You can feel both."

"Yeah. I guess I can." He sidled next to her and leaned against the truck. "It's exhausting trying to earn his love every day."

Mary turned and looked at him. He had a strong profile, with three- or four-days' growth of whiskers on his jaw. "You don't think he loves you?"

"He loves me now that I'm worth three million dollars a year, but maybe he won't love me so much when I don't play anymore."

"Oh," Mary said. "That's too bad." She had no idea how to reassure him because she didn't know what kind of a man Clay's dad was. She found it incomprehensible that anyone would have a hard time loving Clay. He was the most lovable person she'd ever met.

He pushed away from the truck and gave her a more natural smile. She could live for days off the memory of that smile. "You see why I'd much rather talk about goat poop?"

She giggled. "Who *wouldn't* rather talk about goat poop?" Mary eyed her fecal testing kit. "I feel terrible I didn't get you a going-away present."

His eyes danced with their own light. "Don't feel terrible. I'm not offended. You can get me a welcome back present."

Mary cuffed him on the shoulder. "If you're not careful it will be a pile of goat droppings or a jug of ginger urine tea."

They strolled around the barn just as a silver car pulled alongside the broken part of the fence and parked. Dat had temporarily secured the chain-link fence upright with some rope so the goats couldn't escape the yard, but the man who got out of the car had no trouble hopping over the leaning fence and into their yard. It was quite rude how he just came onto their property as if he had a right to be there. In the last two weeks, over a dozen people had taken the same liberties on their farm in pursuit of an autograph from Clay Markham.

Clay heaved a sigh. "I'm sorry, Mary. We're going to have to hang a NO TRESPASSING sign."

"Dat thinks NO TRESPASSING signs are unfriendly."

"Better than this parade of unwelcome guests. I don't mind the fans, but they're intruding on your family, and that's unacceptable."

The man wore a long tan coat and fancy leather shoes that wouldn't have much traction in the snow. Lord willing, he wouldn't slip and break a leg. They didn't need any more accidents on the farm. His hair was jet-black, his face round and youthful. He caught sight of Clay and waved his arm back and forth, as if Clay hadn't noticed him already.

"Oh," Clay groaned softly.

"What's wrong?"

"Leif McIntire. He's a writer for *Pro Day* sports magazine. He's the new guy, and he's trying to prove himself, but he's not making many friends in the locker room. He's nosy and rude and tenacious, like a bull in a china closet."

Mary couldn't swallow past the lump in her throat. She didn't know what "tenacious" meant, but Clay wasn't smiling, and he squared his shoulders as if preparing to be attacked. Leif McIntire barreled through the sagebrush and prickly thistle toward Clay as if he was afraid Clay would escape before he had a chance to talk to him.

Mary's heart lurched painfully in her chest. "I need to go inside," she whispered. As cowardly as it was to abandon Clay, she just couldn't face a bull in a china closet.

Clay didn't seem offended that she wanted to run away. "Yes, go. I'll deal with this."

The house was too far away. Mary turned

and ran to the barn as if someone was chasing her. Fluffy, Blue, and Smiley were huddling around the small space heater and munching on feed. They studied her in the dimness with their big eyes, curious as to why she'd joined them in their cozy corner. Mary stood near the open door, trying to calm her racing heart, ashamed that she was such a scaredy cat. Clay needed her, and here she was, cowering in the barn because she was too afraid to talk to a reporter.

"Clay," she heard Leif say. "You're a hard man to track down."

"Not that hard. You can always call my agent. In fact, it's preferrable. That way you won't unintentionally intrude on my personal time." Clay never ceased to astound her. His voice was friendly and casual, as if he was talking to a fan instead of a bull in a china closet. It seemed nothing ever frightened him or ruffled his feathers.

"I called your agent, and he told me you were on vacation," Leif said. "I had to come down and see this hot tourist spot for myself."

"Well, now you've seen it. Have a nice trip back."

Mary growled to herself. It wasn't polite to eavesdrop, but now she was stuck in the barn until the reporter left. Lord willing, it would be a short conversation, but she didn't hold out a lot of hope. Clay might not like the reporter, but Clay was friendly, and he could talk for hours about baseball. Mary might be here for a while.

"I'm sorry about your head. They say you were at the hospital a couple of weeks ago getting stitches. Can you confirm that?"

"It sounds like you have the information you need. See you soon, Leif." She heard Clay's steps moving closer.

"They say you crashed into this barn and totaled your car," the reporter said. "Were you drunk? Or high?"

Clay stopped in his tracks. "If you want an interview, call my agent and we can set up a time that's convenient for me."

"But this is a hot story, Clay. It will cool down in a few days, and I'll never get traction."

Clay's tone was a little less friendly. "It's not much of a story, Leif, and I'm not in the mood to tell it. But if you want the details, talk to Haley Thorpe at the *County Bugle.* I gave her a short interview."

"Come on, Clay. People want to know why you've stopped showing up at parties and started hanging out with the Amish."

Clay laughed, but Mary could tell he was forcing it. "I didn't know you were writing for the gossip column now."

"This is a sports story, like it or not. Are you playing out some weird fantasy with that Amish girl? Or is she just an easy roll in the hay, no pun intended?"

Mary caught her breath. He was talking about her! In spite of the cold, searing heat crept up her neck.

Clay's voice got soft and low and very unfriendly. "You print anything like that, McIntire, and I'll sue you and your magazine so fast, your head will spin."

"So you're saying I'm getting a little too close to the truth?"

Mary sidled forward to hear Clay's next words. "What you're getting close to is a complete blackout from the entire team. No interviews, no access to the locker room, no VIP treatment. Maybe think about that before you provoke me."

"Don't try that, Clay. I'll just report that you don't believe in freedom of the press. Besides, you don't hold the sway with the team that you used to. They say you're washed-up. They say you have shoulder problems."

"*They* sound like *they* know a lot more about me than I do. Why don't you go talk to *them* and leave me alone?"

"Be straight with me, Clay. What about

Gwen? What would she tell me about your fetishes?"

There was that name again. Clay's old girlfriend. Mary pressed her lips together and ignored the pinprick to her heart.

"I'd like to say it was nice to see you again, Leif, but I'd never lie to a reporter. Have a safe trip back." She heard Clay turn and saw him pass by the barn door on his way to the house. *Ach, du lieva!* He hadn't seen her run into the barn. He must have thought she was in the house.

Should she run after him, or would that rude reporter catch her before she could escape?

"Can I ask you some questions?" Leif McIntire strolled into the barn and stepped right into Mary's personal space.

Mary caught her breath, took a step back, and almost fell over when her foot met with one of Pepper's squeaky toys. The goats started bleating wildly, and Mary reached out and grabbed a post to steady herself. Cousin Peter's scowling face flashed in her mind, and it was all she could do to keep from collapsing to the ground.

Leif held up his hands and gave her what he must have thought looked like a smile. All she saw were fangs and red glowing eyes. "Don't be afraid. I'm just interested in how you know Clay Markham. Are you two dating?"

He kept inching toward her, and Mary released her hold on the post and backed away. Her heart was thumping, and she couldn't get a *gute* breath to save her life. She was desperate to run into the house, but she would have to run past Leif to get there. *Ach,* how long would it take Clay to realize she wasn't in the house?

"Wouldn't you like your name to be in a magazine? You'll be famous."

In what must have been a blessing from Gotte, Apple the goat trotted into the barn and jumped up on Leif, propping her hooves on his thighs and getting mud and manure on his nicely-pleated coat. Never wanting to miss out on the fun, Smiley, Blue, and Fluffy surrounded Leif, in turns nibbling on his coat, jumping up and down playfully, and bleating as if they were singing goat songs in a choir. The noise was deafening, but Mary had never heard a more beautiful sound.

Leif raised his hands high above his head and turned in a complete circle, trying to find a way around the goats and out of the barn. "Go away," he said, nudging Fluffy with his knee. Fluffy was persistent, and she stamped a dirty hoof mark on Leif's nice brown shoes.

Pepper raced into the barn, baring his teeth and barking ferociously with Clay close behind. Mary had never seen Pepper or Clay so angry. The fire in Clay's eyes scared Mary for a second until she remembered Clay was on her side. Then she panicked thinking of what Clay might do to Leif with that kind of anger.

"Leif," Clay yelled. "So help me, if you don't get out of here right now, I'll let this dog tear your throat out."

It was a horrifying, fierce threat, and Leif seemed to resent it. "Never threaten a reporter, Clay. It will come back to bite you, big time."

"This dog will come back to bite you, big time, if you don't get out of here."

Leif found an opening when the goats trotted away to say hello to Clay. Leif skidded on something brown and fresh on the floor but kept his balance as he ran out of the barn.

Clay had no coat or hat or shoes. In his stocking feet, he followed Leif out of the barn. Pepper was close behind, barking as if Leif's pants were on fire. Mary followed Clay and Pepper to make sure no one was planning to throw any punches, and the goats trailed behind her. All seven of them watched Leif climb into his car and drive away. He might have left a little rubber on the road on the way out of town.

Pepper barked one more time for *gute* measure, but he was all bark and no bite, thank Derr Herr.

Clay took her breath away when he threw his arms around her and pulled her to his chest. "Oh, Mary, I'm so sorry. Are you okay? I was so focused on Leif that I thought you'd gone into the house. I'm so sorry."

Surprisingly, Mary's anxiety had all but disappeared, replaced by an unexpected sense of elation. She buried her face in his neck and willed her heart to slow down. "*Ach.* What a horrible man." She thought of Fluffy with a smug grin on her face, stomping on Leif's foot with her hoof, and she started to giggle. The first giggle came out like a cough, and then Mary completely lost control.

Clay nudged her away to look in her face. "I'm so sorry, Mary." The concern on his face turned to puzzlement and then relief. "Shoot, Mary. I thought you were crying."

She laughed so hard, she couldn't talk for a full minute. "*Ach,* bless those goats. They truly do have FOMO."

Clay patted Smiley and Blue on the tops of their heads and made kissing noises with his mouth. "Good girls." He squatted and gave Fluffy some extra attention. "You didn't tell me they were attack goats."

Mary grinned and pressed her palm to her chest. "I didn't know until this moment. They've never had a reason to protect our farm before."

Pepper licked Clay's face, and Clay gave Pepper a big hug. "Good dog. I'm going to bring you some primo doggie treats. You deserve them."

Joanna opened the back door and stuck her head out. "What's going on out here? It sounded like Pepper was chasing prairie dogs. Clay, where's your coat? And your boots?" Joanna ducked back into the house and shut the door without waiting for an answer. It was altogether too cold to be out chitchatting.

Clay lifted one foot. His stocking had a huge hole in the bottom of it. "So much for that pair of socks. I guess it's okay. They never fit very well."

Mary grabbed his elbow. "Let's get in the house before your feet freeze off."

"I'm real sorry. I thought you'd gone into the house, so I just strolled into the kitchen. I took all my winter gear off and left my boots on the rug. You weren't in the kitchen, and I wandered all around the house calling your name. That's when it hit me like a ton of bricks. Pepper was jumping up and down at the back door, and I didn't want to waste time putting on my boots, so I tore out here in my stocking feet." He wrapped his arms around himself. "Um, yes, let's go in the house. It's like ten degrees out here."

"Twenty-seven," Mary said.

"It feels like ten." He rubbed his hands up and down his arms. "I guess I'm not a hardy country boy yet."

"You grew up on a farm."

"Yeah, but it's been a lot of years since I got my hands dirty."

Pepper led the way. Mary herded Clay into the kitchen and made him sit down at the table. Joanna flung the dishtowel over her shoulder. "My floor. My floor. *Ach,* I just mopped! Pepper, get down from that chair."

Mary got out of her winter clothes and hung her coat by the door. Clay peeled off his stockings while Mary set the teapot on the stove to boil. "Hot chocolate, coffee, or tea?"

"Hot chocolate, please, but you really don't have to. I can make my own."

"Of course I have to. You saved me from that awful man and did it in your stocking feet."

Clay cupped his fingers around his neck and grimaced. "Pepper and the goats deserve the hot chocolate more than I do. The goats had things well in hand before I got there."

Mary smiled at the memory. "Yes, they did."

Joanna propped her hands on her hips. "You're going to catch your death of cold, Clay. I'll go fetch a blanket and some clean socks from Dat's drawer." She marched out of the room with Pepper close behind.

Clay massaged his icy foot. "I'm real sorry about that, Mary. He has no right to bother you and your family like that."

"He was quite unpleasant. At least most of the people who come looking for you are nice. Your fans are sometimes pushy, but they're usually polite."

Clay's frown etched itself into his face. "Reporters as a whole are a fairly nice group of people, but some reporters have gotten too cocky. They think they have all the power because if you push back on them, they'll print downright nasty things about you, or flood an article with rumors and speculation and innuendo. It's disgusting and unfair."

"What does innuendo mean?"

Clay took a deep breath and leaned back.

"They say stuff like: 'This rumor we've heard might be true, but Clay Markham isn't talking, so we don't really know if it's true or not. Why doesn't he want to talk about it? What is he hiding?' They make you sound guilty without giving any facts or having to take any responsibility."

"That's exactly what he was doing. Like when he asked you very inappropriate and personal questions about you and me."

Clay couldn't have looked more unhappy. "You heard that."

Mary nodded.

He turned his face away from her. "I'm hurting you and your family by being here."

"What do you mean?"

"How could I have been so selfish? All you folks want is to be left alone, and strangers traipse on and off your property almost every day because of me. Your dad winces every time I open my mouth, and Ada glares at me like she suspects I'm trying to corrupt the whole family. Then a reporter trespasses where he's not welcome, scares you, and makes some disgusting assumptions about us." He scrubbed his hand down the side of his face. "I brought this on all of you. I need to write your dad a check and get out of town. I'm nothing but trouble."

Mary couldn't allow Clay to leave. The

thought made her ill. The sun would never shine again if Clay was gone. "I don't want you to go."

The light behind his eyes faded to darkness. "I hate this, Mary. I just hate it, but for your sake, I have to go."

"Please, don't." She flinched when the tea kettle whistled. She pulled it off the heat. "You can't go." She poured the hot water into a mug and then stirred in some cocoa mix while she grasped for any reason to keep him here. "The work isn't halfway done, and you know Dat won't take your money. You won't learn any lessons if you abandon us like that."

He studied her face, his eyes two pools of longing. "You don't understand, Mary."

"I understand well enough. That reporter scared me to death. That doesn't mean you should leave."

"But . . ." He frowned. "You don't want me to go?"

"No," she whispered, handing him his hot chocolate.

"What about the horrible things Leif said?"

"The Amish have withstood persecution for hundreds of years. This is nothing new."

"But you wouldn't have to withstand anything if I weren't around," he said.

Joanna came back, draped a blanket around Clay's shoulders, and handed him a pair of Dat's stockings.

He gave her a pale smile. "Thanks."

Joanna's gaze flicked between Mary and Clay. "I think Pepper and I should go check on the goats and make sure they're okay." She quickly put on her coat, bonnet, and boots and practically ran out the back door with Pepper in tow. Joanna was a *gute* soul, very perceptive. Mary adored her.

Mary made herself some cocoa and sat next to Clay at the table. "Dat only winces because he's used to doing things one way. He's set in his ways, and getting him to accept a new idea is like trying to stop the river with your arm. Ada thinks she's in charge of the farm and gets touchy because she wants to protect us. She has a *gute* heart. It will take her some time to warm up to you, but when she does, she will be your surest defender and best friend. Next to Dat, you are Pepper's favorite human. He would do anything for you, even charge into a barn to help you fight reporters. And don't even get me started with the goats. They like you better than they like me, and I'm the one who feeds them." She took a sip of the hot chocolate. She hadn't put enough cocoa in, and it was very weak. She wouldn't stop to fix it. "And what about Esther? She's sold more quilts in the last two weeks than she usually sells the whole summer. You're good for business, and you do dishes."

His lips twitched. "I'm glad I can be of service."

"Esther would probably adopt you if you didn't already have family. She adores you."

Clay put down his mug and wrapped his fingers around Mary's wrist. "Oh, my sweet Mary, I'm mostly concerned about you."

My sweet Mary?

She cleared her throat and tucked that endearment away for another day. Now was not the time to get distracted. "I certainly haven't been very brave or very loyal."

He shook his head slowly, never taking his eyes from her face. "I like you just the way you are."

"I tend to get anxious and upset over little things, but that's my problem, not yours." It wasn't Clay's fault at all. It was Peter's.

"I caused the problem. Of course it's my problem, and my leaving is the perfect solution."

"What if that reporter comes back and you're gone? I don't know if Fluffy and Pepper can fend off another attack without you."

Clay chuckled. "Fluffy and Pepper could take on the New York Yankees if they had to." His eyes filled with moisture. She'd never seen him so close to crying. The emotion took her by surprise. "You have no idea how much your friendship has meant to me."

A ribbon of warmth curled up her spine. "Then why are you still talking about leaving? No one, including Ada, wants you to go. If you're leaving for my sake, don't you think it should be my decision?"

He pressed his fingers to his forehead. "I suppose you're right. What do you want me to do?"

"You already know."

His smile was sad and hopeful at the same time. "Are you sure? I can give you the Thanksgiving weekend to think it over. I'll understand if you change your mind."

"I'm not going to change my mind."

He pulled the blanket tighter around his broad shoulders and winced slightly. "You're a very kind person, Mary, and I know that you would put what I want over what you truly want just to make me happy. But I have to let go of my selfishness. Please take the weekend to think about what would be best for you and your family. I'll be gone, and you might find you like it much better without me in your life."

Mary nodded, but she knew she wouldn't need the weekend to decide. She didn't even need one second.

She never wanted a life without Clay in it.

Dread filled her heart. She was going to lose him one way or another, sooner or later.

Chapter 7

Mary paced back and forth in front of the window with both eyes on the highway. Cathy and Esther were late, and everything, everything was going to be ruined if they didn't get here immediately. Joanna, Ada, and Beth sat on the couch comparing the quilt blocks they'd made, but how could Mary think about quilting at a time like this?

Mary let out a breath she'd been holding for about three days when Cathy Larsen's van rolled down the road and stopped in front of the house. Mary's coat was already on. In an effort to save time, she ran outside and opened the back passenger door before Esther had even unbuckled her seatbelt. "Hi, Esther. Hi, Cathy," Mary said as she took Levi Junior out of his car seat and carried him quickly to the house. Lord willing, Esther and Cathy would get the message she was in a hurry.

She went into the house and glanced out the window again. Esther and Cathy hadn't even gotten out of the van yet. *Ach!* Didn't they know this was an emergency?

She slid Junior out of his coat and handed him to Ada. Even though Ada was very attached to cleanliness, she loved babies, even when they spit up or needed a diaper change. Ada exclaimed joyfully when Mary set Junior in her lap, and she immediately began playing with the baby's chubby little fingers.

Esther and Cathy finally made their way to the house with little Winnie beside her mother, skipping through the snow. Mary threw open the door to let them in.

"Mary," Beth scolded. "You're letting out all the warm air. Shut the door."

Mary didn't care. It would take Esther and Cathy less time to walk into the house if there was plenty of space for them to walk.

Cathy trudged into the great room with her bright pink parka and yellow beanie and her purse the size of a feed bag. She stuffed her hand into her coat pocket, pulled out her phone, and looked at her screen. "So, Miss Mary, we are here, as you requested. What is the big emergency?"

As soon as she got Clay's letter this morning, Mary had raced to the neighbor's house, borrowed their cell phone, and sent Cathy a text: THIS IS MARY YODER. PLEASE COME TO OUR HOUSE BEFORE NOON TODAY. IT'S AN EMERGENCY.

WE'LL BE THERE AT 11:30, Cathy had replied.

It was 11:45, almost too late.

Mary was so eager, she actually tugged Cathy's coat off her back and hung it on the hook next to the door. Then she helped Winnie off with her coat and bonnet and hung them next to Cathy's. Esther's lips twitched in amusement as she slowly and deliberately took off her coat and hung it next to Winnie's. Was that a carrot behind her ear or a Cheeto? "You seem to be in a big hurry this morning."

Mary took the wadded-up letter from her pocket, smoothed it out, and handed it to Cathy. "I got this letter from Clay this morning, and I can't make heads or tails of it."

Cathy gazed at the letter, sat down in the rocker, and casually rummaged through her large bag. Mary thought she might scream. Cathy pulled a pair of glasses from the depths of her bag and put them on. "Much better," she said, looking over the rims of her glasses. "Do you mind if I read this out loud?"

Mary shook her head. "I've already read it to them."

Joanna smoothed her hand over the Sugar Bowl quilt block that sat in her lap. "None of us can make it out."

Cathy straightened and began reading while all Mary could do was wring her hands. *"Dear Mary, I meant what I said. If you don't want me to come back, there are no hard feelings. I know how difficult I've made your life."*

"I don't mind," Esther said. "He's very pleasant to have around, and my quilts are selling like hotcakes."

Cathy looked up. "He's trying to be noble, bless his heart." She continued reading. *"I know how hard my being there has been on you, your family, and Esther, even Cathy."* Cathy grunted. "Clay is high maintenance, but I'll admit that car chase was fun."

"Car chase?" Ada said.

"Somebody followed us home from the hospital, and I tried to lose them before we got to Esther's. It got my heart racing."

Mary remembered that day a little differently, but if it made Cathy happy to think she was in a car chase, who was Mary to ruin her memories? "Keep reading," she prompted gently. There was no time for Cathy to lose focus.

Cathy adjusted her glasses and studied Clay's letter. *"Mary, I would do anything to make you happy. My plane gets in at ten on Monday morning. I plan to drive straight to your house, but I have to be sure if you want me to come back tie a yellow ribbon around your mailbox if you don't want me to come back, don't."* Cathy stared at the letter in puzzlement. "He has several flagrant punctuation errors."

Mary groaned in frustration. "Yes! I don't know what to do. Do I tie a ribbon around the mailbox if I want him to come back or do I tie a ribbon if I *don't* want him to come back? It's all so confusing, and I don't want to get it wrong. I just can't get it wrong."

Cathy and Esther and Mary's *schwesteren* pinned their eyes to her face. "We're in big trouble," Ada said.

Beth grabbed Joanna's hand, and her eyes filled with pity. "Big trouble."

Why were they all staring at her? "Of course we're in big trouble. What if we can't figure out what Clay wants me to do? What if he never comes back?"

Cathy narrowed her eyes in Mary's direction. "First of all, the most important question. Mary, what do you want? Do you want

Clay to come back or quit pestering you?"

"I want him to come back, of course."

Ada pressed her lips together. "Of course. But what if the rest of us don't want him to come back?"

Joanna reached out and patted Ada on the leg. Hard. It sounded more like a slap. "Don't be silly, Ada. We all want him to come back. We adore Clay Markham."

Ada shook her head. "It will only lead to heartache."

Mary didn't want to think about heartache or what might happen a month or year from now. She couldn't waste the time or the anxious energy on that thought. "Cathy, you're an Englischer. Can you understand his note?"

"Despite the punctuation errors, it's very clear what he wants you to do."

Mary's heart skipped a beat. "It is?"

Cathy folded Clay's letter in her lap and leaned back in her chair. "It's exactly the type of thing Clay would do. He seems like a pretty romantic guy, even though there's something tragic about his devotion." She huffed out a breath. "He's not very original, but I guess I can give him credit for the grand gesture."

Mary had lost Cathy somewhere after "tragic devotion." She was wasting a lot of words and a lot of time. "So what do I need to do?"

Cathy rocked back and forth. "I can explain everything with a story."

Oh, dear.

"There once was this guy who got sent to prison for three years, and before he got out, he wrote his wife this long letter about how he was getting out of prison, and if she wanted him to come home, she was supposed to tie a yellow ribbon around the oak tree in their front yard. But if she didn't love him anymore, he told her not to tie anything around the tree, and he'd stay on the bus and go away forever. I never understood why he didn't say, 'If you don't want me to come back, tie a black ribbon around the tree.' That way, if there was no ribbon, he would have known that she didn't get his message." Cathy paused as if deep in thought. "That never made sense to me. Anyway, the guy is on the bus, and they pass his house, and everybody starts cheering because there are a hundred yellow ribbons tied around the oak tree instead of just one. He takes it as a message that she wants him to come home real bad. I always wondered how he could count to a hundred so fast. It's literally the very next line in the song."

Mary was breathless with emotion. She

wanted Clay back real bad. She had to go tie yellow ribbons around the whole farm immediately. She strode to the chair and threw her arms around Cathy. "Thank you, a million times over."

Cathy nudged Mary away. "I'm not much for romance, but I do like a good prison story."

"I'm going to tie ribbons around everything, especially at the front of the house so Clay will see when he drives up. But we've got to hurry. He'll be here soon." Mary's excitement deflated like a balloon. "Oh, no. I don't have any yellow ribbon, and there's no time to go buy some."

Ada sighed as if her patience had just run out. "There is almost a whole bolt of yellow fabric in the closet. It's a horrible waste, but you could cut it into strips and make your own ribbon. Clay will never know the difference."

Mary squealed in delight. "Ada, I love you so much."

Ada kissed the baby while still maintaining her sour expression. "Don't say I never did anything for you."

Joanna jumped from the couch. "We're all going to help you make and tie ribbon, aren't we, Ada?"

Ada narrowed her eyes at Joanna. "I was

hoping to talk about our sampler quilt while Esther and Cathy are here."

Joanna gave Ada an irritated smile. "We can talk about our quilt after the ribbons are tied."

Joanna was such a dear. Mary loved her desperately.

The six of them spent the next hour cutting yellow fabric into strips and then tying them around the fence posts, the mailbox, the one tree on their property, the street sign, and the animals. By the time they were finished, Smiley, Blue, Fluffy, and Apple each had a darling bow around their necks. Even Pepper submitted to a yellow bandana. Mary wanted to be absolutely sure Clay knew he was welcome, so she found an unused piece of plywood in the barn and painted a message on it:

COME BACK, CLAY!

If that didn't catch his attention, she didn't know what would.

Once everything was tied up, they actually had time to sit in the great room and talk about their sampler quilt for Mammi Beulah. Mary hadn't made much progress on her Drunkard's Path quilt blocks, but she'd been so busy with Clay, she hadn't taken much time to work on it. It was a little unnerving that she might be living the quilt block instead of making it.

Mary deliberately chose a chair facing the window so she would be able to see the minute Clay pulled up. If by chance he didn't understand the message, she could race outside before he drove away and assure him she wanted him to come back.

Her heart leapt into her throat when his ugly truck pulled behind Cathy's van. She dropped the fabric in her hand, threw on her coat, and ran out the door. Clay was just getting out of his truck, and she was sorely tempted to throw herself into his arms. It wouldn't be proper, especially with her *schwesteren* watching from the window, so she stopped a few feet from him and smiled. "Welcome back," she said.

Pepper stole Mary's hug. He sprinted around the side of the house, his yellow bandana flapping in the wind, and launched himself into Clay's arms. Clay laughed, knelt down, and sank his face into Pepper's fur. "You rowdy dog. Have you been taking care of the family while I've been away? Have you been behaving yourself?"

Clay looked up at Mary, and his expression took her breath away. She had never seen him so happy. All the joy in the world looked as if it had come together on his face. "Hello, Mary." He fingered the bandana tied around Pepper's neck. "I guess this means you want me back."

"You don't need to guess. For sure and certain, that's what it means."

He sniffed and blinked some moisture from his eyes. "It was kind of a cheesy idea, but it just came to me on the way out of town. I mailed the letter right before I left Colorado Springs for Indiana. I'm glad you got it in time."

Just barely.

The goats were never very far behind Pepper. All four of them trotted around the corner of the house and made a beeline for Clay. Clay gave each of them a pat and a nuzzle before standing up and glancing toward the house. "Everybody's watching from that window, aren't they?"

"Everyone but my *dat.* He's getting his hair cut."

"I didn't know Amish got their hair cut."

"The men do. It wouldn't be seemly for them to wear their hair to their shoulders."

"I guess not, but I would think your dad would cut his own hair. He's pretty cheap." His eyes sparkled when he said it, so she wasn't offended. Besides, Dat *was* cheap. The Amish considered it a virtue.

"He goes to his friend's house. His friend cuts Dat's hair, and Dat cuts his hair."

Clay laughed. "That makes sense. So what have you been doing while I've been away?"

Mostly pining for Clay. "I popped John Miller's shoulder back into its socket after he dislocated it in a touch football game. And Erda Sensenig needed two little stitches after slicing her finger when she was making stuffing."

Clay opened his mouth in mock indignation. "You refused to give me stitches."

"I didn't want to make a mistake and mar that beautiful face of yours."

He touched the injured spot on his forehead. "Very funny." He tapped on his truck. "I brought you a coming home present."

"Clay, you don't need to buy me presents."

"I don't need to, but it makes me happy. Besides, this one is for the whole family." He reached into the truck bed and pulled out a small paint can.

"Paint?"

He nodded. "Purple paint. Have you ever heard of the purple paint law?"

"Nae."

"You paint your tree or your fence post or your mailbox, and it's just like putting up a NO TRESPASSING sign on your property. At least, that's how it works in Indiana." He nudged Mary with his elbow. "Your dad might think a NO TRESPASSING sign is unfriendly, but purple paint is about as friendly as you can get."

Mary giggled. "My *dat* will probably think it's too fancy, but it wouldn't hurt to ask. Purple is my favorite color."

"It is? Wow, how lucky could I get, especially since I wear a lot of purple during baseball season." He glanced toward the house again. "Are they still looking?"

"No doubt."

His eyes flashed with amusement. "I'd love to see how the barn has been doing since I've been gone."

Her heart did a little dance. "I tied a ribbon around the shaft of the buggy."

"Well, then. Let's go see it."

They strolled to the back of the house. Mary made sure to go slowly so her *schwesteren* wouldn't wonder why she was so eager. As soon as they were out of sight of the window, Clay took her hand in his. "Is this okay?"

Mary nodded, her face as warm as a potbelly stove.

"Your fingers are like ice. Let's go sit by the heater."

A small solar-powered space heater sat in

the corner of the barn where the goats slept. Goats could handle cold temperatures well, but it got so cold in Byler, and Mary couldn't stand the thought of the goats living in the cold, dark barn in the middle of winter. Clay pulled a bale of hay closer to the heater, and the two of them sat down on it. They had to get close to sit on the bale, and that was just the way Mary liked it.

They both leaned forward and warmed their hands by the space heater. "Did you have a nice Thanksgiving?" Clay asked. "I wish I could have been here."

"I wish that too. Thanksgiving is a very meaningful holiday for the Amish. Our people were early martyrs for the faith in Switzerland. They came to America to avoid religious persecution. This land literally saved their lives."

"What did you have for dinner?"

"*Ach,* all the normal things. Turkey, potatoes, buttered noodles."

He reached over and squeezed her hand. "I love buttered noodles."

"Four kinds of pies, stuffing, deviled eggs, sweet potato casserole."

Clay nodded. "My sisters are good cooks. I mostly stayed out of their way, but they did assign me to make the stuffing."

Mary widened her eyes. "Stuffing is a big job. How did it turn out?"

He chuckled. "Not too big a job. My sisters wouldn't trust me with anything too big. It was stuffing from a box, and it was delicious but a little dry. My main assignment was to play with the nieces."

Mary loved the spark that appeared in Clay's eyes when he talked about his nieces. "We don't have any other family in Colorado, so Esther and her family came here, plus her *schwester* Ivy and Ivy's family."

"I like Ivy," Clay said. "She's been to Esther's house twice since I've been here. She's more unreserved than most Amish women, but Esther says she's found her place in the community and everyone likes her. Esther says Ivy left the church for a time."

Mary nodded. "It's called 'jumping the fence' when an Amish person leaves the community. It's always a great tragedy but also a great joy when someone returns to the church."

Clay eyed her doubtfully. "Esther told me that Winnie is Ivy's daughter but that Esther adopted her."

"I didn't know Ivy back then, but Cathy says Ivy used to be the most unlikeable person in Colorado, and now Cathy likes

Ivy better than just about anybody. From what I've heard, Ivy has really changed, mostly because of Esther."

Clay propped his hands on his knees, laced his fingers together, and stared into the space heater. "That's what love can do. It changes you. Since Ivy has changed, do you think she should have kept Winnie and not given her away to Esther?"

"*Nae,* Winnie has a *gute* home with Levi and Esther. She's much better off."

Clay frowned. "Even if Ivy is her real mother?"

"Even then. Ivy did what was best for her baby. There's no greater love than that."

Clay fell silent. What was he thinking?

She rested her head on his shoulder. "How was your Thanksgiving?"

"I wish I could have been here, but it was good to go away. I wanted you to have time to reconsider."

"I didn't need time to reconsider."

"I love being with my siblings, though Kirk's self-centeredness makes my teeth hurt."

Mary tilted her head to one side. "What do you mean?"

"All he can talk about is himself and medical school and how much smarter he is than the other students. I really don't mind it, though. I love Kirk. He's my brother, and I hope he'll learn a lot about humility when he starts practicing. My dad adores Kirk and hangs on every word that comes out of his mouth. I'm not proud of it, but I guess I'm a little jealous. My dad spent half of Thanksgiving dinner talking about how proud he was of Kirk for actually making something of himself. He spent the other half lecturing me about my poor performance in the last playoff game."

"You know your true fans don't hold that against you."

He glanced at Mary. "That counts my dad out. He's more of a critic than a fan. I sometimes feel like a little kid still fighting for my dad's approval."

"I'm sorry."

He sighed. "You would think I'd be over it by now. I'm thirty-four years old, and I still have hang-ups about my childhood. It's sort of pathetic."

"Don't say that. Emotions can run deep. My *mammi* always says that pain has a long shelf life, like a bottle of home-canned peaches."

Clay's mouth curled at the corners. "My mom has canned fruit in the root cellar that's been there since the Reagan administration." He propped his chin in his hand.

"Amy and I have a joke. The way Dad sees it, Kirk can't do anything wrong, Amy can't do anything right, and I can't do anything at all. Ashlyn kind of got lost in the middle. That's how he always saw us."

"Do you think he still sees you that way?"

"I don't know. He was never happy about my playing baseball until I got a scholarship to play in college. But then I quit school when they drafted me, and he let me know how disappointed he was that I didn't finish my degree. He sort of approves of me now that I'm famous and making lots of money, but if . . . if that ever changes, it will just confirm everything he's always believed about me."

She slipped her hand in his. "Well, that's not what I think of you, and it certainly isn't what most people think. What about Amy? Did she have it worse than you?"

"Amy was above it all. I don't know how she does it. She fought against Dad's expectations and never seemed to let him hold her back. When he criticized her for being ambitious, she went to law school. When he said she wasn't ambitious enough, she quit trying for partner in her law firm and stepped away from her job to be a stay-at-home mom. When he found fault with her pie crust, she laughed and announced he didn't have to eat her pie if he didn't want to. He ate two more pieces."

"Maybe she's learned how not to care."

He drew his brows together. "She's figured out how to let go of the power he has to hurt her feelings. In high school, he wanted her to do 4-H, but she hated the farm. He didn't talk to her for three weeks when she joined the choir. His silent treatment didn't bother her. In fact, she was happy about it. She figured if he wasn't talking to her, at least he wasn't criticizing her. That kind of treatment would have crushed me. It did crush me, and his disapproval still hurts. I wish I could let it go like Amy can."

"You're the oldest son. There are simply more expectations put on you. It's natural to want to make your *dat* proud." Mary nudged him with her shoulder. "You might not believe it, but for sure and certain, your *dat* is proud of you. Maybe he doesn't know how to say it. And, though I can't believe it, maybe he *does* think you're good for nothing. If that's true, then we should pity him, because he's missing out on one of the greatest relationships of his life. Everyone should be lucky enough to know Clay Markham. He is an extraordinary person."

Clay gazed into her eyes and smiled. "You always know how to make me feel better, whether it's giving me a pep talk, saving my life, or making me a glass of ginger urine tea."

Mary laughed. "I didn't save your life, and that tea is one of my best recipes. Don't make fun of it, or I'll never make it for you again."

"I'd like to say I'm disappointed, but it would be a lie." Pepper and the goats sauntered into the barn, and Pepper licked Clay's hand. Clay patted Pepper on the head. "I'm starting on the new chain-link fence tomorrow. They're coming to deliver the supplies first thing in the morning."

"It's a wonderful cold time to be putting up a fence."

He grimaced. "I know, but I've got to look busy, or your *dat* won't let me hang around."

"How long will the fence take?"

"Maybe a week." He grinned mischievously. "If I go really slow, I can probably stretch it to two weeks."

"When you're done with the fence, maybe you could help Dat finish all his projects inside the house before you start on the barn."

His ears perked up at that idea. "Like what in the house?"

"Three steps creak something wonderful.

The stair railing needs to be painted. The kitchen table wobbles, the upstairs shower needs caulking, the downstairs toilet hisses. I'm sure Ada could find ten or eleven other things for you to do."

His smile was warmer than the space heater. "It sounds wonderful."

Mary's heart fluttered like a thousand happy butterflies. "By the time you're done, it will be Christmas. You can come caroling with us to the shut-ins, and there's always a delightful Christmas program at the school."

"I'm in for all of it, but I must warn you that I don't sing, so don't be disappointed by my caroling skills." He stood up. "We should get you inside. Your teeth are chattering."

Were they? She hadn't noticed with the fire blazing brightly inside her chest. "We should. Esther still needs to approve my quilt blocks."

Clay pulled her to her feet. "There's one more thing. I have to go see a doctor in Denver the week before Christmas, but I'll only be gone one day. I just wanted you to know so you won't plan any Christmas parties without me."

"Good to know. No Christmas parties without Clay."

"One more thing. It would be a little bit

of a drive, but what would you think about coming with me to the children's hospital in Aurora for a visit?"

Mary caught her bottom lip between her teeth. "Will there be reporters?"

"Maybe not, if I don't tell anyone I'm coming."

"Can I think about it?"

An unreadable emotion traveled across his face. "Of course. Only if you feel comfortable."

She was such a scaredy cat, but Clay was incredibly understanding. He knew how terrifying her encounter with Leif McIntire had been.

They walked out of the barn. "There's one more thing," Clay said.

She raised her eyebrows. "How many more things are there?"

He chuckled. "Just one more." He stopped walking and pinned her with an intense gaze. "I will never let anything or anyone hurt you."

"I know," she said.

The only risk of hurt was to her own heart, and she had no one to blame but herself.

Chapter 8

Mary's hands felt like icicles. It was always this way milking goats in the winter, but she never got used to it. Her fingers ached constantly from November to March every year. But she wouldn't trade the feeling. She loved the goats, and stiffness was the price she paid for goat's milk and cheese the family could sell to supplement their income. Joanna was not only the best baker in the valley, but she was also an excellent cheesemaker. Everybody helped when Joanna made cheese, but Joanna was always in charge, and her cheese was excellent. A fancy restaurant in Alamosa wanted every bit of goat cheese they made.

Mary put the lid on the milking bucket and slid the rope from Fluffy's legs, which she'd loosely tied there to keep Fluffy from stepping into the milk bucket. "Good girl," she said, patting Fluffy's side. "Thanks for the milk." Fluffy hopped down from the milking stand, and Mary picked up the milking bucket. They'd be making cheese tomorrow for all the Christmas orders they needed to fulfill.

On her way to the house, Mary glanced toward the highway for about the tenth time. Clay had said he'd only be gone for one day, and he was supposed to have been back from Denver last night, and now it was almost dinner time, and he still wasn't back. She was getting a little concerned but also irritated at herself for being concerned. Clay had no obligation to tell her where he was going to be every hour of every day. If he wanted to spend a few days in Denver, he shouldn't have to check with her first or account for his time. He was just the guy who'd crashed into their barn and was working hard to fix the damage he'd done.

Mary pressed her lips together. She could tell herself that lie a thousand times, but it still wouldn't change the way she felt about him. Clay had become the most important person in her life, and she was going to implode when he finally finished his work and left the farm forever. Ada, who was annoyingly perceptive and unafraid to share her opinion no matter how badly it hurt, had come right out and told Mary that she was going to get her heart broken and that it would be better if she told Clay to leave and never come back.

Beth adored Clay, but she was always eager to point out how bad Mary was going to feel when he had to go back to Denver to play ball. Would he go back to his ex-girlfriend? Would he go back to drunk driving? Would he die in a car accident someday without Mary there to help him?

Even Joanna, who liked Clay the best, had her doubts. "*Ach,* Mary," she had said. "This is the road to heartache. Take care, dear *schwester.*"

Mary didn't want to think about what would happen after Clay finished fixing the barn. Most of the time, she did a wonderful-*gute* job of ignoring the problem altogether. What was the point of being sad over things that hadn't happened yet? One of Mamm's favorite sayings was, "Don't borrow trouble." Mary's heart was going to break eventually, and break into a million unfixable pieces, but for now, she was happier than she'd ever been, and worrying about future heartbreak only dimmed the happiness of the present.

December had been *wunderbarr,* and she didn't want to sully any of her memories with fear about what was going to happen. Two weeks ago, Joanna had made Yule Logs, and the family had gone caroling and taken the treats to the shut-ins and widows in the area. Yule Logs were made of thin chocolate sheet cake covered with frosting, then rolled up like a sleeping bag and decorated with icing and Christmas candies.

Clay had eagerly and cheerfully gone caroling with them to every house. Mary smiled to herself. He had told the truth about his singing voice. He wouldn't have been able to carry a tune if it had a handle, but his exuberant singing only made him more endearing. Most of the Englisch neighbors they'd visited knew who Clay was, and one of the widows had a picture of the whole Peaks team taped to her fridge with Clay standing smack dab in the middle of the back row. *Ach,* he was so handsome. The Englischers loved seeing Clay and talking about baseball and the team and Clay in particular. Clay was always so good-natured about the attention, even when Mrs. Clemens lectured him about pitching curveballs when he should have pitched fastballs every time. "That's your bread and butter, young man," she had said. "Don't let those pitching coaches tell you otherwise."

Clay had grinned. "I have to pitch what my manager calls or I'll get in trouble."

Three nights ago, Clay had paid Cathy to drive the whole family into Alamosa to see Christmas lights. Cathy drove them all over town, and they marveled at the clever light and yard displays. When they found a particularly *wunderbarr* house, Clay would ask Cathy to stop. He'd jump out of the van and knock at the door. When someone answered, Clay would hand them a giant chocolate bar and tell them they had been voted best Christmas lights display in the neighborhood.

Neither Mary nor her *schwesteren* dared get out of the van with him, but Clay didn't seem to mind going up to strangers' doors by himself and striking up a conversation. Cathy rolled down the window so they could hear Clay's conversation with whoever answered the door. Sometimes people recognized him and would ask for a picture. All were thrilled that passersby enjoyed their displays. Mary hadn't been able to stop smiling. Even Dat had liked that activity because he said it spread peace on earth and goodwill to the whole county.

That was who Clay was. He loved making people happy.

Mary had spent five glorious weeks with Clay. She would glean every moment of joy from the time she had left.

And stop worrying that he hadn't come back from Denver yet.

It was always easier said than done. That's why Mary glanced toward the highway again just in case Clay drove down the road at that moment. He didn't, and she retreated into the warm house before her fingers froze off.

She handed the milk bucket to Ada and took off her rubber boots and her winter gear while Ada strained the milk into the stainless steel pitcher. "We have enough to make cheese tomorrow, but I don't know if we'll have enough to fill all the orders."

Mary took off her bonnet and hung it on the hook. "I guess we'll do our best."

Ada sighed in exasperation and a bit of I-told-you-so superiority. "You're moping, Mary. I wish you wouldn't mope. How is it going to be when Clay leaves for good? Spring training starts in February."

"What do you know about spring training?"

Ada folded her arms. "Everything I need to know."

Mary picked up the milking bucket and rinsed it in the sink. "I'm twenty-eight years old, Ada. I know what I'm doing, and I choose to be happy now. Is that so wrong?"

To Mary's surprise, Ada stepped next to

her and put a firm arm around her shoulder. "I'm sorry, Mary." The tenderness in her voice was unexpected and unnerving. Mary blinked back some unwelcome tears. "I wasn't thrilled when Clay showed up, but I've grown very fond of him. He's helpful, sincere, and kind, but you know as well as I do that there's only one way this ends. He will move on and break your heart without even trying, then you'll mope around the house for the rest of your life."

Mary sniffed. "Maybe not the rest of my life."

"Lord willing." Ada took the milking bucket from Mary and dried it with a kitchen towel. "I don't try to be harsh on purpose, but if everybody just did what I wanted them to, they'd be much happier." She arched an eyebrow, and Mary laughed.

"*Jah,* I think that too sometimes."

"You do not," Ada protested. "You rarely share your opinion. You don't want to offend anybody."

"I don't like to argue."

"Sometimes I think you'd rather be part of the furniture than have to talk about hard things," Ada said.

"*Jah,* that is true."

Ada set down the milking bucket and gave Mary a hug. "For sure and certain, you haven't talked to Clay about this."

Mary sniffed back more tears. "For sure and certain."

Ada's eyes filled with compassion, with not a hint of the I-told-you-so smugness. "I always try to be realistic, Mary, and I'm sorry that I hurt your feelings, but I'm just looking out for my younger *schwester.*"

"You didn't hurt my feelings. Believe it or not, I've thought long and hard about the consequences of getting attached to Clay Markham."

"Not that I blame you. He's the most handsome man to come within ten miles of Byler in a decade, and he's kind and helpful. He's even sensitive, like a child who's been starved for affection and is trying to earn it one minute at a time."

Ada didn't know about Clay's father, but she had obviously still sensed the scars Clay carried. Mary slumped her shoulders. "He's so easy to love."

Ada's expression filled with pity. "Oh, Mary, I want to protect you, but I can see that it won't matter. You're too far gone to avoid a broken heart."

A wave of sorrow washed over Mary like water rushing down the river. "*Jah,* I am."

Ada moaned her sympathy, took Mary's hand, and pulled her to the table where they both sat. "What can I do to help?"

"There's nothing anyone can do." Mary grabbed a napkin from the holder on the table and blew her nose. "Except, I just want to be happy. In whatever time I have left with Clay, I just want to be happy and not think about what's coming."

Ada frowned and nodded. "You don't need your *schwester* scolding you every five minutes."

"It might help if you didn't say anything," Mary squeaked.

A smile slowly grew on Ada's face. "That took a lot of courage to say. I don't take correction very well."

"You never need to take correction. You're as near perfect as anyone can get."

"That's a thousand miles from the truth, and you know it. What can I do to help you be happy?"

"I'm worried about Clay. He had a doctor appointment yesterday, and he was supposed to be back last night."

Ada glanced at the clock on the wall. "Hmm. What's the worst that could have happened?"

Ada and Mary often played this game because Ada thought Mary worried too much, and it always made Mary feel better. Mary paused. Her worst fear was that Clay had stopped to visit Gwen, the ex-girlfriend, but she wasn't about to share that with Ada. "Maybe the doctor found some dread disease, and they had to operate immediately. He's languishing in the hospital and can't call me because they operated on his throat."

Ada grimaced. "That is definitely the worst that could have happened, but surely he would have gotten a message to you before surgery."

Mary liked to think that was true, even if Clay had to have an operation. "Maybe he ran out of gas, or his truck broke down?"

"It's very likely his truck broke down. That thing always has one foot in the grave. I wouldn't worry about that. Clay makes friends wherever he goes. He's probably got three complete strangers eagerly working on his truck to get it running again."

Mary's lips curled upward. "You're right. Everybody likes Clay. I'm sure he'll be fine."

Ada stood up, never one to be idle for more than a few seconds. "But will you be fine?"

"No pestering me, remember?"

Ada groaned. "Very well. No pestering you. You'll be fine. Clay will be fine. We'll all be fine."

They both jumped when someone

knocked loudly and insistently on the front door. Mary's heart leapt like a mule deer. "It's Clay!" She shot from the chair and ran to the front door. She deflated a bit when she opened to Esther with her two children and Cathy Larsen.

Cathy pushed her way into the house as if she owned it. *Ach, vell.* It was cold outside, and nobody wanted to stand out there for long. "Mary," Cathy said, "you really need to get a phone."

Esther, who had a plain, ordinary pencil behind her ear this afternoon, handed Levi Junior to Mary and took off her coat. "You know she can't justify that with the bishop, Cathy."

Cathy gave Esther a sour look. "Isn't the bishop your father-in-law? What's the point of having powerful relatives if you can't pull a few strings now and then?"

Esther laughed. "I have no idea what you mean by that, Cathy. My father-in-law doesn't bend the rules for anyone. And he's not that kind of a bishop. He doesn't just make commands that we have to follow. The whole *gmayna* has to agree to things."

Ada came from the kitchen and spread her arms wide. "Winnie! Come give Aunt Ada a hug. Would you like a Christmas cookie?"

Winnie tossed her coat on the floor and skipped into Ada's arms.

"Winnie," Esther said, "that's no way to treat your coat. Come and hang it up please."

Winnie pursed her lips and looked at Ada. Ada nodded sternly, and Winnie trudged back into the great room, picked up her coat, and hung it on one of the hooks. Then she turned and catapulted herself into Ada's arms, and they both disappeared into the kitchen.

"Save a Christmas cookie for me," Cathy called. "Hopefully, they're gluten free." After she tugged off her coat and hat, she fished through her giant purse and pulled out her phone. "If you had your own phone, I wouldn't have to be Clay's messenger."

Mary's heart beat double time. "Clay?"

"He sent me this text last night, but I wasn't about to get out of my pajamas to come over and show it to you." She studied her screen as if she'd never seen a phone before then swiped her finger across the screen a few times. "Here it is. *'Cathy, please tell Mary I need to stay in Denver one more night and that I'll be back tomorrow afternoon.'* " She glanced at Mary. "And then he thanks me profusely for delivering this message, even though he couldn't be sure I'd show it to you. He's very trusting. You're lucky I'm not in a contrary mood."

Mary exhaled a breath she felt like she'd been holding for hours. "Thank you, Cathy. You don't know how much that means to me."

"No need to gush. They're inconvenient, but Clay's texts help me stay current on the Amish gossip. There's more. *'Tell her I stopped off at the hospital.'* "

Mary felt as if she'd been beaned in the head with one of Clay's fastballs. "The hospital? What's wrong? Did he have surgery?"

Esther's eyes filled with concern. She took Levi Junior from Mary's arms. "You're pale as a sheet, Mary. *Cum,* sit down."

Mary let Esther lead her to the couch, but she kept her eyes on Cathy. "Is Clay okay?"

Cathy was gazing intently at her phone. "He's fine."

Mary tamped down her annoyance. Cathy wasn't trying to frighten her, and thank Derr Herr, she had driven all the way over here to deliver Clay's message. Mary should be grateful for that.

Cathy swiped her phone screen again. "I was lucky enough to be watching the news last night and recorded this on my phone. I didn't catch the whole thing, but as soon as

I heard Clay's name, I pushed record."

She sat next to Mary and held up her phone so Mary could see the screen. The image was a little blurry because it was Cathy's recording of her television set, but it was clear enough to see a reporter standing in front of a large brick building holding a microphone. *"We haven't seen much of Clay for weeks, but one of his fans spotted him at Children's Hospital Colorado this afternoon bringing a little Christmas cheer to some of his biggest, or should we say littlest, fans."* Clay appeared on the screen. He was signing a baseball and talking to a little girl in a hospital bed. A man and a woman stood next to Clay with giant smiles on their faces. *"Clay visited young cancer patients, signed balls and jerseys, and even announced a hundred-thousand-dollar donation to the hospital. Some fans were unhappy about the way Clay pitched in the Peaks' last playoff game, but to this community, Clay is every bit a hero."*

Mary's heart lurched like a canoe in a violent windstorm, the emotions swirling so fast she wasn't sure which was the strongest. She was relieved and thrilled to see that Clay was alive and well and looking more handsome than ever, even in a blurry video. But she was also a little hurt that Clay had gone to the hospital without her. He'd invited her to go with him, and she'd told him she'd think about it. He'd gone before she'd even given him her answer. The answer probably would have been no, but she would have liked to make that decision instead of having the decision made for her.

Her face burned. She was a coward, and Clay knew it. Surely, he had made the decision not to take her because he hadn't wanted to cause her undue stress or make her feel bad having to say no. Shame lodged in her throat. Clay was off having adventures and helping people and making the world a little brighter, and she was hiding in her house because she didn't like feeling uncomfortable. She liked Clay very much, but she didn't deserve him.

Mary gasped, took the phone from Cathy, and held it closer. A tall, slender woman with long black hair, big, beautiful eyes, and light brown skin sidled into the shot behind Clay, smiling at him like a proud mother. *Or a possessive girlfriend.* The text across the bottom of the screen read, *"Clay Markham and Gwen Rinaldi at Children's Hospital."*

Mary thought she might choke. Had Clay taken Gwen with him because she was his girlfriend or because Mary hadn't had the courage to go? Neither choice made Mary feel better. All she felt was a sense of shock and profound pain. She bit her lip to keep the tears from escaping.

The video ended, and Mary felt increasingly unsteady. "Could you . . . could you play it again?"

Cathy's wrinkles piled on top of each other on her forehead. "Yeah. I saw her too."

Mary couldn't breathe, whether because Cathy had seen a random beautiful woman behind Clay or because Cathy knew Gwen was Clay's girlfriend. "Is that who Clay is dating?" Mary said, nearly choking on her question.

Cathy took the phone from Mary and fiddled with the screen. "Well, according to the gossip, they broke up four months ago, and Gwen was not happy about it. Maybe they've come back together for the good of the children."

Mary was heading for a heart attack. "The children!"

Cathy's frown etched itself deep into her face. "I meant the children at the hospital. As far as I know, Clay doesn't have any children or any past marriages." Cathy showed Mary how to replay the video, and Mary clasped the phone as if it were her only connection to all the answers in the world. "I'd be jealous too," Cathy said.

"Gwen is obviously wearing that dress to attract attention. Who wears sleeveless in the winter? I'd say she and Clay are back together. Professional ball players are known for being fickle."

"Now, Cathy," Esther scolded, glancing at Mary. "Don't jump to conclusions. That's not fair to Clay."

Cathy huffed out a breath. "I know, but I do like the drama. It's exciting to think that I'm witnessing a love triangle in the heart of Amish country."

Mary swallowed past the lump in her throat. There was no love triangle. She had no claim on Clay's heart. He'd made no commitments or promises. He'd been the brightest, most *wunderbarr* part of her life, but that didn't mean he felt the same way. Maybe the affection was all on Mary's side. Clay liked everybody, and everybody liked Clay. Perhaps Clay felt the same way about Mary that he felt about everybody else. It was the only reasonable explanation. Clay was not inconstant or dishonest. It wasn't his fault he was easy to love and hard to let go.

"Hold on," Esther said, staring at Cathy's phone. "Mary, play the video again." Mary slid the little circle back to the beginning of Cathy's video. Esther leaned over her shoulder to watch it. “Pay attention to Clay and the woman. What is her name?”

“Gwen Something,” Cathy said.

“Pay attention to Gwen and Clay.”

Mary watched closely, because if there was anything she needed, it was a reason to still believe.

Esther pointed to Clay. “It’s fuzzy, but look at Clay. He’s smiling and laughing with the little girl and the parents, but it’s almost as if he doesn’t know Gwen is there. Either that or he’s ignoring her.”

Mary studied Clay’s blurry face. He did indeed act as if he was completely unaware Gwen was in the room. Or maybe he was just focused intently on the most important people in the room. “There’s something else too. He looks sad.”

Cathy narrowed her eyes. “What do you mean he looks sad? He’s smiling so wide, you need sunglasses from the glare off his teeth.”

Esther leaned even closer. “You know, I think you’re right, Mary. It’s blurry, but his eyes aren’t dancing like they usually do.”

Cathy folded her arms. “You don’t need to keep reminding me it’s blurry. I did the best I could under the circumstances.”

Esther laughed and patted Cathy on the shoulder. “Of course you did. You have no idea how grateful we are you had the sense to record this."

Cathy nodded. "I'm famous for my common sense."

Mary sent the video back to the beginning again. For sure and certain, Clay wasn't happy. It made her unhappy just thinking about it, but she also felt a glimmer of hope. Wouldn't Clay be happy if he and Gwen were back together? Or maybe he was unhappy about having to come back to Byler to finish fixing the barn? Mary sighed. She was going to tie her stomach into knots if she kept worrying about this. In his text, Clay said he'd be back this afternoon. She could start worrying after that. "When does afternoon end?" Mary asked. She drew in a sharp breath. Did she sound pathetic?

Cathy glanced at her wrist, but she wasn't wearing a watch. "Well, in Scotland, it's already nighttime. It gets dark early there."

Mary stood up when she saw a movement outside the window. "*Ach,* it's him!" She didn't know whether dread or utter happiness was her primary emotion. What if Clay was coming back so he could write a check and get out of Byler? What if he was back for a *gute* long time? She threw on her coat and bonnet and ran outside just as Clay was getting out of his truck. This running out to greet him was starting to become a habit, and she probably looked terribly forward, but she couldn't help it, and she couldn't be anyone but herself. She was ecstatic to see Clay. Why hide her happiness?

Clay was all smiles, but she still saw the sadness in his eyes that had been there on TV. "Mary," he said, "it's so good to see you. Did Cathy give you my message?"

"Yes, but just barely. It was silly, but I got a little worried."

Clay's lips twitched slightly. "It's nice to know that someone worries about me. Sometimes I think you're the only one who really cares. Well, you and my agent."

Now she was getting concerned. How could he believe no one cared? "There are so many people who care, it's impossible to count them all."

He gave in and lowered his head. "I suppose so, but the only one *I* really care about is you." His look was so intense, Mary thought she might float away on a cloud.

A blue tarp sat over the top of his truck bed, and he started working on the rope that held it down. "I brought you some presents."

She slumped her shoulders. "Clay, you don't need to bring me presents every time you leave and every time you come home. It's embarrassing."

He raised his eyebrows. "Embarrassing? Why is it embarrassing? If you mean the fecal testing kit, you don't have to tell anyone about that." He finished untying the knot and pulled back the tarp, revealing six brightly wrapped boxes of various sizes sitting in the truck bed. "I got something for every member of the family and two gifts for you." He seemed so excited that Mary hated the thought of discouraging him, even though she knew that unless it was a three-dollar gift, Ada wouldn't accept anything from him, Beth would be tempted with pride, and Joanna would feel guilty about taking it. Dat would flat-out refuse to take a gift from Clay. Dat had already refused Clay's money. He certainly wasn't going to take Clay's gifts.

Clay seemed to be unaware of her hesitation. He pulled the first box out of the truck. It sounded heavy and expensive. He set it on the dry sidewalk, which Dat had shoveled just yesterday. "This one's for you. You're going to love it."

Mary tried to smile. "Should I wait until Christmas to open this?"

"Not at all. There are more things coming at Christmas."

Ach! That was what Mary was afraid of. How could she kindly decline more gifts without hurting Clay's feelings?

"Open it. You can start using it first thing tomorrow."

Mary reluctantly and carefully peeled back the paper, being careful not to tear it, especially since Clay was going to have to take it back. Would he give it to someone else? A hole gaped in the pit of her stomach. Would someone else be grateful instead of touchy about a gift? There was a cardboard box under the paper with a picture of a strange contraption and GOAT MILKING MACHINE written on the side. "Oh, Clay, this is wonderful," she said, forcing the enthusiasm in her voice. It truly was *wunderbarr,* but a goat milking machine was expensive. She simply couldn't accept it.

"I found it in a farming supply store in Denver, and I had to buy it. This will cut your goat milking time in half."

Jah, it would, and it would save her fingers and hands from the cold every day. The thought made her all the sadder. But how was she going to tell him?

Before she could think of the right, kind thing to say, a red pickup truck pulled behind Clay's truck. Mary threw a questioning look at Clay. Was it another fan? Had he followed Clay from town?

Clay grinned. "His name is Simon, and he came to look at the roof."

"The roof?"

"Both roofs, actually. It's my Christmas present to the whole family. The barn and the house need new shingles, and then Simon is going to install solar panels on both and solar batteries. You'll never have to cut wood or light a fire again."

Oh, no. Mary wanted to crawl into a ball and climb into the cellar. "We can't ask you to do that."

Clay laughed, and the joy in his voice made Mary that much sadder. "You've never asked me for anything. I wanted to do this for you because you've all been so kind to me. I know solar is permitted because almost every Amish farm and house in Byler has solar panels. Your family will have the most, and the neighbors will be super jealous."

Holding a clipboard, a short man with a weathered face and gnarled hands got out of his truck and shook Clay's hand enthusiastically. "Clay, nice to finally meet you. My grandson plays baseball. He's only seven, but he's a big baseball fan."

Clay smiled. "Would your grandson like an autograph?"

"Probably, though I don't think he knows who you are. His favorite player is Isaac Paredes because he's from Hermosillo where my father was born."

Clay cocked an eyebrow. "That's sort of refreshing."

The man turned and smiled at Mary, and she was moved by the kindness in his eyes. Clay seemed to attract the best sorts of people to him. "Hello. I'm Simon Gonzalez. I own Brillo Solar and Roofing company in Alamosa, but we serve the entire San Luis area."

"It's . . . nice to meet you," Mary stuttered. *Nice to meet you, and I'm very sorry, but my* dat *will never agree to a new roof.*

Simon pulled a pen from his pocket. "So, let's take a look at what you have in mind, Clay, and I'll work up an estimate. Now is a good time to put solar in. The prices are low, and my men need the work during the winter months."

Mary would have rather done an hour-long interview with Leif McIntire than say what she had to say, but it was wrong to waste Simon's time and even more wrong to let Clay go on thinking the family would accept his gifts. She took a deep breath. "Mr. Gonzalez, I'm so sorry you came all the way out here, but we don't have any plans for a new roof, and I wouldn't want you taking all this time on an estimate." She reached out a shaky hand. "It was very nice to meet you."

Simon glanced at Clay in puzzlement, but his expression was nothing compared to the look on Clay's face. The light completely went out of his eyes, and his smile was the most painful thing she'd ever seen. "I'm planning on paying for it. You know that, don't you?"

"Yes," she whispered. "But we're not getting a new roof."

"Are you sure, Mary?" he said, but it wasn't a question. It was a statement of utter defeat.

She had expected him to be disappointed, but this was something much worse. It sounded too much like despair. Mary wrung her hands. "I'm . . . sure. I'm sorry. Can we talk about it later?"

Again, Simon looked to Clay, but Clay, it seemed, had nothing to say.

Mary hated the abject silence that had overtaken them. "I'm sorry again that you came all the way out here."

Simon cleared his throat. "Okay. I appreciate that." He slid his pen back in his pocket and glanced at Clay doubtfully a third time. "If you change your mind, give me a call.

You've got my number."

Clay nodded dumbly.

Mary felt sick to her stomach, and it didn't make her feel better knowing she'd done the right thing. Or had she? Clay's expression made her question every decision she'd ever made.

Simon got in his truck and drove away, and Clay and Mary stood in silence until he disappeared down the road.

"Clay . . ." she whispered.

Clay propped his hand on the side of his truck. "I've ruined everything, haven't I?"

"You haven't ruined anything."

"You don't even want the goat milker, do you? I can see it on your face."

Mary took a deep breath, but it did nothing to soothe the tightness in her chest. "It's not that I don't want it, but we're a simple family. Possessions tempt us to be proud. We don't want to be better than anyone in the neighborhood. We just want to be good neighbors."

Clay stared out at the pasture. "These things would make your lives so much easier. Why won't you let me do this for you?"

"It is not your place to buy us nice things or pay for solar panels or a new roof. You're a stranger to us. It would be wrong to take these elaborate gifts."

His eyes flashed with a yearning so profound, Mary forgot how to breathe. "You think of me as a stranger?"

"That's not what I mean. You're not family, and you're not Amish. You don't understand our ways."

Clay reacted as if she'd smacked him across the face. She felt the sting of his pain right in the center of her chest. She had obviously said the wrong thing and made it worse. "We still love you, Clay. We just can't accept your very generous gifts."

He covered his mouth with his hand and pressed his fingers into his jaw, his eyes deep caverns of loss and pain. Mary had no idea what to do with all that grief. The emotion suddenly left his eyes, and he squared his shoulders and stiffened like a post. "I suppose I'd better get these gifts back to the store. You never know what their return policy is like."

She opened her mouth, but before she could utter a word, he tossed the goat milker into the back of the truck, jumped into the cab, and drove away as if every dog in the county was chasing him. The tarp flapped behind the truck in the wind and cracked like a sharp whip behind him.

What had she done?

Chapter 9

Mary trembled, and it wasn't from the cold. She had been so eager to see Clay, and in a matter of ten minutes, she had somehow driven him away. Would he ever come back? Her knees felt like jelly as she dragged herself back to the house where Esther and Cathy were waiting for her. No doubt they'd seen the entire scene between her and Clay. Overcome with shame and confusion, she ran breathlessly into Esther's arms and let the tears flow.

Cathy sat on the couch just where Mary had left her, holding Levi Junior in her arms. "What in the world did you do, Mary? I've never seen Clay hightail it out of here so fast. He left skid marks on the road."

Mary sobbed into Esther's neck. "I don't know."

Esther patted her on the back. "What did he say? Who was that other man?"

"Clay asked him to come take a look at

our roof. Clay wants to pay to have it reshingled and solar panels put in. He also bought gifts for all of us. I told him we couldn't accept any of it."

Cathy sighed. "I can't understand you Amish. If Clay wanted to pay to have a new roof put on my house, I'd say yes and throw him a party."

Esther draped her arm around Mary's shoulder. "It's not the Amish way, Cathy. We're a plain and simple people. Extravagant gifts aren't appropriate."

Cathy bounced Levi Junior in her arms. "It seems Clay didn't take that too well."

Mary groaned. "He was upset. I tried to explain, but I somehow made him feel worse. Now he's going back to Denver to return all the gifts, and I'm afraid he won't come back."

Esther nodded sympathetically. "*Ach,* I'm so sorry, Mary, but don't you worry. He'll be back."

"How can you be sure?"

"Because he left a drawer full of baseballs at my house."

Mary giggled in spite of herself. "A drawer full of baseballs?"

"People ask him to sign his autograph so often, he keeps a stash of balls at the quilt shop just in case."

Mary found the thought of Clay's stash of baseballs oddly comforting. "I guess he has to come back and get those at least."

Cathy snorted her disagreement. "He could just leave them there. It's not like he can't afford to buy more, especially now that he doesn't have to pay for a roof."

Cathy was very *gute* at crushing people's hopes and dreams.

Cathy pinned Mary with a stern gaze. "If you think you've driven him away for good, just put that thought right out of your mind. A man who would drive four hours one way to see you won't give up that easy. Mark my words. He's disappointed, but not defeated. He'll be back, or my name's not Cathy Larsen."

Um, okay. Maybe Cathy wasn't so bad after all.

Cathy pressed a button on her phone and talked into it. "Call Clay Markham," she said.

Mary nearly jumped out of her skin. "What are you doing?"

Cathy looked at Mary as if she was crazy. "You want Clay to come back, don't you?"

"Yes."

"Well, if you had your own phone, you could call him yourself, but since you don't, you need me to call him for you."

Mary drew her brows together. "But what if he doesn't want to come back?"

"Then it won't hurt to remind him why he does."

Ach, vell. That was true.

Cathy put the phone to her ear and waited. "He's not answering. I'll leave a message." Long pause. "Clay? First of all, I want to commend you for not answering your phone. You're driving, and you don't have hands-free in that ancient truck of yours. I hope you have both hands on the wheel and both eyes on the road. But you need to know a few things, Clay Markham."

Esther waved to Cathy to get her attention and shook her head vigorously.

Cathy puckered her lips as if she'd just eaten a lemon. "Okay. Fine. I was going to give you a long speech, Clay, but instead just call me as soon as you can. There are people here who want to talk to you, and pouting is not attractive."

Mary was completely mortified, but if it was possible to die of embarrassment, she'd have been dead already.

Cathy pressed her screen. "Now we wait, but if he's going all the way back to Denver, it will be at least four hours before he calls me back, and I'll be in my pajamas watching *The Bachelor* reruns." She dropped her phone into her purse. "So if he calls, I'll have to get back to you in the morning."

"I don't think I can bear to wait that long," Mary whispered.

Esther put her arm around Mary. "Why don't you come to my house? You can help me make dinner, and if Clay comes by to get his balls, you'll be waiting for him."

Mary felt a glimmer of hope. "I don't want to impose."

Esther waved away her doubts. "Stuff and nonsense. I could always use an extra pair of hands for dinner duty."

Mary retrieved Winnie from the kitchen where she was helping Ada knead dough. Mary told Ada where she was going and why, and Ada kept a straight face, even if disapproval oozed from her pores like sweat. She couldn't help herself. Ada tried to stall for time by insisting that she badly needed Winnie's help to finish the bread, and Winnie felt so important, she refused to leave before the bread was in pans and on the counter rising.

When the bread was rising, Winnie finally agreed to go. They buckled the kids in the van, and Mary sat between their car seats, chewing her fingernails and watching the road just in case Clay passed in his truck. When they were almost to Esther's house,

Cathy's phone rang through the speakers in her van. Cathy had hands-free.

Cathy pressed a button on her steering wheel. "Hello?" she said.

The most beautiful sound in the world came through Cathy's speakers. "I don't pout," Clay said.

Cathy glanced back at Mary and put her finger to her lips. Mary put her hand over her mouth just in case. "You drove away in a huff," Cathy said. "I'd call that pouting."

"Whatever," Clay said. "What did you want to say to me?"

"Are you going to Denver tonight?"

His voice got softer. "I don't know." He sounded lonely. He shouldn't be driving in that condition. "Still deciding. I stopped in Alamosa at a little Mexican restaurant to drown my sorrows in salsa."

"What sorrows?" Cathy asked. "Are you drunk?"

Mary held her breath. No, Clay. Don't drown your sorrows in alcohol.

"It's four in the afternoon. I'm not drunk yet." Clay fell silent, and Mary clenched her teeth. Wasn't he going to explain what *yet* meant? "What did you want to say to me, Cathy?"

Cathy gave Esther an exasperated look.

"You should at least come back to get your balls."

Clay sighed deeply. "I'll talk to you later, Cathy. Thanks for the riveting conversation." Then a click and nothing.

Something heavy and anxious pressed on Mary's chest. "We've got to stop him. If he tries to drive to Denver when he's drunk, for sure and certain, he'll get in another accident, and he could die this time."

Cathy looked into her rearview mirror. "He's drunk. He didn't even care about his baseballs."

Mary grabbed the back of Cathy's seat. "Please take me to Alamosa. I've got to stop him. Esther, I'm sorry, but this is more important than helping you make dinner."

"Of course it is," Esther said. "Let's go find Clay."

They were almost to Esther's house, and Mary wasn't about to inconvenience Esther with a trip into Alamosa. "Please don't worry about me, Esther. *Die kinner* need you. I . . . I think I can find Clay on my own and talk him out of going to Denver tonight."

Esther furrowed her brow. "Are you sure? I feel like I'm abandoning you."

Cathy turned down Esther's road. "Don't worry. I'll stick with Mary and help her find him. Force him into the van if I have to."

Mary was five foot six, and Cathy was eighty-four years old. They wouldn't be able to force Clay to do anything. But maybe Cathy could distract him while Mary stole the keys to his truck.

Cathy pulled up to Esther's house, and Esther gave Mary one last uncertain look before taking her children and disappearing into the house. Mary's heart pounded in her chest as she moved to the front passenger seat and Cathy pulled onto the road.

"We just have one very large problem," Cathy said, taking a right turn a little too sharply. "There are four or five Mexican restaurants in Alamosa. We don't know which one Clay went to."

Mary bit her bottom lip, more determined than ever. "We'll just have to keep looking until we find the right one." And hope they didn't get there before Clay left.

Clay had said he was at a little Mexican restaurant, so Cathy drove to the smallest Mexican restaurant in Alamosa first. Clay's truck wasn't in the parking lot. Cathy grabbed her phone and touched the screen. "I say we go from smallest to biggest, even though Clay might have called the restaurant 'little' to throw us off the scent."

"Why don't we try to next closest one first?"

Cathy nodded. "Even better idea. That will save us some time."

The second restaurant didn't open until five, which was about fifteen minutes away. Cathy diligently drove to the next restaurant where, thank Derr Herr, Clay's truck sat by itself in the parking lot. Mary had never loved the sight of that truck as much as she did at this moment. "Stop, Cathy. There's his truck."

Cathy pulled into the parking spot next to Clay's truck. "Should I wait here or come in with you? I don't think you can drag him out of the restaurant by yourself, especially if he's a little tipsy."

Mary unbuckled her seatbelt and opened her door. "I want to go in by myself. I'm the one who hurt Clay's feelings. I need to make it right."

"That's true. It is all your fault."

Mary slid out of Cathy's van. "I don't know how long this will take. He might not want to come out."

"You could be there a long time if you get him talking about his wounded inner child or something like that." Cathy glanced in her rearview mirror. "If you can't get him to come out, wave to me from the window, and I'll go to Walmart. They've always got some good Christmas deals. Clay can call me when you're ready for me to come back."

Cathy must have really liked Walmart.

Mary pursed her lips. "Okay, I'll either be back here in a few minutes, or wave to you from that window and you can leave."

She walked into a *gute* size atrium decorated with piñatas and sombreros with lively music blaring from a speaker on the ceiling. Despite the music, the place was quiet, no hostess at the front stand, no servers bustling back and forth. To her left were three steps up that looked like they led to the main restaurant. She went up the stairs and peeked into the long, spacious room that was the main restaurant. All the tables were empty except for one in the corner where two women were eating and visiting quietly. Mary frowned. Clay wasn't there. But he had to be. His truck was parked out front, and surely there wasn't another truck in the entire world like Clay's.

Another dining area was separated from the main room with a wall with arched openings. Hoping she wouldn't get in trouble for exploring, Mary tiptoed into the separate dining area. Her heart leaped for joy and anxiety. It was Clay. Even though his back was to the entrance, there was no mistaking the broad shoulders and messy short hair that she longed to run her fingers through. Clay, looking as lonely as a puppy in a dog pound, sat slumped over in a corner booth with his fingers wrapped around a glass of brown liquid. Was it alcohol? How much had he already drunk?

She practically ran to his table, hoping to stop him from taking even one more sip. "Don't do it, Clay." She winced. Her voice sounded breathless and desperate.

Clay looked up at her with a blank expression, as if he'd turned off his feelings and it was too much work to turn them back on again. "Hey. You look real pretty," he said flatly.

Mary didn't want to be rude, and she didn't want to offend him, but she was too upset to pussyfoot around his feelings. "Are you drunk?"

His left eye twitched slightly, and he looked down at the glass he was holding. "I guess I shouldn't be offended by that question since I once crashed into your barn, but I kinda thought maybe you knew me better than that." There was no emotion in his voice, no light in his eyes, none of that sweetness and charm that were as natural to him as breathing.

Mary had never seen him so empty, and she'd seen him at his worst. Even on the night of the accident, his smile had melted her defenses. Clay was broken, and even though it was unintentional, she was the one who'd broken him. "Come with me, Clay. Let's go home and talk about it."

He took a sip of whatever was in his glass. "Talk about what?"

"Talk about what I did to make you so upset. I'm wonderful sorry, Clay."

His expression softened a little around the edges. "You didn't do anything wrong, Mary. It's me. It's always been me."

"I don't think so."

He picked up his glass and swirled it in a circle. "Dr Pepper, full strength. Lots of carbs, lots of calories, lots of caffeine. I'm living on the edge."

Mary felt like the worst person in the world. "I shouldn't have jumped to conclusions."

"I don't blame you. It's me. It's always been me."

"Stop saying that."

He didn't argue. Just took another drink, as if it took too much energy to disagree with her.

"Come back to Esther's with me. Let's talk about it."

He leaned back against the bench. “I’m not up to it, Mary.” One side of his mouth curled upward, and for a second, she saw the real Clay in there. “It’s nothing personal. I just want to be alone.” He turned his body and looked toward the entrance. “How did you get here?”

She probably shouldn’t mention that Cathy was waiting outside to drive him home just in case he’d had too much to drink. “Cathy drove me. I was worried.”

“No need to worry about me. I’m pretty good at taking care of myself. Three million a year buys a lot of independence.”

“Won’t you come back to the farm with me tonight? Fluffy learned a new trick.”

Clay stared into his glass. “Fluffy is a smart goat.”

Mary stood next to his table with no idea what to do next. Should she summon Cathy and drag Clay out of here?

Her heart skipped when Clay reached out and caressed her hand. “Don’t worry about me, Mary. Have Cathy drive you back. I’ll go to Denver, return these gifts, and see you in a couple of days. Probably.”

Mary didn’t like that “probably.” In fact, she wouldn’t stand for it. This was going to take longer than she had hoped, and Cathy might as well be at Walmart finishing her

Christmas shopping. Without a word, Mary strolled into the main dining area and looked out one of the windows that faced the parking lot. She waved to Cathy, but Cathy was looking at her phone and didn't see her. Mary knocked on the window with little hope that Cathy would hear her. She finally marched outside and knocked on the passenger side window. Cathy looked up from her phone. Mary gave her a goodbye wave and backed away toward the restaurant doors. Cathy got the message and gave Mary a thumbs up.

Mary went back into the restaurant and, after a few minutes of looking into probably forbidden rooms, found someone who worked there — apparently the only employee in the whole restaurant. It was a younger boy stocking the salsa. "Could you get me a cup of coffee?" she asked him.

He nodded enthusiastically, scooped some guacamole from a nearby bowl into a plastic cup, and handed it to Mary. Mary looked at the cup of green mush. *Ach, vell,* this was better than nothing. She found a spoon at the salsa bar, carried her spoon and cup of guacamole to Clay's private little space, and slid into the booth across the table from him.

His look of surprise was the first recognizable emotion she'd seen from him since she got here. "I thought you'd left."

"I guess I shouldn't be offended since I once abandoned you to a nasty reporter, but I kinda thought maybe you knew me better than that. What kind of a person would I be if I just left you here like this? You need me. I'm not leaving."

He drew his brows together in irritation. "You won't let me help you, Mary. Why should I let you help me?"

"That's an absurd thing to say. I let you help me every day. You fixed our fence. You're fixing our barn."

He turned his face away. "I'm not going to argue with you. You can't understand."

Mary huffed out a breath. "Why do you think I wouldn't understand? I understand that I did something to hurt you. I understand that you would never do anything to intentionally hurt me. I understand that you have feelings that run very deep. I want to make it right."

"I said it's not your fault. It's me. The problem is me."

Mary pounded her fist on the table and raised her voice. "Stop saying that." In horror, she clapped her hand over her mouth. She never raised her voice. She even scared herself.

Clay stared at her for a second, then cracked a smile. "Well. That was refreshing. I don't think I've ever actually seen you angry before."

"There's more where that came from," she mumbled in complete mortification. If she hadn't been determined to make Clay talk, she would have slinked out of the restaurant in shame, never to return again.

Clay eyed her as if expecting another outburst, then pointed to her strange cup of guacamole and twitched his lips into a half smile. "You gonna drink that?"

Clay was as elusive as a prairie dog, but Mary wasn't going to let him get away with being charming. She stabbed her spoon into the cup. "Talk to me."

He immediately retreated behind his soda. "What do you want me to say?"

"Whatever you want. Just don't make me angry again."

He chuckled. "I wouldn't dare. I never want to witness such a violent outburst again."

"Now you're just being difficult."

Clay raised his gaze to her face and looked at her, really looked at her. The sincerity in his eyes took her breath away. "Am I nothing more than a stranger to you, Mary?"

Ach. Her heart sank. "No wonder you

sped away."

"It's not your fault, Mary. I'm the problem."

She narrowed her eyes and shook her spoon in his direction. "Stop it."

He blew a puff of air from between his lips. "Okay, okay. Whatever you say."

"You know I didn't mean it that way, when I said you were a stranger."

He leaned forward. "Mary, if I *knew* you didn't mean it that way, I wouldn't be so upset, and that's the honest truth."

Mary was too ashamed to look at him. "I didn't mean it, but I feel terrible that I said it."

"I'm foolish to believe you and your family could ever need me for anything. Foolish for thinking I could be an important person in your life."

If only he knew how important he was in her life! She drew in a shaky breath. "Clay, you are not a stranger to me in any sense of the word, and it was a stupid thing to say. You mean the world to me." She tripped over the words. "The world to . . . to all of us. Our lives have been so much richer since we met you." Mary didn't dare go closer to the truth. Clay was everything to her, like the sun to the earth, the stars to the night sky, but what good would come of telling him that?

He ran his finger down the side of his glass. "Then why won't you let me help you? Why won't you let me buy you a few nice gifts that would make your life easier?"

"It's not our way."

He sat back and folded his arms, his face a mask of disinterest. "When you reject the gift, you reject the giver."

The pain in his voice sent a shard of glass right to Mary's heart. "Is that what you think?"

He focused on his glass again. "That's what I think."

She stared at him in astonishment. "Clay . . . that's . . . nothing could be further from the truth. I've told you about Amish Christmases. I get Dat a pair of socks or a new pair of suspenders. Joanna bakes everyone a plate of cookies. Ada makes stationery. I can't remember who said it, but fancy things aren't gifts. They're apologies for gifts."

"Thoreau," Clay murmured.

"You give us the gift of yourself every day. You fix things around the house, you play with the goats, you literally mend fences. When you walk in the door, the whole house lights up with happiness. You couldn't give us a greater gift. You don't need to buy us presents to prove how important you are to us. We already know."

He gazed at her intently and blinked some moisture from his eyes. "I don't know what to say."

"Say you'll come to the house and have a slice of Ada's bread."

Clay curled his fingers around his glass and turned his face toward the window. "Money is everything to my dad. It's how he shows love. It's how he apologizes. It's how he receives love. He can't bring himself to give me a hug, but in high school, if I got straight As, he'd give me twenty dollars. One time he got really mad at me and slapped me a good one upside the head. The force sent me flying into a shelf, and I banged my eyebrow and had to get stitches. The next morning there was a brand-new mitt on my chest of drawers. It was Dad's way of saying sorry."

Mary bit her tongue so she wouldn't start crying.

"In high school, if I pitched a good game and we won, he'd take the whole team out for ice cream. If we lost, he'd yell at me and tell me I would never amount to anything, then he'd refuse to talk to me for days. He treated Kirk better because Kirk was smart, and he won the science fair and the spelling bee and the DAR writing contest. Kirk got rich just from all the twenties Dad was throwing his way. I wasn't jealous of Kirk, but I sure envied the approval he got from Dad."

Mary nearly cried out thinking of younger Clay longing for a scrap of affection from his dad. "That breaks my heart."

He reached out and laid his hand tenderly over hers. "I don't want you to spend one minute feeling bad about this. It's my story, not yours, and it's gotten better since I started pitching in the Majors. The second year of my contract, I bought him a truck for Christmas." His eyes flashed with pain. "That was the first time in my life he ever told me he was proud of me."

A tear rolled down Mary's cheek. "For what it's worth, I'm proud of you."

He smiled sadly. "It's worth a lot." He exhaled and leaned his elbows on the table. "It's been this pull ever since I was little. Everybody wants something from me. First, it was my parents, then my coach, my teammates, my fans. Even my supposed girlfriend was using me to launch her acting career."

Mary swallowed hard. "Your girlfriend?"

"Her name is Gwen. For a guy who makes millions of dollars a year, I was pretty naive. I liked her, but she really wanted to date me because she thought it would help her acting career, plus she liked all the gifts I showered on her." He grimaced sheepishly. "I guess it worked. She now opens suitcases on a game show."

Mary blurted out her question before she lost the courage. "So. So you broke up with her?"

He studied her face. "Yeah. It was a shallow relationship. She told the papers I was a jerk, but she was just going for the publicity. I gave her a designer purse as a breakup gift. If she had been as mad as she said she was, she wouldn't have kept it."

Mary's throat constricted, but she *had* to mention it. "Cathy showed me the news report of you at the hospital. Gwen was there."

He rolled his eyes. "She caught word that I was going to be there and sort of sneaked onto the cameras. I couldn't very well ask her to leave, or the papers would have believed I was a jerk. But some people got the impression that we're still together. You weren't one of them, were you?"

Mary coughed weakly. "It might have crossed my mind."

He shook his head, a look of puzzled amusement on his face. "I guess you didn't know, but believe me, Gwen and I are finished. She's too much like my dad, and I was tired of buying her love."

Mary could have stood up and done a tap dance. "Your fans adore you, even when you don't win games. That will never change."

His smile was warmer, like the sun shining through a window. "I love my fans, and so far, they like me, but a few more bad games and they'll start booing instead of cheering." He clamped his eyes shut, grimaced, and opened them again. "You and your dad are some of the first people I've met who don't want anything from me, and I don't know what to do about that. I'm useless to you."

Mary pounded on the table again, but with much less force than the first time. "You are not useless. Don't ever say that."

He clutched his hands to his chest in mock horror. "You're frightening when you're angry."

"You should be frightened. I won't allow you to say such terrible things about yourself. Besides, I'm the useless one." She lowered her head and watched him out of the corner of her eye. "You didn't take me with you to the children's hospital."

"Did you want to go?"

"I don't know."

"I know how you hate attention and get

anxious around a lot of people. I thought it would cause you too much anxiety, so I decided to go without you."

She clasped her hands together. "I wondered if you were embarrassed to be seen with me. Gwen is much prettier than I am."

His mouth fell open. "Gwen is pretty like a bedazzled grocery bag is pretty. You're pretty like a bush full of roses or an orange sunset. You should be the one who's embarrassed to be seen with me. I lost that last playoff game, remember?"

Mary didn't know what a bedazzled grocery bag was, but she warmed to Clay's compliment. "*Ach,* Clay, can you be serious for more than five minutes at a time?"

He raised his hand. "I'm being completely serious, but I should have checked with you before I visited that hospital. It's not going anywhere. We can go visit up there anytime you want."

Mary stretched her lips across her teeth. "Um, I'll keep that in mind, but I'm still not sure if I want to go."

Clay's laugh echoed through the restaurant. "So you felt bad about being left out, but not bad enough to come next time?"

"That's correct."

He gave her an affectionate smile. "You don't know how hard it is to owe you and your family so much but not be allowed to pay you back. You won't even let me use my money to make your life easier."

"Well, you know, Clay, after this conversation, we'll never be able to accept another gift from you ever again. I never want you to wonder if we only like you for your money or your fame."

"But that really does make me feel useless." Mary pounded her fist on the table, and Clay laughed. "Okay. I won't say that anymore." But she could see he wasn't convinced. "I knew you didn't care about how famous I am because you didn't know who I was. You didn't ask for my autograph." Something like regret traveled across his face. "Pretty soon, no one will want my autograph. What happens when I can't do it anymore? When the money stops coming in and my career ends, I'll be use . . . I won't be worth a dime."

Mary wanted to grab him by the shoulders and shake some sense into him. "Everyone matters. Everyone is precious in Gotte's sight. You are worthy whether you play baseball or not."

"I wish I could believe it." Clay frowned and ran his hand down the side of his face. The light went out of his eyes. "There's something else. I went to see a specialist while I was in Denver. He says I've got permanent nerve damage in my elbow and without surgery, my career is over."

Mary felt dizzy. "Oh, Clay."

He propped his elbows on the table and covered his eyes with his hands. "Even with surgery, there's an eighty percent chance my career is over anyway. That's why I struggled in the last playoff game. I can't throw without excruciating pain, but nobody else knows but the doctor and you."

She laid a hand on his arm. "I'm so sorry."

To her shock, he pressed his hand to his eyes and started to sob. "If I don't have baseball, then I truly am nothing. Useless. Useless." He glanced up, his eyes shining with raw anguish. "Don't get mad at me, Mary. I can't bear your disapproval right now."

Mary was devastated that Clay might lose something he loved so much and devastated that he could believe such things about himself. With burning eyes and an aching heart, she scooted off her bench and slid in next to Clay, wrapping her arm around his shoulder and tugging him close.

He leaned into her, resting his forehead against hers. "I used to believe in God, Mary. I used to think He was watching out for me, but then my elbow started deteriorating. I prayed every night for healing and got silence. I've tried to live a good life. I'm not perfect, but I try to treat everyone with kindness. I've quit drinking, I don't smoke, I donate lots of money to charity, but God won't heal me."

Mary wasn't going to argue with Clay, not for all the goat milking machines in the world, but Clay's view of Gotte was wrong, and someday she'd tell him. Today, he needed her comfort, and *ach*! It felt so nice to be needed by the man who had everything.

"The day before I crashed into your barn, I'd gone to a different doctor. The look on his face told me everything I needed to know. After I left the doctor, my dad called me and yelled at me for losing the game. It was the same day the nasty article about Gwen and me came out in the paper. That night, the team we had beat three times this year won the first game of the World Series. It just hit me all at once. All I could think about was getting out of Denver, away from reporters and fans and my life. I drove south with no particular destination in mind, and I saw this sign for the sand dunes, so I got off the highway and drove into Alamosa. I couldn't find the sand dunes, so I found a bar." He glanced at her. "You might not believe it, but before then, I hadn't had a drink in over a year."

"I believe it," Mary said.

"I drank until I couldn't remember my own name, let alone my failures as a pitcher and a man. The next thing I remember was waking up with my head hugging the steering wheel and a beautiful Amish girl in a nightgown sitting next to me in my wrecked car."

Mary believed everything except the "beautiful" part. "I wouldn't have guessed you were so low, Clay. You treated me and Dat and my sisters with kindness and respect. You were so good to your fans, even the man who yelled at you in the waiting room at the hospital. You are a good man. I know just by watching how you treat people. God has not abandoned you."

"I'm mad at Him. I've given Him the silent treatment for weeks. Of course He's abandoned me."

"Of course He hasn't. He brought you to a family who didn't call the police when you were driving drunk. He saved you from serious injury when you crashed into our barn. He saw to it that Dat bought two fire extinguishers a week before the accident because they were on sale."

Clay's lips twitched in amusement. "They

were on sale?"

Mary grinned playfully. "The only time Dat will spend money is if it's on sale. God even arranged for a place for you to stay in Byler. And don't forget the ginger tea."

He flashed a reluctant smile. "I will never forget."

She tenderly curled her fingers around his arm. "Maybe you can't see it, but God brought you to us, as sure as I'm sitting here right now."

He laid his hand over hers. "I've very glad you're sitting here right now."

"Do you mind if I mildly scold you?"

"Of course I mind, but you look so pretty right now that I can't tell you no."

Mary laughed softly. "You are very charming, Clay Markham, but I won't let it distract me. Do you remember when we went to the hospital? There was a vending machine in the hall, and you bought me a bag of chips."

"You were nervous. Chips always make me feel better."

"Proving once again how kind you are." Mary propped her elbow on the table and rested her chin in her hand. "The Bible tells us that God is love. Do you agree with that?"

He shrugged. "I guess."

"Probably my favorite scripture ever is Isaiah 54:10: 'For the mountains shall depart, and the hills be removed; but my kindness shall not depart from thee.' You're just a man, Clay, but you know how to be kind. Just think about God being God. He is kinder than all the people in this world put together. I don't know why bad things happen to people, even people who love God, but if God is good and God is love, then He is kind, and He is eager to bless us."

Clay wiped some moisture from his cheek. "It doesn't seem like He's eager to bless me."

"Mostly because you're not noticing his blessings. The only reason some people think they're blessed and others don't is because the ones who think they're blessed notice their blessings. Have you even noticed your blessings lately? Have you expressed gratitude to God for saving your life?"

"*You* saved my life."

Mary shook her head. "I got you out of the car. God saved your life. Have you thanked Him?"

Clay winced. "Is this the part where you scold me?"

"Yes, it is."

He cocked his eyebrow. "I guess I deserve that, but I'm having a hard time being grateful for anything. I'm feeling real sorry for myself."

"You can feel sorry for yourself, but I don't see that it accomplishes very much."

"It helps me justify my anger at God."

She huffed out a breath. "It sounds like you're going in circles now."

"Definitely." He took the last gulp of his Dr. Pepper. "Hmm. Watery. I don't mean to be difficult, but what does this have to do with vending machines?"

Mary nodded. "Well, God is not a vending machine."

He stared at her blankly. "God is not a vending machine. That's probably profound, but I don't get it."

"Some people think that if they obey the commandments, God will give them what they want. But God isn't up in heaven taking orders like the guy at your favorite fast-food restaurant."

"Chick-fil-A," Clay said.

Mary giggled. "God doesn't work like a vending machine. We obey the commandments and try to be good because of our love for Him, not because of what we think we can get from Him."

"But you just said He's eager to bless us."

"Yes, but with what we need, not necessarily with what we want and *not* because we complete some checklist of commandments. Your dad sort of thought of you like a vending machine. He thought if he put in money and gifts, he'd get love in return."

Clay formed his lips into an O. "That's deep, Mary. I can't keep up."

She patted him on the arm. "Just remember the vending machine, and you'll be fine."

He chuckled. "I'd rather think of Chick-fil-A."

She gazed at him intently, hoping he saw the honesty in her eyes. "So will you come back and spend Christmas with us?"

He scrunched his lips to one side of his face. "As long as you don't mind a washed-up, useless, injured baseball player eating your Christmas dinner."

Mary pounded on the table. "Clay, stop saying that."

He held up his hands as if stopping traffic and smiled. "I'm just kidding! I had to say it, Mary. I wanted to see you pound on the table one more time."

Chapter 10

Mary's teeth chattered and her hands shook violently, as if she was experiencing her own private earthquake. Clay noticed. He reached over and took her hand in his, giving her that smile Mary couldn't resist. "Cold?"

"Nervous."

"I don't mean to make you feel bad," he said, "but I'm the one who's supposed to be nervous." He pressed the back of her hand to his lips and kissed it softly. "It's going to be okay, Mary. This doctor is one of the best in the country for elbows and shoulders."

Cathy pulled into the parking space outside the hospital outpatient wing. "No need to be nervous. We said a prayer before we left Byler, and God will be watching over Clay while he's under the knife. If he dies, we'll feel better knowing it was God's will."

Clay winked at Mary. "Thanks, Cathy. You

know exactly what to say to make me feel better."

Mary tried to smile so Clay would quit worrying about her, but all she could muster was a faint curl of her lips. She was worried about Clay's surgery, for sure and certain, but she was ashamed that she was more worried about encountering a crowd of fans and reporters. *Ach!* She hated crowds, she hated attention, and she hated nosy Englischers who wanted to pry into her life. How was Clay so calm in those situations?

She needed to get control of the shivering. Clay needed her today more than ever, and she had to show him confidence and strength so he could focus on himself and not worry about her. Unfortunately, he worried about her a lot. Two days before Christmas, that reporter, Leif McIntire, had shown up on the farm again, even though Clay had painted every fence pole on the farm purple. Come to find out, Colorado didn't have a purple pole law, and Leif walked right into the barn without a care in the world. She wasn't sure how Leif had managed to sneak past Clay on his way to the barn, but Leif had stormed into the barn and startled Mary as she was milking the last goat. She had gasped, thrown her arms around Smiley's neck, and tried to make herself as small as possible, even though Leif could see her and she knew she wasn't fooling anybody.

Leif seemed to have learned his lesson since the last time he'd come to the farm. He wore sturdy rubber boots, a pair of jeans, and a coat that looked about forty years old. He also carried that ubiquitous notepad and pen and didn't even pause to take a breath before he started asking questions. "What's your name?" he had said first thing. "Can I at least get your name and age for my story?" When Mary didn't reply, he narrowed his eyes. "Look, ma'am, I'm willing to pay you five thousand dollars if you'll tell me everything about your relationship with Clay Markham. What do you say? The Amish angle is really popular right now, and I think it could be a feature story."

Mary had squeezed Smiley's neck tighter. "I don't want your money."

Leif held his pen to the notebook as if expecting her to say something very interesting. "Do you Amish believe in sex before marriage? Are you disobeying the commandments by dating Clay? Are you in — what's that called? — Rum-spring-er? Amish girls have a reputation for being wild. Is that why Clay is dating you?"

Mary's heart had felt like it was trying to

claw its way out of her chest. She wanted to stand up, face that reporter eye-to-eye, and order him to leave the property, but she'd cowered like a water-logged kitten using Smiley as a shield. Her terror was only matched by her shame.

Thank Derr Herr, Clay had seen Leif's car. He had come into the barn and gone straight to Mary, taking her hand and pulling her up. With his arm firmly around her, he'd faced Leif and given him a look that could have curdled goat's milk. "Leif," he said, with a mildness that Mary would not have thought possible. "Please go away and leave my friends alone."

Probably remembering what had happened last time with Pepper and the goats, Leif had backed away without argument and left the property without another glance in Clay's direction. As soon as she heard him drive away, Mary had run out behind the barn and vomited into the sagebrush. It had been a very unpleasant day, and Clay had been livid.

No one should be livid two days before Christmas.

Clay had called to complain to someone at *Pro Day* where Leif worked, but he told Mary he didn't know if it would do any good. He again apologized to Mary and Dat and Ada that he had brought so much trouble to the family, but Dat didn't seem bothered. "Next time he comes," Dat had said, "let's invite him in for a cup of *kaffee.* Gotte said to do good to those who despitefully use you."

If she encountered Leif McIntire at the hospital, Gotte would probably want Mary to buy Leif a cup of *kaffee,* but if she never saw him again, she could have the *gute* intention without having to follow through with it. Lord willing, Leif was in New York or California pestering some other baseball player and would never find out she was at the hospital with Clay.

Clay pulled a beanie over his ears. "If I die, at least I got to spend Christmas with the Yoders. That was the last thing on my bucket list."

In spite of Leif McIntire, Christmas with Clay had been the best holiday of Mary's life. There was the annual Christmas program at the school, which was one of Mary's favorite things every year. Clay had never seen anything like it and thought it was *wunderbarr.*

They had spent Christmas Eve with just the family, singing carols and reminiscing about Mamm. Like Joanna, Mamm had been known in the community for her baking, and there were lots of stories about delicious desserts Mamm had made and the many people Mamm had served while she was alive. Everybody who knew Mamm loved her. Clay enjoyed hearing the stories about Mamm's many adventures sneaking over to neighbors and leaving baked goods on their porch and running away. One time, Mamm and Ada had left something at the Millers' house and had encountered a skunk on the way home. Dat had filled a galvanized tub in the barn, and Mamm and Ada burned their clothes and each took an hour-long bath before Mamm would step in the house.

On Christmas Day they had exchanged gifts, and Clay's presents were less expensive than his earlier gifts and much more appropriate. Mary had given him a new pair of stockings to replace the ones he'd ruined while chasing Leif off their farm, and he had given her a new milking bucket because Blue had kicked a hole in the old one. He'd given Ada a little solar-powered calculator, because she did the household budget. Joanna got a silicone oven mitt that Clay said was recommended by all the famous cooks on TV. Beth got a book about all the bird species in Colorado and a little pair of binoculars for bird watching.

Dat got the goat milking machine, and when he gave Clay a questioning look, Clay insisted that the milking machine hadn't cost very much and that it would benefit the whole family. Dat agreed to keep it, but only because Clay had worked so hard the last six weeks.

Since they didn't have family in Colorado, they had invited the four other single women in the district to join them for Christmas brunch, and then they went to a singing at the bishop's house in the afternoon on Christmas Day. Mostly, Mary savored the time she had with Clay and took every opportunity to just sit with him and bask in his warm glow.

Cathy turned off the van and turned around so she was looking at Clay and Mary sitting on the bench behind her. "Clay, take off your coat and roll up your sleeves."

Clay looked sideways at Mary. "Um, why?"

Cathy rummaged in her enormous purse. "Just do it. You'll thank me later."

Clay was used to Cathy's oddities by now, and he slipped his coat off his shoulders. He didn't need to roll up his sleeves because he was wearing a short-sleeved black T-shirt.

Cathy pulled a Sharpie from her purse and took off the lid. "Now, which elbow are they operating on?"

Clay pointed to his right arm.

"Lean over so I can reach it," Cathy said.

Clay did as he was told, and Cathy took his arm in her hand and pressed the pen to his forearm. He drew back. "What are you doing?"

"I had a cousin who went in to get his deviated septum fixed and came out without his appendix."

Clay narrowed his eyes. "I thought it was your aunt who went in for a melanoma and come out without her gallbladder."

Cathy puckered her lips and nodded. "That happened too. I'm going to mark your arm so the doctors know which elbow to operate on. You'll be asleep, and you won't be able to stop them if they cut into the wrong one."

Clay's lips twitched upward slightly, and he leaned forward and let Cathy take his arm again. "Okay. I guess it can't hurt, and it's nice to know you care enough to want to help me."

"Of course I care. You need to help us win a World Series next year." Cathy drew two arrows, one above his elbow and one below his elbow, each pointing to his elbow. Then she wrote, "Operate on this elbow," up his arm. She released his arm and motioned toward his left arm. "Hand me that one."

With a good-natured sigh, Clay stretched out his left arm. Cathy wrote, "Not this arm. Stay away" both above and below Clay's elbow. "You can't be too careful," she said. "Those doctors just want your money."

Clay put his coat back on and winked at Mary. "I like to believe they're trying to help people."

Cathy dropped the Sharpie into her purse. "You can believe that if it makes you feel better."

"It does."

Clay nodded to Mary. "You know you don't have to come in with me. You can just drop me off, and I'll text Cathy when I'm ready to be picked up. They have a really cool nature and science museum. You and Cathy could go look around while you're waiting."

Mary gave him a steady, confident look, even though she felt neither steady nor confident. He shouldn't have to doubt her loyalty or worry about her welfare while he was in surgery. "I'm going to be fine. I can read the magazines in the waiting room and buy anything I want from the vending machine." She pulled a twenty-dollar bill from her pocket. "Dat gave me some money."

Clay's face lit up like a yard full of Christmas lights. "I know how you like vending machines, but I'll really be okay without you."

Mary's smile faltered. That was what she was afraid of. She'd been dreading the day Clay would leave almost since the first time she met him. "I need to be there for you. You need to see a friendly face when you wake up." That was a silly thing to say. Everybody loved Clay. After ten minutes, every nurse on the floor would be Clay's best friend and half of them would want to date him.

Clay seemed to like her answer. "I know it's hard for you, but I'm real glad you're going to be there. Thanks."

"Text me when you're ready to be picked up," Cathy said. "I'm going shopping."

Clay and Mary walked quickly into the hospital and up to the front desk. Clay had told the team manager and owner about his surgery, but he didn't want anyone else to know. He told Mary he was hoping to keep the drama to a minimum, at least until after surgery.

They checked in, and a very nice nurse who looked to be in her fifties ushered them into the back to get Clay prepped for surgery. The nurse and the doctor both laughed when they saw Cathy's markings on Clay's arms, but they didn't seem offended or annoyed.

When they asked Clay to get into a hospital gown, that was Mary's cue to leave. Clay in a hospital gown was just a little too intimate and private for a shy Amish girl, not to mention the fact that Dat would never approve. He'd only agreed to let Mary come with Clay to the hospital because he was so fond of Clay and so trusting of Mary.

Mary squeezed Clay's hand and said goodbye. He gave her a look that took Mary's breath away, as if every *gute* thing lived in Mary's face. "It's going to be okay, Mary. Don't worry about me. Just hang out in the waiting room. If anyone bothers you, find one of the nurses to help you, okay?"

"Okay," Mary whispered, her heart jumping in her chest like a team of skittish horses. Why was she suddenly so breathless?

Clay handed Mary his phone. "Take this, and call Cathy if you need anything."

She pressed her lips together. He still felt like he had to take care of her, even though he was the one going into surgery. "I'll be praying for you," she said, willing her voice not to shake. Clay should not have to worry about her and her irrational anxieties. "God won't abandon you, and neither will I."

The look he gave her could have turned winter into spring. "Thanks, Mary. That means a lot to me."

Mary walked out of the surgery prep room, and the nurse gave her a black plastic disk about the size of one of Joanna's kitchen timers. "When Clay is in recovery, we'll page you with this," she said. "It will buzz and light up, and then you can come back to the recovery room and talk to the doctor."

Mary's chest was too tight to say a word to the nice nurse, who pointed her in the direction of the waiting room. She held the disk in front of her like a compass as she found a seat in the corner of the waiting room where it was least likely she'd be noticed. Keeping the pager firmly in one hand, she thumbed through some magazines and did her best not to think about Clay and his elbow and the disappointment he would feel if the surgery didn't work.

She closed her eyes and said a prayer for Clay. There wasn't anything else she could do.

Sitting on the table under three other magazines was a sports magazine with a baseball player on the cover. It wasn't Clay, but the ball player wore a Colorado Peaks uniform. Was he a teammate of Clay's? She opened the magazine and read the article. It was about some of the "bright spots" of the Peaks' defense. The article mentioned that Clay pitched for the Peaks but didn't say anything nice about him. Mary's mouth went dry when she noticed who had written the article: Leif McIntire. *Ach!* He was here even when he wasn't.

After about ten minutes, there was some sort of commotion at the front entrance. Mary glanced up, and her chest tightened like a clamp. A huge man on crutches hobbled in, followed by seven or eight other people, one of whom was Leif McIntire! Leif was the last person in the door, and everybody seemed to be ignoring him, or trying. Like Clay had said, Leif was like a bull in a china closet, and he was yelling out questions, apparently to the giant of a man on crutches. The man on crutches went up to the front desk to check in, and Leif, with his little notebook and pen, called to him. "Lamar, is it true you injured your knee when you kicked the Gatorade cooler in the San Francisco game?"

Lamar, the big guy on crutches, glanced back over his shoulder. "Come on," he said. "I'm going in for surgery. Have some decency, and leave people alone."

Mary sank in her chair and lifted the magazine so it covered her face. She could only hope that Leif wouldn't see her or that he was too engrossed in harassing Lamar to care about the Amish girl hiding in the corner. She gulped in several deep breaths so she wouldn't faint, squeezed her eyes shut, and prayed that Leif wouldn't notice her. She thought about running for the nurse, but she would have had to pass Leif and Lamar and all his friends to get there, and she just couldn't muster the courage to do it.

The commotion died down after a few minutes when they took Lamar back to get prepped for surgery. Or at least that's what probably happened. Mary still had her face buried in the magazine, and her eyes were tightly closed, but her ears still worked. The front entrance slid open and shut several times, and Leif quit shouting. Lord willing, he'd left the building.

"Hey, I wrote that article."

This time, Mary really was going to have a heart attack, because that was Leif's voice not five feet away from her. *Ach!* Why hadn't she used the home and garden magazine as a shield? She slowly, ever so slowly, lowered the magazine from her face.

"It's you!" He sat down in the chair across

from her and acted as if he was going to be there for a while.

She truly was going to throw up right there in the hospital waiting room. "I'll call the police," she said, her voice shaking like a match in the wind.

Leif smiled and held up his hands. "Okay, okay, no need to get touchy. You surprised me, that's all."

Mary set down the magazine and folded her arms around her waist. She was most definitely going to throw up.

Leif narrowed his eyes. "Why are you here?"

Mary pressed her lips together. She wouldn't give Leif the satisfaction of a reply. Clay told her it was better to stay silent. Besides, even if she'd wanted to say something, she wouldn't have been able to speak if her life depended on it.

Leif stared at her for a long second, then to her surprise, he stood up, pulled out his phone, and walked away to make a phone call. Mary exhaled the breath she'd been holding. Maybe Dat would call her a coward, but it didn't matter that she was supposed to love her enemies. She would never, ever buy Leif a cup of *kaffee.*

Mary made herself as small as possible and watched Leif's every move. His first phone call lasted maybe thirty seconds. Then he called at least three other people, talking too softly for Mary to hear anything. Did he suspect she was here for Clay? Mary winced in self-condemnation. It would be all her fault if Clay's secret got out.

After about fifteen minutes, Leif came to rest in a chair on the opposite side of the waiting room, and Mary relaxed slightly. Leif was in the same building, but he wasn't bothering her — *ach, vell,* his presence bothered her, but he wasn't asking any personal questions or even trying to convince her to do an interview. But Mary couldn't be comfortable. She clutched the black disk, willing it to light up so she could go back to the recovery room and leave Leif behind her.

Trying to calm her nerves, she picked up the baseball magazine again and started thumbing through it, not really seeing anything on the pages. Leif was on the other side of the room looking at his phone, but she got the sense that he was acutely aware of her and her every move. She should go find a nurse. That was what Clay would have wanted her to do.

A thin, graceful woman wearing a beanie, sunglasses, and an electric-blue parka strolled into the waiting room, swinging her hips as if she was knocking obstacles out of the way. Mary frowned. She looked vaguely familiar, but Mary couldn't place her. Was it someone she'd met in Alamosa the first time she and Clay had gone to the hospital? Mary's throat tightened as the woman came straight toward her and sat down in the seat across from her, the one where Leif had sat a few minutes before.

She nodded to Mary, then settled in the seat as if waiting for someone, but she never took off her glasses, her beanie, or her coat. That was odd. Mary held her breath. The woman had beautiful brown skin, but Mary couldn't tell the color of her hair because it was all tucked up under her beanie. She couldn't really see her eyes either behind those sunglasses. The woman smiled at Mary. She had perfectly straight white teeth, but her smile was fake and unattractive. "Are you a Mennonite or something?"

Mary felt uneasy, but she didn't want to be rude. "Um, Amish."

The woman nodded. "I read all about the Amish on Wikipedia. You don't believe in cars or electricity. Or, like, sex before marriage."

Mary's throat tightened. It was a wildly inappropriate thing to say. Who was this woman, and why had she focused in on

Mary? Mary truly didn't know what to say. Her heart knocked against her chest. *Love your enemies. Do good to those who despitefully use you and even those whom you're suspicious of.* "Are you hungry? Do you want me to buy you something from the vending machine?"

The woman put her hand over her mouth to cover a laugh. "You're so cute, but no thanks."

"You're so cute" sounded like an insult.

Mary tightened her fingers around the black disk and willed the light to start flashing. Nothing.

The woman leaned back and crossed her legs. "Have you seen *Breaking Amish* on TV? The girls can be as wild as they want before they're baptized." Mary felt as if she were being accused of something but wasn't sure what or why. Hostility oozed from the woman's pores like sweat.

"We don't watch TV," was Mary's weak response. Couldn't this woman just go away and leave Mary alone?

The woman pointed to the magazine Mary was still clutching in one hand. "You like baseball?"

Mary had no idea what the "right" answer might be, so she chose the truth. "I don't know much about it."

The woman tilted her head to one side, as if to get a better look at Mary. "I love baseball. My boyfriend is one of the Peaks players." She leaned forward, and her lips twisted in disdain. "His name is Clay Markham. Do you know him?"

Mary reared back. How could she have been so stupid? How could she not have recognized Gwen Rinaldi? *You are not Clay's girlfriend,* Mary wanted to scream, but she was struck mute by the sheer weight of the situation.

Gwen's eyes flashed with triumph. "You know him pretty well, don't you?"

Gwen glanced back at Leif. Mary hadn't noticed before, but he had abandoned his phone and was watching their conversation with intense focus. Had he called Gwen to come to the hospital to get the interview Mary had refused to give him? It was a dizzying realization. And Clay wasn't here to help her.

Gwen took off her sunglasses as if to get a better look at Mary. "The real question is: Why is a guy like Clay hanging out with an Amish girl? Is it a rebound relationship? Leif thinks Clay wants, you know, a casual hook up." She glared at Mary. "Are you having sex? It's against your commandments, isn't it?"

Mary felt lightheaded, Gwen's questions cutting off her air supply. With all the strength she could muster, she got to her feet and moved toward the front desk.

Gwen got up and followed her. "I'm insulted that Clay's rebound girlfriend is an ugly, boring Amish girl. It's obvious he's trying to make me jealous, send a message he'd rather date anyone but me. He's definitely scraping the bottom of the barrel."

Mary couldn't breathe. She showed her disk to the woman at the front desk. "Could . . . I . . . could I go back and see Clay now?"

The woman was engrossed in something on her phone. She glanced up at Mary. "I'm sorry. It's not buzzing yet. You just have to be patient."

Mary nearly collapsed right there at the front desk. She had to get out of there, away from Gwen and Leif and all the hurtful, hateful things Gwen was throwing at her. Her coat and bonnet were draped over the arm of her chair, but she couldn't retrieve them without going near Gwen. It was better to freeze to death than suffer one more insult or indignity. She abandoned her things and hurried out the entrance doors, the disk still in her hand.

"You're pretty naive," Gwen yelled to her.

"There's only one thing Clay wants from a girl like you."

Cold air washed over Mary like water from an icy lake when she stepped outside, but she didn't pause or change her mind. She walked quickly in no particular direction, and it wasn't until she was sure no one was following her that she burst into tears. For a *gute* fifteen minutes, she walked around the streets of Denver until her nose stung and her fingers ached with cold. Hoping no one had followed her, she ducked into a coffee shop and gulped in a breath of warm, moist, delicious air. The coffee shop was empty except for a middle-aged man standing at the counter looking at a receipt.

He glanced up and flinched as if he'd seen a ghost. She must have been a frightful sight. He bustled around to the front of the counter and put his arm around her. It was a friendly, fatherly arm, and she didn't pull away. "Goodness, dear girl. Where is your coat? Sit here, and I'll pour you a nice cup of coffee." He led her to a booth and poured her some coffee from a pot sitting near the register. "What's your name? Are you lost? Can I call someone for you?"

Mary gasped. She had left Clay's phone in the waiting room in her coat pocket. She pulled a napkin from the dispenser, pressed it to her mouth, and started sobbing.

The man sat across from her in the booth. "It's okay, honey. How can I help?"

"I left his phone at the hospital," she managed to say between sobs.

The man leaned closer. "Do you have someone in the hospital?"

"Yes. He's getting surgery, and he gave me his phone to call Cathy when he's done, but I left it because Gwen said I was ugly and naive, and Leif was right there listening in. I had to get out of there."

The man nodded sympathetically. "Of course you did."

Mary took a deep breath and a sip of coffee. It felt deliciously warm going down. She sighed. The man was being so kind, even though he surely had no idea what she was talking about. "I'm sorry. I'm not making much sense. My friend Cathy dropped me and my friend off at the hospital for his surgery." She set the disk on the table. "They gave me this disk and said it would buzz when the surgery was over. My friend gave me his phone so that I could call Cathy after the surgery and she could pick us up. But I left his phone at the hospital, and Cathy will never know when to pick us up."

"Do you know Cathy's phone number?"

Mary nodded. That was one she had

memorized.

The man pulled a cell phone from his pocket. "You are welcome to use my phone to call her. My name's Ron Gallagher. Would you like a donut?"

Mary wiped her eyes and tried for a smile. It probably looked more like a pathetic cry for help. "I left my money at the hospital in my coat pocket." Gwen would probably steal it. She'd probably steal Clay's phone too.

Ron waved away her concern. "It's free. A donut makes everything better."

"That's very nice of you."

"You've obviously had a very bad day, and it's good karma to help a stranger. I need all the blessings I can get."

Mary gazed at him in concern. "Is everything okay?"

Ron propped his chin in his hand. "I'm fine. My wife's been sick, and the coffee shop isn't doing so well. There's a national chain coffee company that just opened up a block to the west. It's hard to compete with five hundred different selections."

"I'm sorry. Is your wife going to be okay?"

He nodded. "I think so. They finally narrowed it down to pancreatitis, which is serious but treatable. We are hopeful now that she has a diagnosis."

Mary didn't know why she suddenly felt so brave. "Would you like me to pray with you?"

Ron's eyes pooled with moisture. "I would appreciate that very much."

Mary's face warmed considerably. "I'm not accustomed to praying out loud. Could you . . . could you pray?"

"Of course. There's a lot of power in two people coming together to talk to God."

Ron bowed his head and closed his eyes, and Mary did the same. He said a beautiful prayer asking God to help his wife and the coffee shop and Mary. Mary was especially grateful for that prayer for her. Ron wasn't Amish, but for sure and certain, God had heard that prayer.

Ron stood and brought Mary a donut and his cell phone. "Here, why don't you call your friend?"

He punched in the password, and Mary entered Cathy's phone number. "If this is a scammer, hang up right now," Cathy said when she answered.

"Cathy, this is Mary."

"Mary? Whose phone is this?"

Mary glanced at Ron who'd gone behind the counter. "It belongs to the coffee shop, I guess. I . . . I'm not at the hospital. That horrible reporter found me and then he called Clay's old girlfriend, and she came over and was mean to me, and the nurse wouldn't let me go back to Clay's room."

"I have no idea what you're talking about. Where are you? Did you just leave poor Clay there all alone? That's how people disappear and end up on the missing persons list."

Mary pressed her fingers over her mouth as her own shame nearly strangled her. She had been determined to be strong and brave and loyal. Instead, she'd run away and left Clay all by himself at the hospital. "I . . . she said some nasty things, and I didn't know what to do. I panicked."

"I feel your pain, girl, but it wasn't very nice to leave Clay by himself. He needs to see a friendly face when he wakes up." Cathy heaved a sigh. "I suppose it will have to be me, even though I haven't had a friendly face for thirty years. Clay will just have to take what he gets. It'll take a few minutes to get dressed, then I'll head over to the hospital."

Mary almost didn't dare ask. "Get dressed?"

"I'm in the dressing room trying on swimming suits. I wouldn't recommend it at my age. It has totally ruined my self-esteem." Mary heard some shuffling on Cathy's end.

"Wherever you are, stay put. I'll go comfort Clay, and when they release him, we'll come find you."

"But the disk hasn't buzzed yet."

Cathy grunted. "Maybe it has. You're probably out of range. Try not to worry. I'll take care of it."

"I'm at Bean There, Donut That Coffee Shop," Mary said.

"Clever name but kind of dumb."

Mary had never felt so useless or so low. Clay needed her, and she was cowering in a coffee shop half a mile away because Clay's old girlfriend had hurt her feelings. But it hadn't seemed so minor at the time, and even as ashamed as she was, Mary couldn't bear to go back there and face Gwen Rinaldi and Leif McIntire. The tears gushed down her face. She'd let Clay down, and the embarrassment was unbearable.

"Cathy?" she squeaked. "Will you get my coat and bonnet and Clay's phone and my twenty dollars? They're in the waiting room, unless Gwen stole them."

"Gwen better not be there when I get to the hospital, or she'll get a lecture she'll never forget. I'll call this number if I run into any trouble. If worse comes to worst, Clay might have to bail me out of jail."

Mary's heart jumped. "Jail?"

"Things could get rough with this Gwen person. I don't back down to bullies, and I won't stand for people to be rude to my friends."

Lord willing, Gwen would be long gone before Cathy showed up. There was nothing quite so formidable as an eighty-four-year-old woman with a chip on her shoulder and a purse the size of a small country. Mary wished she were anywhere near as brave as Cathy was.

Chapter 11

Mary stared out the window while Ron waited on a customer. She'd talked to Cathy two hours ago and had called her every ten minutes after that, but Cathy hadn't answered any of Mary's calls except the first one. Maybe she had been arrested. Mary chewed on her fingernail. She should have walked back to the hospital long ago. Surely Gwen had left after Mary was gone. Surely there was nothing to fear.

Mary hung her head. She was so disappointed in herself. What would Clay think? He was always so kind and understanding, but after she'd abandoned him, she wouldn't blame him if he never trusted her again.

The black disk had never vibrated or lit up. That either meant she was out of range, or Clay was still in surgery. Lord willing, he wasn't still in surgery. Why wouldn't Cathy answer her phone?

Mary had wiped tables and washed dishes for Ron while she waited, but for the last fifteen minutes, she'd been staring out into the street watching for Cathy's van. It started to snow, and Mary nibbled on another fingernail. Would the roads get slippery? Would Cathy be able to navigate the van in the city? Would she and Clay get into a car accident?

Having worried herself into a tizzy, Mary turned from the window as Ron's customer strolled out the door. "I'm sorry, Ron, but can I use your phone again? I just don't know what's happened to Cathy."

Ron wiped his hands on a dishtowel and pulled his phone from his pocket. "Sure thing. I'm sorry they're not here yet. I guess if she doesn't answer, you could call the hospital directly, though I doubt they'd tell you anything. Patient privacy laws and all that."

Mary took Ron's phone and punched in Cathy's number. No answer. "Ron, would you help me look up the number for the hospital?"

The bell above the door rang, and Mary whirled around as Clay stumbled into the coffee shop. His face was lined with worry, and his right arm was wrapped from wrist to armpit in a fat white bandage. She caught her breath and her heart fell to her toes as he clamped his fingers around the nearest chair to keep himself up. He looked worse than the morning after the car accident when he'd sat on the floor making friends with the toilet. He was pale and shaky and having a hard time keeping his balance. After a short pause at the chair, he strode to her side with purpose, reached out his *gute* hand, and put his arm around Mary's shoulders, pulling her in for a one-armed embrace. She buried her face in his neck and let his warmth envelope her while also doing her best to keep the two of them upright. "Mary, Mary, I'm so sorry. Cathy told me what happened. Are you okay? I can't believe you walked all this way without a coat. Oh, Mary, I'm so sorry."

Mary's shame was deeper than a Colorado well. "Sit down, sit down," she said, pulling out the nearest chair and pushing him into it." He didn't resist, but he clamped his hand around Mary's wrist and tugged her to sit next to him. "I'm the one who's sorry, Clay. I abandoned you at the hospital. That's how people disappear and end up on the missing persons list."

Clay chuckled and squeezed her hand. "You've been talking to Cathy, who is waiting outside and told me to hurry."

Mary reached out and laid her hand on Clay's forehead. "You look terrible. How do you feel?"

"Like I could use some ginger urine tea right now. Anesthesia makes me sick."

"That's terrible."

"I think I'm done throwing up for the day. At least that's what the nurse told me."

Mary closed her eyes as a river of remorse washed over her. "I'm so sorry I abandoned you. I should have stood up to them, but I just couldn't. My heart was beating so fast, I felt like I was going to die."

"You didn't abandon me. You were attacked and did the only sensible thing you could have done." He gave her a soft look. "Though I wish you would have taken your coat."

"Me too, but I would have had to get past Gwen to get my things, and I just couldn't."

Clay furrowed his brow. "What did she say to you?"

Mary shrugged weakly. "Just the normal jealous girlfriend things. She called me ugly and then implied some terrible things about me and you."

Clay swiped his hand across his mouth. "How dare she?"

"I . . . should have at least rescued my coat, but I was upset. I'm such a chicken."

"You're not a chicken. Gwen and Leif were out of line, and no one could expect you to know how to deal with either of them."

Mary pressed her hand to her chest to suppress the sharp ache that grew there. "I'm still ashamed I didn't have the courage to stay with you."

Clay propped his good elbow on the table and cradled his forehead in his hand. "Mary, there's no shame in being who you are. Gwen is aggressive and pushy, and I'm very glad you're not like her."

"Still, I should have been there. I didn't even get to talk to the doctor. How did the surgery go?"

Clay gave her an exhausted smile. "He said it went well, but we won't really know for a few weeks. I'm hopeful." His smile faded. "But the one I'm really worried about is you. I'm so sorry about Gwen and Leif. Leif was still there in the waiting room when Cathy and I left the hospital, and it was all I could do not to punch him, but my left hand has always been weaker. It probably wouldn't have hurt at all."

"I'm glad you didn't punch him."

"I'm glad too. It would have felt so good, but it's never worth it, and that is not who I am."

Mary grabbed his hand. “I guess you don’t know how good of a person you are unless you’re occasionally tempted to do the wrong thing.”

His jaw twitched with tension. “I do know that you’ve had nothing but trouble since I came into your life. I’m sorry. I didn’t know Gwen could be so mean-spirited.”

Mary had forgotten all about Ron standing behind the counter until he cleared his throat. They both glanced at him. His eyes were wide, his jaw slack. “Um, hi. Um, this is your friend who had to get surgery?”

Clay grinned at Ron, even though he couldn’t have been feeling very cheerful. He was so *gute* to his fans. “Yeah. I’m sorry to just storm in here like this, but I was worried about Mary.”

Ron lit up like a candle. “You can storm into my place any time and any way you want.”

Mary stood up. “Clay, this is Ron. He was wonderful nice. He gave me free coffee and donuts and let me use his phone and stay here out of the cold.”

“I’m so grateful,” Clay said.

He tried to stand up, but Ron protested. “No, don’t get up.”

Clay sank back into the chair. “I’d like to shake your hand.”

Ron came out from behind the counter and shook Clay's left hand gently. Clay moved like every bone in his body hurt. "It's so nice to meet you, Clay. I'm a big Peaks fan."

Clay's eyes shone with gratitude. "Well, now I'm a big Ron fan. Thank you for helping Mary out."

Ron was clearly thrilled to be talking to Clay Markham. "It was nothing." He motioned to Clay's right arm. "So, you got surgery?"

Ach! Mary felt worse than ever. Clay had wanted to keep it a secret, but the secret was out because of her.

Clay brushed his hand down his bandaged arm. "Yeah. My elbow has been real sore. The doctor repaired some damage."

"I never would have guessed. You pitched so good in the last game."

Clay raised his eyebrows. "I'm not sure what game you were watching, but I gave up two home runs."

Ron shook his head. "It's Seaman's fault. No manager should ever call a fastball right over the plate for Edgar Navarro. It was a bad strategy."

"My speed was off."

"That's nonsense," Ron said. "You did everything humanly possible. Seaman made a coaching mistake. And Navarro is the best hitter in the league."

Clay's Adam's apple bobbed up and down, and the light behind his eyes softened. It was the expression he always got when something deeply touched him. "Thanks, Ron. That really means a lot to me. To tell you the truth, I've been feeling sort of washed-up." He lifted his right arm. "This has been the worst thing. A pitcher with a bad arm."

Ron sat down on the other side of Clay. "Nobody in their right mind would say you're washed-up, but is another year or two of pitching worth the pain or your quality of life? The life span of a pitcher in the Majors isn't long."

Clay didn't seem to like hearing that. He'd said as much to Mary that night at the Mexican restaurant. "But who am I if I can't pitch? It's been my whole life for twenty-five years."

Ron pulled a napkin from the dispenser and swiped it across the table. "It's okay to start thinking about life after baseball. It doesn't mean you're washed-up. Your life will still be important. It has to be. You're less than halfway done. Pitching in the Major Leagues can't be all there is."

Clay looked down at his hand. "I guess

that's true."

A muted van horn sounded long and loud outside the window. Mary glanced out to the street. Cathy sat in her van leaning on her horn with a very irritated look on her face.

Clay winced. "I told her I'd hurry, and here we are shooting the breeze."

"We need to get you home," Mary said. "You need to rest."

Clay pressed his hand to his forehead. "Yes, I do. I'm not feeling so good."

Ron stood up. "I'd ask for your autograph, but it looks like you won't be signing many baseballs in the near future."

Clay let Mary help him stand, and he leaned heavily into her. "I'm coming back into town next week, and I promise to stop by and say hello, take a few photos if you want. I'm real grateful for what you did for Mary."

Cathy must have been sitting on the steering wheel. The horn didn't stop.

Ron laughed. "I hope you're not in too much trouble. It was nice talking to you."

"I'd say we're in big trouble," Clay said, "but what can Cathy do to a disabled baseball player and an Amish girl?"

"You'd be surprised," Mary said. She

hooked her elbow around Clay's good arm and dragged him out the door.

Chapter 12

Mary didn't usually ride her bike in the winter. The roads were icy, and the wind stung her face, even if she wrapped a scarf over her mouth. But the January wind couldn't stop her this year. She needed to take care of Clay, to prove to him that she was loyal and courageous and capable and would never abandon him again. Of course it was easy to resolve to be brave when Clay was staying at Esther's house and reporters didn't ever come onto Esther's property.

For two mornings in a row, Mary had ridden her bike to Esther's house to be with Clay and take care of him after his surgery. She wore long stockings and sweatpants under her dress, plus a fleece sweater and long underwear as well as her coat, her bonnet, and a scarf tied over her ears and one wrapped around her neck and face. She was sufficiently warm and seriously worried.

Clay didn't seem to be getting better. He

said his elbow hurt worse than ever, and the pain pills the doctor had prescribed hadn't helped. Last night, he'd seemed lethargic and uncomfortable. Mary had ridden home in the dark, and Esther had promised to keep an eye on him until Mary returned in the morning.

It was eight a.m., but Mary had been up at five pacing the floor, worried sick about Clay. She walked her bike up Esther's sidewalk and propped it against one of the tall bushes next to Esther's porch. She knocked softly on Esther's door, even though Esther's children never slept past 6:30. Winnie opened the door, her face smeared with purple jam, and smiled at Mary. "*Hallo.* Mamm says *cum reu.*"

Winnie took Mary's gloved hand and led her into the kitchen, where Esther was doing dishes and Levi Junior was lying on a soft, fluffy blanket in the middle of the kitchen floor.

Esther glanced at Mary, and her eyes flashed with distress. Mary's stomach lurched. "What's wrong. Is Clay all right? Is he still asleep?"

Esther pressed her lips into a hard line. "He's gone."

The floor fell out from under her. "Gone?"

"Winnie, don't lay on your *bruder.* He got

up this morning at the crack of dawn, and someone came to pick him up." Esther pulled a piece of paper from her pocket. "This is for you, but he said I could read it."

Mary took the paper from Esther and unfolded it.

> "Mary, I think I've got an infection. I called an Uber to take me to Denver to see my doctor. One of the players, Freddie Smith, and his wife are going to meet me at the hospital. I'll text Cathy to let you know how I'm doing. Clay."

Mary sank into one of Esther's kitchen chairs, fighting for a deep breath.

Esther slipped into the chair next to her and laid a hand on top of Mary's arm. "I'm sure he's going to be okay."

"He left me behind," Mary murmured.

Esther eyed Mary with concern. "He didn't want you to worry."

Mary took a deep, shuddering breath. "He can't depend on me. I've let him down too many times before. This time, he didn't even ask."

"That is the furthest thing from his mind." Esther fingered the celery stick tucked behind her ear. "For sure and certain, he didn't want to inconvenience you."

The bitter truth sank clear to her bones. "He knows I don't see him as an inconvenience. He also knows I panic, that I can't keep a clear head. He called a teammate because he knows he can't count on me." A soft sob escaped Mary's lips. "He doesn't trust me, and for *gute* reason. I've done nothing but let him down."

"You took him in and nursed him back to health after the accident. That doesn't sound like someone who let him down. Winnie, stop kissing Junior's head. You're going to smother him."

Mary wiped the tears from her cheeks. "Anyone would have done that. But when it was really important, I cared more about myself than Clay. He was in surgery, and I just walked right out of the hospital."

Esther reached out and wrapped her arms around Mary's shoulders. "*Ach,* Mary, I'm so sorry, but you have nothing to be ashamed of. This is who you are. Clay and I like you just the way you are."

Mary snorted and startled the baby. "It's not *gute* enough, not if I can't be there for Clay when he needs me."

"The doctor will take *gute* care of him. Clay doesn't need you."

"That's what I'm most afraid of," Mary

said, before disintegrating into a puddle of tears.

Mary poured the feed into the goats' little trough and petted Smiley on the head. She felt as if she'd been sleepwalking through the last two weeks. Clay had been in the hospital for three days, followed by recovery and intensive physical therapy in Denver. He had sent Cathy four texts a day keeping everyone updated on his progress, but Cathy wasn't about to interrupt her own life to bring messages to Mary four times a day. Communication had been frustrating and sporadic.

Mary had never been so tempted to get her own cell phone.

Every day, she thought about asking Cathy to drive her to Denver, but it was obvious Clay didn't want her there, and that thought hurt her heart more than anything. He hadn't finished fixing the barn, but Mary was beginning to wonder if Clay would ever come back. She tried not to think too hard about it, because such thoughts always brought her perilously close to the edge of despair.

Spring training started in less than two weeks, and even if Clay came back to finish the barn, he wouldn't stay long, and she might never see him again. The lump in Mary's throat felt like a jagged boulder.

Should she have gone to Denver? Maybe, but she feared she'd let Clay down again. Worse than that, she couldn't bear to face him, couldn't bear it if all she saw in his eyes was pity or, worse, indifference. If he truly wanted to see her again, it had to be his choice, not hers. So she waited, hoping Clay still thought about her, hoping he didn't think he was better off without her.

Mary nuzzled her face against Fluffy's neck and brushed her hand down Blue's back. Then suddenly, Clay was there, standing just inside the barn door as if he'd never left. Mary caught her breath, and without thinking about how Clay would react, she threw herself into his arms and burst into tears. To her relief, he acted as if he'd been expecting it, even hoping for it. He wrapped his strong arms around her and lifted her off the ground. "*Ach,* Clay! Don't do that. You're going to hurt your elbow."

He gently set her on her feet, his smile fading when he noticed her tears. "Mary, I'm so sorry!"

She pulled a tissue from her coat pocket and wiped her eyes even though she was by no means done crying. "I was afraid you'd never come back."

He gazed at her, a muted sadness in his expression. "Of course I came back. This is where my heart is."

Mary ignored the warmth traveling up her arms. "You left me."

He winced. "I know. I knew you'd be hurt."

"I'm not hurt. I'm ashamed. Very ashamed."

Clay pulled her to him. "There's nothing to be ashamed of. I knew it would be better for you if you didn't have to go. You hate reporters and ex-girlfriends and crowds, and I didn't want to have to worry about you."

"I let you down," Mary sobbed. "You needed me, and I failed you. The truth is, you couldn't trust me to take care of you, and I'm ashamed."

He nudged her chin up. "Mary, there's no reason to be ashamed. You've lived a very sheltered life. You have no idea how to handle worldly, sophisticated people who attack and bully you. I don't expect you to."

"But I abandoned you. I told you I'd be there after surgery, and I ran like a scared bunny rabbit. I left when you needed me the most."

His lips twitched upward. "I like bunny rabbits."

"But that's why you didn't ask me to go

with you to Denver. You don't think you can trust me."

He brushed an errant strand of hair from her face. "Mary, I like you just the way you are."

She sniffed. "That's not good enough." Not for a man like Clay Markham. "I want to be good enough for you, and I never will."

An emotion raw and uncertain traveled across his face. "You're too good for me, Mary."

"Ha, ha," she said with a moan.

"Nothing funny about it," he murmured.

She rested her head in the crook of his neck. "How is your elbow? How was Denver? What did the doctor say?"

"The elbow is getting better, but I'm going to miss spring training. I can't even throw a change-up. Denver was cold and lonely, and my doctor said we just have to wait and see. I'm trying not to think about it too hard or I get depressed."

"I like you just the way you are," she said, then looked up and grinned.

He rolled his eyes. "That's good because this is all there is." Fluffy and Blue sniffed at Clay's pants. He squatted and patted both of them on the head. "I'm afraid I won't be able to finish the barn until my elbow is fully healed. Who knows when that will be."

"I don't mind." She wouldn't mind if the barn never got finished as long as Clay kept coming around to work on it.

"I'm pretty much useless for a few months."

Mary narrowed her eyes in mock irritation. "Don't say that, or I'll have to find a table to pound on."

He laughed. "I guess not totally useless. I've been invited to go visit some underprivileged elementary and high schools in Denver next week and give them sort of a pep talk. Would you want to come with me?"

The question caught her off guard, and her heart skipped a beat. "I . . . I could do that." She realized her mistake as soon as the words were out of her mouth. This was a chance to prove herself a true friend. She couldn't hesitate. "Um, I mean, I really want to. I'd love to come."

It was too late. Clay had seen her uncertainty. His face fell. "You don't have to come. I just, I just like being with you."

"No, really, Clay. I can do it. Surely Leif and Gwen won't be there."

He nudged her away from him, turned his back, and stared out the open barn door.

"You don't trust me to protect you."

Mary frowned. "It's not that." She reached out to put a hand on his shoulder, and he stepped away to avoid her touch. It stung as if he'd slapped her hand away.

"You don't need or want my money, you don't care how famous I am, and you don't trust me to protect you. There is absolutely nothing I have that you will accept. I'm useless to you, Mary." He lifted his right hand slowly and stared at it. "I'm useless to the whole world."

There was such despair in his voice, she couldn't scold him. Once again, she had done something to make him doubt her. She wanted to weep. "Clay, that's not true. I trust you. Of course, I trust you. The problem is inside me. It has nothing to do with you."

"It has everything to do with me. You don't believe in me. You don't trust that I mean what I say, that I will never let any harm come to you. And for good reason. I failed you at the hospital. You should never have had to deal with Leif and Gwen."

"You were in surgery."

"I should have thought it through. I know things you don't. I should have asked the nurses to find you a private room instead of letting you go to the waiting room. All you've tried to do is support me, and I've made your life miserable. It's no wonder you don't trust me, but it still hurts that you don't."

Clay deserved nothing less than the truth, but she didn't know if she had the courage to give it to him, especially since he might hear it, walk out that barn door, and never look back. Mary took a ragged breath, and the cold air cut sharp against her throat. She moved up behind Clay and wrapped her arms around him so her hands were pressed against his chest. He seemed to relax in her embrace. "Does this hurt your elbow?"

"No. It feels wonderful."

Could he feel her heart's wild rhythm through the back of his coat? She pressed her head against his shoulder blade. "I'm going to tell you something that you're not going to like and I don't want to tell."

"Okay?" he said, the hesitation evident in his voice. "If you're going to tell me you don't want to see me anymore, I don't think I can bear it."

Mary's knees turned to jelly. He didn't want to give up on her. She felt the bittersweet happiness of it down to her toes. "You might not want to see me anymore after what I have to tell you." She released him and sat down on the little milking stool she used to milk the goats. He turned and looked at her, his eyes filled with an emotion Mary couldn't define. Hope? Sorrow? Love?

It couldn't be love.

Clay Markham couldn't love a plain, shy Amish girl, and she most certainly shouldn't love him. She was Amish, he wasn't. End of story.

Ada would insist that was the end of the story.

Dat would say that was the end of the story.

Even Joanna would agree that was the end of the story.

"It wonders me," Mary said, "if you could sit over there on the workbench and not look at me."

"Not look at you?"

Mary swallowed the bile in her throat. "It's a terrible story." And she didn't want to see the horror or the shock or the condemnation in his eyes.

Clay strode to the workbench, but instead of sitting on it, he dragged it closer to her with his left hand. He sat down, braced his elbows on his knees, and took both of Mary's hands. "I won't look away, Mary. Ever."

She shivered at the truth in his eyes. "Okay."

He squeezed her hands tighter. "I'm ready to hear anything you want to tell me."

Clay's look was both comforting and unnerving, but this was no time to get distracted. "We have family in Iowa. I think I told you."

"Yes."

"Aunt Gloria is my mother's sister, and she was furious when Dat moved us to Colorado. Aunt Gloria wasn't here when Mamm died, and she blames Dat for robbing her of a sister. She doesn't have a kind word to say to him, so he has avoided Aunt Gloria ever since Mamm died. That's why he didn't go to the wedding."

Clay's eyebrow twitched slightly. "You didn't go to the wedding either."

Mary exhaled a deep breath. "Not because of Aunt Gloria, but because of Cousin Peter."

"Aunt Gloria's son?"

"No, Peter is one of my cousins on Dat's side." She closed her eyes and worked up the courage to keep going. "I was seventeen years old when we took a trip to Iowa to visit family. We stayed at Aunt Ruth and Uncle Menno's house while we were there. Peter was twenty-two and engaged to a very nice girl in the district." Mary licked her dry lips. "I don't even remember why I was alone in the barn, but Peter . . . he, um, he attacked me."

Lines of shock and horror etched themselves deep into Clay's face. "He attacked you?"

"I didn't have the courage to cry out or fight him. I was so surprised and horrified, I just went limp. It was like I was paralyzed." She shuddered. "I shouldn't have let him do it. I'm so sorry, Clay. I know I shouldn't have let him do it."

Clay groaned and slid off the bench, kneeling next to her stool. He wrapped his arms around her like a blanket and held on so tightly, Mary wouldn't have been able to fall if she'd tried to. "I've got you," he whispered. "You're safe."

"I should have resisted. Maybe he thought I wanted it."

"No, Mary. You have no fault in this." He pulled away and pinned her with a fiery gaze. "Peter bears all the responsibility, not you. Don't ever believe it happened because of you. Peter is an evil man. You are blameless. Do you understand?"

"Every time I go anywhere where there are strangers or lots of people, I feel the fear all over again. The way Peter looked at me, the violation of trust, the sheer terror of the moment. It broke me. I was never the same again. I never felt safe. Peter destroyed my peace. That first time Leif McIntire strolled into our barn like he owned it, memories of that terrible day crashed into me like a runaway horse."

Mary felt something moist against her cheek. Clay was crying. "I'm so sorry, my dear, sweet Mary. I'm so sorry."

They sat for a few minutes in silence, both of them weeping, sharing the pain of an unspeakable act.

"After it happened, I was so ashamed. I just wanted to come back to Colorado and forget about it, but then I thought of other women who could be hurt by Peter. I couldn't let him ruin more lives the way he had ruined mine. The day before we left Iowa, Mamm and I went to Uncle Menno and told him about his son. He kicked us out of his house. I don't know how I found the courage after that, but I went with Mamm to Peter's fiancé, and I told her the whole story. Her name is Priscilla."

Clay smoothed his hand down her arm. "That's the bravest thing I've ever heard anyone do."

"She didn't believe me."

"She didn't?"

"Or maybe she didn't *want* to believe me. To learn something like that about your fiancé was, I'm sure, sickening. I didn't want to upset Priscilla or ruin her wedding plans. I just wanted to warn her. I don't know what I was thinking. First, she told me it was a lie, then she claimed I had tempted Peter beyond his ability to resist." The heat crawled up Mary's neck. She hadn't relived the accusations for many years. "There was nothing else I could have done, but after we left Iowa, Priscilla told everyone I was spreading lies about Peter to cover my own sin. Peter played innocent, and the entire district in Iowa turned against me and my family. I got letters from Iowa admonishing me to repent. Uncle Menno refused to allow us in his home ever again. Some Amish in Iowa wrote our bishop encouraging him to put me under the ban, but I hadn't been baptized yet. I'm glad I wasn't in Iowa. Our community here in Colorado is more forgiving."

"But, Mary, there was nothing to forgive. You did nothing wrong."

"I upset the balance of things in the community. We don't talk about such things. It's not the Amish way."

Clay swiped his hand down the side of his face. "Peter upset the balance of things by taking what he had no right to take. Mary, I'm so sorry. This makes me sick."

It made Mary sick too. "*Jah.* It's okay if you want to go away and never come back. I've been damaged, ruined for life."

His eyes flashed with raw anger. "That couldn't be further from the truth. Peter stole something very precious from you, but you are not damaged or ruined. It was one moment in time that you are forced to carry with you for the rest of your life. Mary, you get mad at me when I say I'm useless. I'm not going to let you believe the same thing about yourself."

"But I don't."

"Yes, you do. You've framed it a different way in your mind, but you believe you are somehow not good enough because your Cousin Peter did something terrible to you. Don't let him determine your worth as a person. Don't give him that kind of power over your life." He took her face in his hands. "Peter doesn't deserve one more minute of your life than he already took from you."

Hope brightened a corner of her mind. Clay knew her secret, and he was still here. "I wish I could shrug off the memories like taking off a coat. It's so easy to say, so hard to do."

He grimaced. "That is painfully true. Just look at where I still am with my dad. I don't know that I have hope of ever forgiving him, ever moving on from his influence. But at least I'm aware of how it colors the way I live my life."

Mary slung her arm around Clay's neck. "I feel so much better knowing you know and that you don't blame me."

"Never, never, never. You are that much more precious to me because of what I know." He took her hand and kissed her knuckles one by one. She trembled at his gentleness. "So is Peter living happily ever after in Iowa with Priscilla and ten Amish children?"

Mary couldn't contain a small smile. "Priscilla didn't marry him. I'm not sure if it was because of me or because she eventually saw for herself the kind of man he is. Maybe what I did influenced some girls to avoid him — I hope so. Priscilla married someone else a year after the attack. Peter finally convinced someone to marry him last year. He was thirty-three years old. I hope he feels remorse. I hope he never did it again. I hope he has changed for the better. I have forgiven him, but I haven't forgotten."

"Of course not. How could you ever

forget?" He gave her a sad smile. "I don't know if this will help, but I swear his name will never cross my lips again."

"It never crossed your lips before."

He nodded in mock earnestness. "For that, I am very grateful."

She giggled, then gave him a serious look. "So, now you know why I get anxious over nothing. It's not because I believe you can't protect me."

"I won't argue that you have every reason to be anxious, and I'll try not to take it personally, but I still feel the need to be useful to you. I just wish I knew what I could do."

She pressed her palm to his cheek. "Just be who you are. That is more than good enough."

He grinned. "You always know the right thing to say, even if I don't believe you."

She protested loudly and gave him the stink eye. "Then there's nothing more to do but find a table and pound on it."

Chapter 13

Ada set the basket of sliced bread on the table. "Where's Clay? He's got four minutes or he's late. I'm not holding dinner for him."

Mary turned away to hide a smile. Ada talked tough, but she would let dinner grow cold before she would start without Clay. The *gute* news for Ada was that Clay was never late, though tonight he was cutting it a little close.

"Maybe that truck finally broke down," Beth said, putting a serving spoon in the bowl of corn.

Joanna pointed to the oven. "Should I pull out the chicken, or wait for Clay to come?"

Dat sat down and picked up his napkin. "Pull it out. I'm starving, and since when do we eat on Clay's schedule?"

Beth snorted her amusement. "Since November."

Beth was right about that. Since Clay had

shown up on the farm, it seemed that all of them, Dat included, had centered their lives around Clay. Of course, Mary revolved around Clay like the Earth revolved around the sun, but the entire family very much had Clay in their hearts all the time.

It was the second week of February, and Clay spent weekdays in Denver working with the pitching coach and doing rehab on his elbow. He would drive back to Byler on Friday nights and spend Saturdays and Sundays with the family. He didn't spend nearly enough time in Byler to suit Mary, but she was doing her best to get used to Clay being gone. She wasn't blind, though she wanted to ignore the hard truth. Once Clay's elbow was better, he would be in Denver full time, playing ball, making lots of money, signing autographs, and forgetting about Mary Yoder.

Joanna glanced at the clock just as Clay walked into the kitchen, flashing that beautiful smile. He didn't knock anymore because everyone considered him part of the family.

Mary's heart still leaped out of her chest every time Clay came to the farm. He was so handsome, so strong. He had a gentle spirit and a kind heart that Mary found impossible to resist. What was she going to do without him? Could she live on the *memory* of Clay for the rest of her life?

"Am I late?" Clay asked as he grabbed the bowl of chowchow from Ada's hands and set it on the table.

"We almost ate without you," Ada grumbled.

He smiled sheepishly. "I had a little trouble getting my truck started."

"I told you," Beth said.

"And," Clay said, taking five small wrapped boxes out of his pocket, "I had to wrap these presents for you." He handed the presents to each of the *schwesteren,* Dat, and finally Mary.

Dat held his box as if there was something poison inside. Ada frowned. Even Joanna looked as if she didn't know what to say. Mary's heart sank. "Clay, you don't have to . . ."

Clay chuckled, his eyes flashing with amusement. "I'll be crushed if you don't accept them. Please open them before dinner gets cold."

Mary glanced doubtfully at Joanna, who glanced doubtfully back. *If you reject the gift, you reject the giver,* Clay had said. *Ach,* Mary thought they were past this.

There was nothing to do but open it and then try to manage Clay's disappointment. She tore the paper and opened the box.

Inside it was a tiny baseball on a hook and chain. It couldn't have been worth more than five dollars.

Clay flashed those white teeth. "I'll spoil the surprise for the rest of you. I got you all the same thing. I saw them at the team store and thought they were cute. They are also cheap, small, completely useless, and acceptable as a gift for stubborn Amish people."

"We're not stubborn," Dat said, "just resolute."

Clay raised his eyebrows. "Whatever." He took Mary's baseball and wound it around his fingers. "They're keychains. Since none of you have cars, I don't know what you will do with them, but I just had to buy them. I guess you could say they were an impulse purchase."

Mary looked at Dat. "Can we keep them, Dat?"

Dat was the one who had insisted that Clay repair the fence and barn, and he genuinely liked Clay, even though Clay disagreed with him about improvements to the farm, but Clay was an Englischer, and Dat scrutinized everything he did. Dat took his keychain out of the box and examined the baseball as if he'd never seen anything like it before. "I have two keys, one to our house and one to the toolshed. I suppose I could put my keys on this keychain. It doesn't seem too fancy."

Clay nodded. "I don't think anyone would accuse you of being proud."

Dat stroked his beard. "I suppose not."

Ada opened her box, and Mary could tell she was trying not to smile. "I could hang this on the handle of my cleaning bucket to remind me that things could be worse."

Clay cocked his eyebrow. "Worse?"

"I haven't mopped the floor once since you've been here. It's been a nice break. You don't mop correctly, and sometimes I have to go back and re-mop, but at least you're trying. It could be worse."

Clay laughed. "Glad I could help."

Joanna held hers up. The baseball swung back and forth on the chain. "I'm going to hang mine on the oven handle." She smiled at Clay. "I'll think of you every time I bake something."

Clay pressed his palm to his chest. "I'm honored," he said, with a teasing glint in his eyes. "What are you going to do with yours, Beth?"

Beth fingered the tiny baseball. "Would it be weird to hang it around Fluffy's neck?"

"Yes," Ada said. "The other goats will try to eat it."

"No, they won't. They'll taste it, but they're too smart to eat it."

"What about you, Mary?" Joanna asked.

It might have been silly, but Mary never wanted to be anywhere without her tiny baseball. "I think I'll just keep it in my pocket."

Clay's eyes danced with delight. "I have to admit, I didn't think you would accept these. That gives me hope. I'm working my way up to the big stuff."

Mary shook her finger at Clay. "Don't even think about it. We don't want to have to keep hurting your feelings."

He chuckled and held up his hands as if she was pointing a gun at him. "Okay, I was just teasing. I know your limits. I just wanted to test them to make sure."

"Cum," Ada said. "Dinner is five minutes late. I'm blaming Clay if the chicken is dry."

"You can blame me for everything, especially the chicken."

When he'd first started eating with them, Clay found the whole idea of silent prayer strange. "How do you know when to open your eyes? What if there's someone who prays for twenty minutes? Do you all have to sit and wait?" he had asked. Ada had not-so-patiently explained to him about silent prayer, that *Handt nunna* meant "hands down." When Dat said *"Handt nunna,"* everyone put their hands in their laps and bowed their heads, and they all knew when prayer was over when they heard Dat pick up his fork and clink it against the plate. Clay had raised his eyebrows. "So your dad gets to decide how long the prayer lasts? It's good he's a man of few words."

Now Clay was very comfortable with the idea of silent prayer. One time, Mary had peeked at him while everyone's eyes were closed, and his eyes were tightly shut and his lips moving as he formed the words in his mind. Mary liked that he took it seriously. Maybe the family was helping his faith grow just by going about their daily lives.

After prayer, Ada carved the roasted chicken and served everybody their favorite pieces. Clay liked dark meat. Mary preferred white. For sure and certain, Ada made the best roast chicken in Colorado, but Mary would never tell her that. Ada avoided anything that sounded like a compliment. Like the rest of them, she didn't want to hear something that might tempt her to be proud.

Clay's regular place at the table was right next to Mary. He handed her the chowchow. "I went to Ron's place this week," he said.

Dat poured himself a glass of water. "Who is Ron?"

"He's the man I was telling you about, Dat. The one who owns the coffee shop I went to in Denver. He was really excited to meet Clay."

Clay grinned. "He was very kind to Mary, and he makes a mean cup of coffee."

Beth tilted her head to one side. "Why is it mcan?"

"It's a compliment. Ron makes really good coffee. His wife has been sick, but she's doing better. Ron's a good guy. I've told all my teammates and everyone at the front office about his coffee shop. Hopefully, business will pick up for him."

Dat nodded. "I appreciate that he was kind to my Ladybug. Too many people just look out for themselves, like that reporter who keeps bothering us."

Clay's fork stopped halfway to his mouth. "Leif has been here since Christmas?"

Mary frowned. She hadn't seen Leif McIntire since that horrible day at the hospital. Had he come to the farm after that?

Dat slowly chewed his food, looking mildly irritated but also a little amused. "Two days ago."

Ada widened her eyes. "Where was I?"

"You were all at Esther Kiem's house working on quilt squares. I invited him in and made him a cup of *kaffee.*"

Mary gaped at her *schwesteren.* They all looked as bewildered as she felt. "Why didn't you tell us?"

"I don't talk about my aches and pains or how many cavities I've had filled. Why would I talk about that unpleasant man?"

Clay looked crushed. "He was unpleasant to you?"

"What did he say?" Ada asked. "Did you brew the French roast or the cheap stuff?"

A smile bloomed on Joanna's face. "It was kind of you to invite him in for *kaffee.*"

Dat waved away the praise. "I told Mary she should invite him in and make him a cup of *kaffee* next time he came. I try to practice what I preach."

"What did he say?" Mary blurted out. "What did you say? Was he rude? Did he bring Clay's girlfriend?"

Dat ignored Mary's questions and jabbed his fork in Clay's direction. "All my fence posts are purple, and they didn't do a thing to keep that man off my property."

Clay grinned sheepishly. "But they look pretty."

Mary was the most patient person she knew, next to Clay, but her curiosity was about to kill her. "Dat, what did he say?"

Dat set his fork down and leaned back in his chair. "He liked the coffee." Dat nodded to Ada. "I used the French roast. I didn't want to be anything less than completely hospitable."

Mary resisted the urge to growl. "What did he say?"

"I hope you threw him out on his ear," Clay hissed.

"I was tempted," Dat said. "He wanted to know about you and Mary, and I refused to answer any questions. I complimented him on his nice, thick hair, and I got the impression he thought I was strange."

Clay burst into laughter. "I hope he felt very uncomfortable."

Dat nodded thoughtfully. "No doubt."

"Though, I don't think Leif is capable of feeling discomfort." Clay narrowed his eyes. "He doesn't seem to feel shame, anyway."

The lines around Dat's eyes etched themselves deeper into his face. "I finally had to invite him to leave. You can ask an enemy to supper, but when he starts to break the dishes, you have to show him the door."

Mary gasped. "He started breaking dishes."

"No, Ladybug. It's just an expression. He said some things I found deeply offensive, and I don't suffer fools."

Mary swallowed past the lump in her throat. "What . . . what did he say?"

Dat reached over and patted her arm. "That is none of your concern. Lord willing, he won't come back, and if he does, I'll serve him the cheap coffee."

"I'm sorry," Clay said, spreading the same butter on his roll over and over again. "I'm so sorry. I've brought this on all of you." He glanced at Mary, regret shining in his eyes. "Especially you."

Dat wasn't near as upset as Clay was. "I don't blame you. We Amish like a little excitement now and then. It gives us something to gossip about during the long winter months. That reporter is the most exciting thing that has happened to us since you came along, Clay."

Clay seemed to perk up, as if Dat had paid him a nice compliment. "I hope I've been helpful in some small way, because I've brought a lot of trouble too."

Dat cleared his throat and took a drink of water. "I'm glad you're here tonight, Clay. There's something I need to say."

Clay smiled at Mary and set her heart racing. "I'm glad I'm here too."

Dat paused and looked from Mary to Clay and back again. "I know that sometimes I can be proud and stubborn, and I need to repent."

Clay shook his head. "You don't have to apologize, Try. I shouldn't have suggested the new siding or the new roof or anything but chain-link fencing. Or the purple paint."

Dat grunted his disapproval. "The purple paint was your worst idea. The vinyl fencing was almost as bad. There is no other choice but chain-link."

Clay laughed and held up his hands in surrender. "I promise I won't try to talk you into it ever again."

"I'm most certainly not going to apologize for standing up to your vinyl fencing idea, but I do need to repent for something else. Do you remember what I told you the morning after the accident?"

Clay tapped his finger to his lips and looked up at the ceiling. "You said you didn't trust me and that I needed to put on a shirt."

Beth frowned in confusion. "You weren't wearing a shirt when you hit our barn?"

Mary's face got warm at the memory of Clay's muscular chest and arms and the fact that Dat had said "bare chest" right out loud that morning. "He was fully dressed the night of the accident, Beth. But we had to wash his shirt because it was covered in blood." Beth didn't need to know how Clay's shirt had gotten off his back and into the laundry.

By the funny look on Beth's face, it was obvious she was piecing together that very thing.

Dat studied Clay's face. "I told you that you wouldn't learn a lesson by just writing me a check for the damage you did to our barn."

"And you were absolutely right. I needed to learn a lesson."

"I didn't know if you were really sorry for what you'd done or if you were just saying what you thought I wanted to hear. I wanted to test your sincerity, and I didn't want to make it easy for you, especially since it seemed your life was heading in a bad direction. I thought the hard work might do you some good."

Clay propped his chin in his hand. "It did. I'm very grateful that you cared enough to want to help me."

Dat shook his head. "It would be pure pride if I took any credit for changing or helping you, Clay. It is you who have helped us. You've proven yourself sincere and honorable, and we have come to depend on you. Our fence is fixed, the wobbly railing is secure, and there isn't one hinge on the whole farm that creaks."

"He handles rude reporters," Joanna said, "and he's brought a lot of business to Esther's quilt shop."

Mary's smile sputtered to nothing. "He cleaned up the fire extinguisher foam inside and outside the barn."

Ada dabbed at her mouth with a napkin. "The upstairs toilet doesn't leak anymore, and he cleans out the wood stove three times a week."

"And he mucks out the barn whenever I ask him to," Beth said. "I hate mucking out."

Dat turned to Beth. "You've taken advantage of Clay's *gute* heart, Beth. I'm afraid we all have."

Mary's heart skipped. Had Clay hung around for so long only out of the goodness of his heart? Had she taken advantage of that?

Beth caught her bottom lip between her teeth. "I haven't taken advantage. I just hate mucking out, and Clay doesn't mind at all."

Clay grinned. "Anything for you, Beth." He took another roll. "You've all done so much for me. I wanted to repay you."

Dat nodded. "You have made amends several times over, and I should have told you long before now. I'm sorry for that. As far as I'm concerned, your debt is paid. You should be allowed to get back to your own life without our farm hanging about your neck like a chain."

Mary couldn't breathe. Joanna glanced at her, concern saturating her features. Beth looked as if she was going to be ill, and Ada's mouth drooped into a deep frown. Clay peered at Dat under heavy eyelids. Mary couldn't begin to guess what he was thinking. Was he overjoyed to finally be free of his obligation? Would he miss Mary even a tiny bit?

Dat didn't seem to notice the pall that had descended over the kitchen table. "You've barely had any time to rehab your elbow. You've already missed spring training, and Cathy tells me baseball season is coming up soon. She says you need to concentrate on getting your arm back into shape."

Clay pressed his lips into a hard line. "So . . . you don't want me to come work on the farm anymore?" The tone of his voice gave Mary a little hope. She didn't want him to be sad, but he sounded reluctant to leave.

"It's not a matter of wanting," Dat said. "We've been selfish, and I'm repenting right now. For sure and certain, we'll miss you."

Clay's brows met in the middle of his

forehead. "I haven't fixed the fire damage to the barn. It needs to be sanded and painted, and to really do a good job, I should probably reinforce the wood on that corner."

Joanna nodded so hard she fanned up a breeze. "He promised to fix the water pump, and you wouldn't want him to go back on his promise."

"Swear not at all," Dat said, as if that absolved Clay of any promises he'd made to the family.

Ada skewered a piece of chicken with her fork. "I really can't make cheese without him. He's the only one strong enough to stir a whole pot of curds."

Dat didn't budge. "You've never had trouble stirring it all by yourself before."

"I really hate to muck out," Beth mumbled.

Joanna gave Mary an encouraging look. Mary found her voice. "Clay is the fastest milker in the family. I can't possibly manage without him."

A light turned on behind Clay's eyes. "You . . . you can't manage without me?"

"I wouldn't dream of it," Mary said breathlessly.

Dat gazed at the faces turned toward him. "But don't you want to rehab your elbow?"

Clay laced his fingers together in his lap.

"I spend five days a week in rehab. My elbow is getting stronger, and the trainer is hopeful. I don't want to overdo the rehab, or I'll make it worse. I have all this time on the weekends. Why can't I spend it here and finish the job I started?"

Dat's lips twitched. "Are you sure? Don't you have a thousand more important things to do?"

Clay glanced at Mary. "No, nothing more important."

Dat sighed. "Well, then, I suppose you can keep coming. I've enjoyed having you around, even though you try to talk me into things I don't need or want."

Clay seemed immensely pleased. "I've learned my lesson. I can't give you anything bigger than a keychain, and I can't suggest any improvements more expensive than a box of screws."

Dat cracked a smile. "And don't you forget it."

Did Dat have any idea how absolutely elated Mary was? Did he have any inkling about what Mary felt for Clay? Of course not. If Dat knew how much Mary adored Clay, he would have given Clay his mini baseball back and never let him set foot on the farm again.

Chapter 14

Mary sat at Esther's kitchen table working on her quilt blocks for Mammi Beulah's quilt. She'd decided on a simple pink fabric with a white background. It was going to be so beautiful, especially combined with all her *schwesteren*'s quilt blocks. Mammi Beulah was going to love it.

"Now that you know how to make the Drunkard's Path quilt block, you should make a whole quilt of it," Esther said. "It makes such a cute pattern all together in a quilt."

Mary smoothed her hand down the quilt block she'd just finished ironing. "I do like it."

"You could make one for Clay, since it was his drunkard's path that brought him to you." Esther pulled a plastic spoon from behind her ear and handed it to Levi Junior, who was sitting in the highchair. Winnie was playing with a set of blocks on the floor.

"Or, if you want, I could sell it in my shop."

Mary clipped an errant thread. "I'd like to see that."

Esther smiled. "I think your favorite thing in my quilt shop will always be Clay Markham, but one of your quilts would probably make you happy too."

Mary giggled. "I have to admit, Clay is the best thing about your quilt shop."

"He says his elbow is getting better. I'm happy for him." Esther glanced doubtfully at Mary. "But maybe not so happy for you."

"It really does feel like we're coming to the end." Mary couldn't muster one ounce of cheer in her voice.

"I can't imagine Clay is very happy about that either."

Mary slumped her shoulders. "We never talk about it. I just want to postpone the sadness, I guess."

Esther pressed her lips together and nodded. "We don't have to talk about it. What will be, will be. We accept Gotte's will and move on."

Mary's lips curled upward even as pain pricked her heart. "When I first met him, Clay couldn't agree with that. He said, 'What if we don't think God is doing a very good job?' I told him to stop talking like that or Gotte would smite him. He said that's why he didn't go to church because he was afraid Gotte would smite him."

"That's not true," Esther said.

"I know. Gotte doesn't smite people for saying bad things about Him."

Esther picked up the spoon Levi Junior had tossed on the floor. "I mean Clay goes to church every Sunday."

"*Ach, vell,* every other Sunday with us. I think he kind of likes it."

"Nae," Esther said. "Before we met him, if he wasn't playing ball, he went to church every week. He told me because I said I was concerned for his salvation."

Mary drew her brows together. "I didn't know that."

"For sure and certain, he was mad at Gotte and stopped talking to Him for a while, but at least for the last year or so he's gone to church."

"Why wouldn't he tell me that?"

Esther shrugged. "Maybe he didn't want to sound like a hypocrite. You saw him at his worst that first night."

"I did. He was a mess." She breathed in the memory of Clay, with tousled hair and a green-tinged face, sitting on the floor with his arm around the toilet as if it were his best friend. She would cherish that memory forever, even though he would probably prefer to forget all about it.

A loud knocking came at Esther's door, and before Esther could get up to answer it, they heard the door open. Someone tromped down the hall to the kitchen. "Mary Yoder, you need a cell phone. I've half a mind to buy you one out of the money I've been saving for a cruise." Cathy Larsen came around the corner and pulled off her bright pink beanie. Her short hair floated out in every direction, carried in the air by static electricity.

Mary jumped to her feet. "Is everything okay?"

Cathy took off her coat and peeled off her gloves. "Is everything okay? I was in the middle of *Jeopardy!* when the mail came, and now I'll never know who won." She held out the magazine in her hand and turned to a page inside. "*Pro Day* magazine. Look at this."

Clay Markham, with a bandage on his head, smiled back at her from a full-page photo.

Her heart skipped a beat. Cathy scowled and moved her thumb so Mary could see the whole picture. Mary felt dizzy, like she was standing on a precipice looking over the edge into nothingness. There was Mary in the picture standing next to Clay, peering at someone off camera.

She snatched the magazine from Cathy's hand. "What is this? I don't . . . how did they get that picture?"

Cathy pointed to the blurry image of a van in the background. "I didn't give anyone permission to take a picture of my van, but there it is. That was on the day I drove you and Clay to the emergency room for stitches."

The title of the article stole Mary's breath. "The Secret Life of Clay Markham, the Sex, the Booze, and the Lies." She used to think "naked" was an embarrassing word. "Sex" was even worse, especially right alongside the photo of her. What would people think? What would Ada say? Or Dat? Mary thought she might pass out with shame.

Esther's eyes were wide as saucers. "Mary, this is . . ."

"Terrible?" Cathy said. "Embarrassing? Nauseating? I consider myself pro-free speech, but this reporter deserves a raging bladder infection."

Mary narrowed her eyes and looked at the name below the title. Of course, the reporter was Leif McIntire. He'd told Clay that Clay would regret not giving him a story. Now he'd gotten his revenge, and Mary was going to throw up. She scanned the article.

There was a picture of Clay's old girlfriend, Gwen, in the bottom corner sitting next to Clay at what looked like a fancy dinner, each smiling as if they loved each other very much, each holding up a glass of wine or champagne or something. Mary didn't really know the difference.

She read the first few lines of the article. "Clay Markham, party animal and starting pitcher for the Colorado Peaks, has a new address, a new girlfriend, and a secret, and the people who love him best are worried he's lost his mind. Or is this fascination with a new woman some sort of weird sexual fetish? Will any ball club sign him after this?" Mary's face felt as if it was on fire. Leif was talking about her, and the implications were stunning and horrible.

Cathy snatched the magazine away from her. "Good heavens, Mary, don't read it. It will give you a stroke."

"I want to know what they're saying about me," she said, barely able to draw a breath. She sank into her chair.

"No, you don't. This kind of trash shouldn't have been written. It most certainly shouldn't be read by anyone."

Esther took the magazine from Cathy. *"Ach, du lieva,"* she murmured.

Cathy yanked the magazine away from Esther. "You shouldn't be reading it either. The last time you lost your temper, you broke your big toe kicking the side of the house."

Esther hissed and folded her arms. "It was just a bruise."

Mary's heart cracked in a thousand different places. "Does Clay know?" It was the dumbest question she'd ever asked. Of course Clay knew, and surely he blamed her. She shouldn't have gone with him to the emergency room. They should have hidden his mangled car better than they had. She shouldn't have shown her face at the hospital when he went in to have surgery. She'd drawn unnecessary attention to him and, for sure and certain, had hurt his career, his reputation, and his chances of pitching for another season. How he must hate her!

Cathy shoved the magazine into her monstrous purse and took out her cell phone. "I'm sure Clay knows, but he's not answering my calls or my texts. I've texted him seven times and called him twice. It's radio silence."

The lump in Mary's throat was a jagged stone. Clay always answered Cathy's phone calls, even if he was in physical therapy.

Cathy sighed. "He's probably pouting.

That boy is a pouter."

"He's not a pouter," Mary mumbled. It took a lot to upset Clay, and his anger was usually associated with Leif McIntire.

Mary couldn't bear trying to guess how Clay was feeling. If he hated her, she wanted to hear it from him. If he was hurt, she wanted to apologize. "Cathy, will you please try to call him again? I've got to talk to him."

Cathy pressed her phone screen, put the phone to her ear, and waited. Mary held her breath as the seconds ticked away. He wasn't answering. After a few seconds, Cathy said, "Hello, Clay, this is Cathy. You can't pout forever, and Mary wants to talk to you. Call as soon as you get this message, because I'm not going to come back over here in an hour during *Wheel of Fortune.* My number is 555-903-9809." Cathy frowned. "I guess I don't have to leave my number, but it's just a habit. At the doctor, they ask for your cell number, your birthday, your blood type, and then want to know how depressed you think you are. It's annoying."

Mary was desperate to talk to Clay but was also dreading what he would say to her. Would he decide this was the end of his visits to Byler? Would he decide he was better off without her? If he wanted her out of his life, he wouldn't be mean about it, because unkindness wasn't in his nature, but in the end, the result would be the same.

They sat together at the table for about ten minutes, watching Levi Junior and Winnie play and not talking about the only thing that was on all their minds. Mary thought she might go crazy waiting for Clay to call.

Thank Derr Herr Cathy wasn't a patient person. She huffed out a breath and pulled her phone from her purse. "He's either on the phone with his agent or he's still ignoring me. I'm going to text him again." Cathy wasn't a very fast texter. Mary caught her bottom lip between her teeth, wishing she had her own phone so she could text Clay with her thumbs instead of the way Cathy was doing it, one finger at a time. Cathy set her phone on the table. "That should get his attention."

"What did you say?"

"I told him that you need to talk to him now and that he is a coward and a pouter. If you want results with Clay, you have to question his manhood." Sure enough, not one minute later, Cathy's phone rang. Cathy pointed to Mary. "You see. It works every time."

Cathy handed the phone to Mary, and Mary swiped the little white circle that Cathy had shown her how to use. "Clay?"

"Mary?" His voice was flat, but at least he had called her.

Relief washed over her. "Clay, I'm sorry about the article. I never meant to make trouble for you."

Clay was silent for a few seconds. "Trouble for me? I can't believe you're saying that. I can't believe you even want to talk to me. None of this is your fault. I am the one who has made trouble for you and your whole family." His voice cracked. "That article is disgusting, and I can't imagine what you are going through right now. I'm so sorry."

She should have known Clay would take full responsibility and not blame her at all. "I'm doing okay," was all she could think to say. Even now, Clay was more concerned about her feelings than his career or his life. Her heart swelled thinking of the goodness of this man. "It was inappropriate to print that photo of me, but please don't worry about it."

"But I do. This never would have happened if I hadn't crashed into your barn. Those things he wrote . . . I can't even . . .

I can't face you knowing what I've done to you."

"What have you done but bring me more happiness than I could possibly hold?"

"Oh, Mary, you're so good. I don't deserve you." His voice shook with emotion. "I want you to know that I've never lied to you, but I didn't dare tell you the complete truth. I was going to tell you everything eventually, but I was afraid you'd reject me, so I kept all my secrets to myself. I don't blame you if you hate me. I hate myself, not only for what he wrote about me, but for what he wrote about you and Peter."

Mary's heart stopped completely. "Peter?" she choked out.

"Yes, didn't you . . . ?" he stuttered. "Didn't you read the article?"

"Cathy wouldn't let me."

Another long, weighty pause. "Oh, Mary." The anguish in his voice made her flinch. He sobbed into the phone. "Oh, Mary."

"Clay, please don't cry." Cathy and Esther watched Mary's face with keen interest. Mary pressed her lips together and gave them a panicked look. Clay sounded as if he was about to disintegrate into dust. "It's going to be okay."

"No, it's not, and I was an idiot to hope that I could ever be good enough for a girl like you."

"That's not true, Clay. You are infinitely too good for me."

He groaned, and she could hear him moving around, maybe pacing the floor. "I love you with my whole heart, Mary Yoder, but I'm getting out of your life. I've caused enough damage."

Mary pressed her fist against her chest to keep her heart from shattering. "Please don't say that, Clay."

"Will you promise me one thing? Don't read that article. I want you to remember me and you the way we were before we ever met Leif McIntire. Will you do that for me, Mary?"

Mary couldn't catch her breath. This couldn't be the end. "I won't promise anything unless you promise me I'll see you this weekend."

"I'm real sorry, Mary, but you won't hear from me again." The phone went dead.

Mary's heart tried to claw its way out of her chest. She frantically dialed Clay's cell number, but all she got was his voicemail. She hit the END button and tried again. Again, the call went straight to Clay's voicemail. After the fifth attempt, she wanted to cry until she melted into a puddle on the linoleum floor.

Esther's eyes filled with compassion, and she pulled Mary into her embrace.

Mary blubbered for almost ten minutes while Esther handed her tissue after tissue, and Cathy took Levi Junior into the bedroom for his afternoon nap. Sensing something was wrong, Winnie climbed onto Mary's lap and patted her cheek tenderly, trying to make everything all better.

Esther propped her chin in her hand and gazed doubtfully at Mary. "So I guess that's that."

Something about the finality of Esther's words pricked Mary's heart. "It's what Clay thinks is best."

Cathy came back from the bedroom and pulled out a chair at the table. She leaned toward Mary as if she was sharing a secret. "It's nauseating how self-sacrificing that boy is. You're better off without him."

Everything inside Mary revolted against that thought. "I will never be better off without Clay."

Cathy's lips curled upward, either in a grimace or a smile. Mary could never tell the difference. "Then what are you going to do about it?"

What was she going to do about it?

"There's nothing I can do. Clay ended it. I must accept Gotte's will and move on with my life." Fresh tears sprang to her eyes. *What was she going to do about it?* What a useless question. She'd never had enough courage to *do* anything. If her horrible experience with Peter had taught her anything, it was that she was better off safe at home, not talking to strangers and not putting herself through the anxiety.

Esther glanced at Cathy. Her lips twitched as she fingered the spaghetti noodle tucked behind her ear. "It's definitely safer that way." Had Esther read her mind? Esther pulled Winnie from Mary's lap and cuddled Winnie in her arms. "With Clay out of your life, there will be no more reporters to deal with, no more ex-girlfriends to make you anxious, no more pictures in magazines."

Cathy nodded eagerly, even though Cathy rarely seemed eager or enthusiastic about anything. "This is really the only way if you want to avoid more heartache. No more frantic trips to Mexican restaurants or cold rides in that old truck. I won't have to miss another episode of *The Bachelor* or *Jeopardy!* to bring you one of Clay's texts. This is turning out to be a great day after all."

Cathy and Esther were just trying to make her feel better, but it wasn't working. She loved every minute she had spent with Clay, even if they were fending off reporters or talking to fans or riding in that old truck that didn't have a heater.

Mary smoothed her hand down her finished quilt block, Drunkard's Path. Cathy had said there was a little magic in every stitch someone sewed into a quilt block. Mary didn't believe in magic, but she did believe that Gotte had a plan. Had Gotte guided Clay's path even when he was drunk? Of all the barns in the valley Clay could have run into, why had he driven right up to Mary's back door? And what if there had never been any trouble with Cousin Peter? Mary would have gone to the wedding, and Dat would have called an ambulance instead of letting Clay spend the night. Had Gotte put Mary exactly where she needed to be?

An unfamiliar emotion seized Mary by the throat and left her breathless. Was it raw anger or fierce courage or both? She didn't know. All she *did* know was that she refused to trade Clay for a little bit of safety and peace of mind. If Gotte had indeed put Clay in her path, who was she to let her fear control her? If she wasn't willing to fight for him, then there was no power in her love. She pounded her fist on the table and made Esther jump. "No!" she shouted.

Cathy puckered her lips as if she'd just

eaten a lemon, rind and all. "What part of what I just said do you object to?"

"I won't lose Clay, and I don't care how noble he thinks he's being. I'm going to fight for him, for us, because I love him with my whole heart."

Cathy's expression didn't change except for her right eyebrow which inched upward. "This isn't like you, Mary." She narrowed her eyes. "I like it. It's about time you stopped acting like a baby."

Mary's mouth dropped open. "A baby? I'm not acting like a baby."

"Clay pouts, and you think you're helpless."

Ach, Cathy didn't know how to tell the truth without adding a tablespoon of vinegar. "Well, I'm not helpless now." Mary held out her hand. "Let me read that article."

Cathy picked up her purse from the floor and clutched it to her chest. "You can't handle the truth."

"You just said I was acting like a baby. Well, I'm going to start behaving like a grown-up, and I want to read that article."

Cathy tightened her arms around her purse. "I was just teasing you about being a baby. If you read this, you'll feel the need to power wash your eyes afterwards."

"If you don't let me read your copy, I'll

just find another one."

Cathy glared at Mary. "It's too bad you Amish are allowed to shop at Walmart." She sighed and held her breath out so long, Mary feared Cathy would pass out from lack of air. "Not that I don't trust you, but I don't trust you. Promise me you won't hate Clay after you read it. I've grown quite fond of him, even though he's a pouter and a mediocre pitcher. He doesn't need your disdain."

Esther gave Cathy an arch look. "Have you ever known Mary to be disdainful of anyone?"

Cathy's eyebrows loomed over her stormy face. "There's a first time for everything, and you haven't read the article either. Don't judge me for judging Mary."

Mary hesitated. Could there be anything in that article that would convince her to stop loving Clay? Should she do as Clay wished: hold on to the memory of how they were before Leif McIntire ever came into their lives?

Nae, she couldn't do that. For sure and certain, she would hear about the contents of the article from Ada or Dat or someone else in the district, and it wasn't possible that she could ever stop loving Clay, no matter what he'd done. She would not abandon him the way she had at the hospital the day of his surgery.

How could she fight for Clay if she didn't know what she was up against? She stretched her hand across the table. "Let me read it."

Cathy scrunched up her face until she looked like a dried apple with eyes. "Don't say I didn't warn you." She pulled the magazine from her purse and handed it to Mary. "I'm sorry. It's going to hurt."

Mary pressed her lips together and thumbed through the magazine until she found the page with her photo on it. With Winnie still on her lap, Esther leaned over so she could see the page. "Can I read too?"

"*Jah.* I'll read it out loud."

"Don't do that," Cathy said. "You'll die of embarrassment before you get to the end of the first paragraph."

"Cathy's right," Esther said. "Besides, I don't want Winnie to hear it."

Mary held the page so Esther could see it, took a deep breath, and started to read.

" 'Clay Markham, Colorado Peaks' on-again, off-again starting pitcher, is well-known for drinking his body weight in alcohol, partying hard with his thousands of friends, and changing girlfriends as often as most people change their clothes. His relationship with Gwen Rinaldi lasted all of six months. According to Gwen, Clay told her she wasn't famous enough for him, and he dumped her. This penchant for finding a new girlfriend every few months has taken a bizarre and sordid turn. Clay is now dating an Amish girl, and we can't help but wonder why. Clay has been spending a significant amount of time hanging out with an entire family of Amish girls, all old enough to date him.'

"And believe it or not, it gets weirder. Mary Yoder, Clay's Amish girlfriend, once had an affair with her engaged Amish cousin."

Mary thought she was going to be sick. Every word, every attack on Clay's character, every mention of her family made her want to throw up. The suggestion about her and Peter nearly choked her.

" 'Clay, who can drink anyone under the table, claims he's been sober for over a year — we'd like to think so after six weeks in rehab — but Clay met Mary Yoder when he crashed his car into the Yoders' barn while allegedly driving drunk. He was seen at a hospital in Alamosa a few days later for an undisclosed injury from the accident.

" 'Is Clay Markham trying to renovate his image by dating an Amish girl, or is he living out some strange fantasy at the expense of the Yoder family?

" 'Clay is good at hiding things. He was good at hiding his drinking, good at hiding his elbow surgery, and even better at hiding his daughter from all of us. *Pro Day* just learned that three years ago, Clay and actress Paige Templeton had a daughter together and then gave her up for adoption.' "

Mary reared back as if she'd been slapped. She glanced at Esther, who must have just read the same passage. She was pale as a ghost. Mary's blood ran cold. "He has a daughter?" She looked at Cathy for confirmation.

Cathy's forehead wrinkles bunched on top of each other. "Don't ask me. Everything I know is in that article. Maybe it isn't true." She pointed to Mary. "There's at least one lie about Mary in there."

"Jah," Mary coughed out. "At least one."

"I think he does have a daughter," Esther murmured.

"Why do you say that?" Cathy asked.

"We had a conversation about Winnie. Clay wanted to know if I thought Winnie was happy, if she was better off not being raised by her real mother. I told him that I'm Winnie's real mother and that Ivy did a very unselfish thing by letting me adopt her daughter. He seemed very interested in my opinion."

Clay had a daughter? Mary couldn't comprehend such a thing.

Cathy narrowed her eyes in Mary's direction, as if accusing her of something she hadn't done yet. "What are you going to do if all that stuff about Clay is true? Does it change the way you feel about him?"

Mary's heart felt wrung out like a wet dishrag, twisted beyond recognition and strangled tightly in Leif McIntire's fists. She drew in several breaths just to relieve the pressure on her chest. She had been through most of these emotions already. When Clay had crashed into her life, she had assumed many things about him: he was a drunk, he was a selfish Englischer, his soul was tarnished beyond repair. And then she had come to know him for who he truly was. His past mistakes didn't matter to her. Mary set the magazine on the table. "It does change the way I feel about him. I love him even more than I did before."

Cathy wasn't prone to smiling, but now she smiled so wide, Mary could count all her molars. "I seriously thought you would ask me to delete Clay's number from my phone. It makes me happy when people exceed my expectations."

Mary gave Cathy a feeble smile. It was all she could muster, considering how devastated she felt for Clay and for herself. "I know who Clay is, and he is bright, beautiful, and full of love. He wouldn't hurt a fly or a nasty reporter, and he has the kindest heart I have ever known." She swiped her hand across her cheek to clear the tears that had started to fall. "But he doesn't feel worthy."

"I like Clay," Cathy said, "but he's kind of dumb. He's handsome, rich, and talented, but he doesn't think he deserves anyone's love."

Esther wrapped her arms tightly around Winnie. "My sister Ivy was the same way. She left home and lived with an abusive boyfriend because she didn't think she deserved any better. I could finally forgive her when I realized that Jesus would never condemn her, and neither should I. And she gave me the greatest gift anyone could have given me. She let me adopt Winnie."

Mary drew in a shuddering breath. "Clay has carried these secrets and heavy burdens by himself because he's never been able to trust my love. When things got hard, I ran away instead of standing by him. I've never given him reason to trust me. I've let fear overcome my love."

Esther squeezed Mary's hand. She felt the warmth of it all the way up her arm. "Clay thinks he can take care of himself, but he depends on you more than you know."

"He's trying to protect me from things he can't protect me from. That's why he thinks I would be better off if he were out of my life." A wave of painful emotions washed over her, smacking her in the face and leaving her gasping for air. But then her love for Clay pushed her upward into the light. She closed her eyes and pressed her lips together. "I'm not going to let him do it. He can't push me out of his life that easily. It's time to stop shrinking. I'm going to show him I'm strong and brave and faithful." At the moment, she didn't feel strong or brave. She felt very much like she was going to lose her lunch.

"What are you going to do?"

Mary stood up. Her knees felt like jelly, and a sharp ache stabbed at her gut. She braced herself against the table and picked up the magazine. "I'm going to call a reporter."

Chapter 15

Mary stood outside the Bean There, Done That Coffee Shop, her heart drumming an uneven rhythm against her chest, making her breathless and panicky and ill all at the same time. She had already peeled off her jacket, but she was still sweating as if it were a hot day in the middle of July even though it was early May, and the air was chilly. She had anticipated that this wasn't going to be easy, but she hadn't realized how anxious she would feel or how tempted she would be to run down the street and keep going until she reached California. The only thing that kept her feet planted right there was her love for Clay and her need to set things right. She didn't regret her decision, but she was genuinely concerned that she might have a heart attack before she could deliver her speech.

Haley Thorpe, the *County Bugle* reporter she and Clay had met outside the emergency room last November, had suggested a press conference combined with a Facebook Live event, both things that Mary had never heard of, but Haley seemed pretty confident about them, and Mary trusted her. A press conference was when you had something to say, and you invited reporters to come and listen. A Facebook Live event was when you filmed yourself talking and then people watched it on Facebook.

It was Mary's worst nightmare.

Haley said they needed to do both because she was certain that no one would come to the press conference and she wanted to get the message out to as many people as possible. "We can put this on Twitter, Twitch, and Insta too," Haley had said. It sounded like she knew what she was doing, and Mary didn't know anything.

Mary wasn't concerned about how many views her speech had as long as Clay saw it. She didn't even care how the bishop was going to react or what he would do. She would gladly submit to the consequences of her actions because Clay was the only one who mattered.

Mary paced back and forth in front of the coffee shop where Haley had set up a microphone and a video camera for the speech. Haley fiddled with the camera while

Ron Gallagher from the coffee shop stood next to Haley, staring at her phone and trying to get the camera to "sync" with it. Cathy huddled with Ron and Haley, but she didn't seem to be helping much. "What happens if you press that button?" Cathy said.

Neither Ron nor Haley answered her, but Ron pulled the phone closer to his body as if to keep Cathy from touching it.

Mary wished she could help, but she knew nothing about cell phones, cameras, the internet, or Facebook. She was as helpless as she was anxious.

Mary wrung her hands. Would Clay even see the press conference? Everything depended on Clay knowing she was willing to fight for him, for them.

After she had read that article two weeks ago, she'd bought a cheap cell phone and a cheap cell plan and had called and texted Clay every few hours for twelve days. He hadn't responded to her or Cathy, and Mary's heart had broken all over again every day. Last week, Cathy had driven Mary to Clay's house in Denver, but he lived in a gated community, and Mary couldn't even get close. One of the neighbors told Mary that Clay was in Hawaii.

Ach, she was so mad at him, she could spit.

And so sad, she could have mopped the floor with her tears.

And so in love with him, she would disintegrate into a pile of ashes if she had lost him.

Of course, she hadn't expected Clay to make it easy for her. She had to prove her love by being willing to fight for it. She had called Haley Thorpe and asked for help setting the record straight about her and Clay. Haley had enthusiastically agreed to help. She said Mary's story was every reporter's dream.

Mary had texted Clay ten minutes ago about the press conference with a link to the Facebook Live event. She hadn't wanted him to know sooner because he would have found some way to stop her, thinking he needed to protect her, and she wasn't about to let anything derail her plan. She had no expectation that he would show up — he might be in Hawaii for all she knew — but she prayed with all her heart that he would see it. Maybe it would change his mind about her.

She swallowed past the lump in her throat. Maybe it wouldn't.

Cathy abandoned Ron and Haley and

sidled close to Mary. She wore a lime green jacket with "I'd agree with you, but then we'd both be wrong" written across the front, dark green pants, and bright white shoes that looked like they'd just come out of the box. "Take a deep breath, Mary. You're a little green around the gills, and if you throw up, you'll ruin everything."

Cathy was always such a ray of sunshine.

Mary couldn't reassure Cathy of anything, because she wasn't altogether sure herself that she wouldn't throw up or pass out or suffocate before she even got a word out.

Cathy patted her on the shoulder. "But don't worry. If you throw up, I'll finish your speech for you." She pulled a piece of paper from her jacket pocket. "I've prepared a few words about global warming and the high cost of breakfast cereal."

Mary squared her shoulders. She was not going to waste her press conference on breakfast cereal. "Okay, Cathy. I'll keep that in mind." Lord willing, Cathy didn't notice the panicked hitch in her voice.

About three minutes before they were scheduled to start, a woman who looked like she might be a reporter strolled up to the coffee shop. *Ach, vell,* one reporter was better than none. Mary gave her a wan smile, too nervous to do much more than concentrate on breathing.

With only about one minute to go, three vans simultaneously pulled up in front of the coffee shop. Mary's pulse raced as three cameramen got out of the vans as well as three more reporters. It was looking more like a press conference and feeling more like an inevitable heart attack. Four other people appeared from various directions, one holding a camera and a microphone, one wielding a notebook and a pen. Seven or eight people joined their group, probably just curious about what was going on at the Bean There, Donut That Coffee Shop.

Mary now had a proper audience, whether she wanted one or not.

Haley gave Cathy the signal, and Cathy walked toward the X that Haley had chalked out for her on the sidewalk. Haley had told Cathy that Cathy needed to stand on that spot during the press conference so they could triangulate the sound of Mary's voice. Mary suspected Haley had made the whole thing up so Cathy wouldn't try to insert herself into Mary's speech. With her giant purse over her shoulder, Cathy ambled to her X and folded her arms, looking like she was ready for an attack from any direction. Haley left Ron in charge of the camera and scooted next to Mary at the microphone.

"You ready?" she whispered breathlessly.

Mary nodded, even though she wasn't sure she had the power of speech.

Haley looked at the group of people, then smiled into the camera as if she was doing an advertisement for toothpaste. "Hello and welcome. My name is Haley Thorpe. I am a reporter for the *County Bugle* in Alamosa. This is my friend Mary Yoder. Because of the unflattering article about her and Clay Markham in *Pro Day,* Mary asked me to help her put together a press conference so that she can address some of the issues from the article and set the record straight about her character and her relationship with Mr. Markham."

Four or five more people gathered at the back of the group, including, to Mary's surprise, Leif McIntire, wearing an impeccable gray-blue suit with a crisp white shirt and silver tie. An invisible hand clamped around Mary's throat. There was the man who had caused so much trouble. The man who had written those nasty things about her and Clay. The man she needed to forgive. But forgiveness wasn't at the top of her list right now. Her only goal was to show Clay that she was willing to fight for him and that it wasn't his job to protect her. It wasn't his fault that he was famous, and she wouldn't allow her anxieties to keep them apart.

Haley stepped back, and Mary pulled her paper from her apron pocket. She had written everything down because she didn't want to forget anything, and she would rather look at the paper than into so many curious faces. Haley had helped her with some of the words, but everything was what Mary wanted to say. Unfortunately, her hands were shaking so badly, she could barely read what she'd written. "My name is Mary Yoder. I was mentioned in a recent article about Clay Markham in *Pro Day* magazine. I want to correct some of the misinformation in the article. This story was irresponsible and has hurt my family, my community, and my reputation." She dared to glance at Leif McIntire. His hands were stuffed in his pants pockets, and he gazed defiantly at Mary, obviously unwilling to admit he had done anything wrong.

Ach, her hands shook, and her voice trembled like a flame in the wind. She seriously doubted she could get through the whole speech. Taking a deep breath, she thought of how much she loved Clay. "We Amish are very private people, and we consider photos to be graven images. The magazine knew how offensive it would be to me and my community to put a photo of me in the article without my permission. I hope they will correct the mistake in any future articles about the Amish." She looked up at the reporters standing in the front. They didn't look bored or mad or disdainful. They certainly didn't act superior like Leif McIntire always did when he looked at her. "Clay Markham is my friend and a friend of my family, and that is all I have to say about our relationship. I have done nothing wrong, and Clay has never treated me or my sisters with anything but kindness and respect. We are blessed that he came into our lives the way he did." She cleared her throat. "One night in late October, Clay crashed his car into our barn, and he has spent almost seven months working on our farm to fix the damage and make amends for what he did. He didn't have to erect a new fence or repaint the barn or clean up the dried fire extinguisher foam, but he did. He didn't have to help my *dat* plant alfalfa or drive me to the grocery store or mop our floor."

Now she had come to the hardest part. Haley had reassured Mary that she was very brave, but Mary didn't even know if she was capable of saying the words in front of all these people. What would Dat think? What would her *schwesteren* and cousins and community think? Would they hate her? Would they feel sorry for her? She tightened her fingers around her paper and did her best to quell the trembling. "I did not have an affair with my cousin. I . . ." She couldn't catch her breath. The weight of that horrible day in Peter's barn pressed down on her chest. It was very possible she would pass out before she got the words out of her mouth. "I am the victim of a sexual assault."

A slight murmur traveled around the group of onlookers. Her vision blurred, and her legs went numb. Hopefully, Haley would catch her when she fell. Suddenly a tall, broad figure aggressively pushed through the crowd and wrapped his strong arms around her. "Mary," he whispered. "It's okay. I've got you."

She had never heard a more beautiful sound in her life.

Clay, his eyes flashing with anger and pain, turned and scanned the small group of people, keeping one arm firmly around her shoulders. "We're done here. Please direct all further questions to my agent."

Maybe it was her determination to be brave or maybe it was the strength that Clay's presence lent her, but Mary refused to move. She ignored her wobbly knees and pushed Clay away from her with all the force she could muster. "No, Clay. Not this time."

Surprise mixed with anxiety on his face. "Mary, you don't have to do this. This is my fight. It never should have been yours."

She squared her shoulders. "You don't have to protect me."

The sadness in his eyes almost undid her. "Yes, I do."

Mary got on her tippy toes and kissed Clay on the cheek right there in front of the cameras and everybody. It was the boldest thing she had ever done. Ada would be appalled. Beth would be insulted. The bishop would have something to say about it. Lord willing, Dat wouldn't have a stroke. "I need to do this, Clay," she whispered, "for me and for us. It's my turn to protect you. Please don't make a fuss about it."

"But . . ."

"I would appreciate it if you stood right here so you can catch me if I faint."

Several emotions traveled across his face in succession. By the firm set of his chin, she could tell he wanted to protest. A desire to protect her was followed closely by uncertainty, then resignation, then deep affection. "Why do you think I need your protection? I'm pretty sure I can bench press at least two-hundred pounds more than you can."

"I said, don't make a fuss."

He didn't smile, but he moved to the side so he was no longer between Mary and the growing crowd of people. There was so much love in his eyes, she thought she might be able to fly. "I've got your back, Mary."

Clay kept his arm around her as Mary stepped closer to the microphone. Her hands stopped shaking, her breathing slowed to normal, and she suddenly wasn't afraid anymore. She smoothed out her paper, which had gotten crumpled while she had been trying to convince Clay that she was brave. "Clay has made mistakes, but I am a Christian and I believe we are all sinners and come short of the glory of God. Maybe you can't look past Clay's mistakes, but your short-sightedness says more about you than it does about Clay. I know Clay's heart."

She had never been so grateful that she'd called Haley Thorpe. Haley had done hours of research for Mary. "Did you know that last year Clay made over fifty visits to children's hospitals and cancer centers? Clay has donated millions, *millions,* of dollars to veterans' organizations, education foundations, and Operation Underground

Railroad, which is a group that works to free children from human trafficking. Clay has signed thousands of autographs, made countless public appearances, and is beloved by thousands of fans because he treats people with respect and kindness."

Clay bent down and whispered in her ear. "Okay. That's enough. I'm a nice guy, but I'm not a saint."

Mary giggled softly and spoke louder into the microphone. "I prefer to look past the mistakes and see the amazing, beautiful man Clay is."

One of the reporters smiled wryly. "He's definitely beautiful."

The onlookers laughed, all except Leif McIntire, who wore a smug, I-don't-care look on his face. Mary wouldn't have expected anything different.

Another reporter pointed his pen at Clay and grinned teasingly. "Hey, Clay, when do think you'll be nominated for the Nobel Prize for philanthropy?"

Clay rolled his eyes and swatted the question away. "Okay, okay. Are you done yet?"

The reporter laughed. "I was just wondering. Mary Yoder thinks you're the best thing since sliced bread."

Clay groaned. "I'm not even the best thing since moldy bread, Phil. Will you all go away now and leave us in peace? Be sure to get a cup of coffee and a donut from Bean There, Donut That before you leave."

"One more question," said one of the reporters in the front row. "Are you and Mary a thing?"

Mary couldn't look at Clay, even though her attention was riveted to his answer. Clay tightened his arm around her. "That," he said, "is none of your business."

CHAPTER 16

Clay took Mary's hand and motioned to Ron, who waved them into the coffee shop. Clay nodded and led Mary to a spacious storage room behind the front counter. After shutting the door, he let go of her hand and took three steps away from her. "I can't believe you did that."

At that moment, Mary didn't care what the bishop or Ada or even Dat might think. She wanted to spend the rest of her life next to Clay, preferably held tightly in his arms, and she wasn't going to wait one more minute. The surprise on Clay's face was adorable as she catapulted herself into his arms, threw her hands around his neck, and kissed him with all the emotions she'd been suffocating for weeks. Clay quickly got over his shock and wrapped his arms all the way around her and tugged her closer to him.

He kissed her back with an intense gentleness that Mary hadn't thought possible, and suddenly, her whole life fell into place. She found everything she didn't know she was missing and felt loved in a way she didn't know was possible.

"Oh, Mary," he said. "I love you so much. Can you forgive me? Can you ever love me?"

"Ever love you? Clay, I have loved you since the day I met you, and there is nothing to forgive. Let's leave mistakes in the past and never look back."

He kissed her again with all the fervor of someone who has recovered a lost treasure. Mary was completely swept away by her love for him.

He drew her closer, if that was possible, and touched his forehead to hers. "I can't believe you called a press conference."

Mary's relief made her giddy. She giggled like a little girl. "I can't believe it either."

Clay pulled away, huffed out a breath, and scrubbed his hand through his hair. "As soon as I got your text, I raced over here to try to stop you, but you'd already started talking. I was sick, Mary, just sick that you would put yourself through that for me. I pulled my hoodie over my head and sneaked to the back of the crowd because I thought it would be worse for you if I interrupted. But then you started shaking so badly I seriously thought you were going to have a seizure." His lips twitched upward. "I had to save you. I didn't realize it was you who was trying to save me."

"I wanted to show you that you are worth defending. I couldn't let them get away with printing lies about you."

Clay hung his head. "They didn't print any lies about me. Only about you." He looked into her eyes, and the pain on his face was raw and jagged. "Everything is true, Mary. I'm not the man you think I am. I'm for sure not the man you deserve."

Mary felt as if a shard of glass had lodged in her heart. She hated to see Clay so broken. "Didn't I tell you we were going to leave all that in the past? You have nothing to explain or apologize for."

"Yes, I do."

Mary frowned. "It won't change how I feel about you."

He stiffened as if an icy wind had just blown past his heart. "You're too good for me, Mary."

"That's not true."

Clay's eyes flashed with anger. Mary drew back in surprise. Hadn't they just kissed and declared their love for each other? "Please don't pretend you're not curious."

"The past is in the past," she stuttered. It

wasn't what he wanted to hear, but it truly was how she felt.

He turned his back on her and propped his hand on one of the upper storage shelves. "My mom never stood up for herself. She was always the noble one, the good one, the long-suffering one." He gave Mary a sideways glance. "The martyr. My dad was always the bad guy." He hung his head. "Mary, I don't want to always be the bad guy."

Mary furrowed her brow. "What do you mean?"

"I know you think it's noble to be forgiving, to leave the past in the past. It's your Christian duty to forgive, and kindness comes naturally to you. You try to do what you think Jesus would do. It's one of the things I love most about you." He ran his fingers through his hair. "But I don't want to be the undeserving one who always needs forgiveness and you to be the noble one who constantly has to forgive." He lifted his chin. "You stood up for me today, but now you need to stand up for yourself. Don't settle for a man you can't respect. I don't want your pity, and I don't want to wear myself out trying to deserve you every day. That's one of the reasons I decided to get out of your life. I'm not worthy of you, and it's too hard to keep pretending."

Emotions swirled inside Mary's head like a swarm of bees. She was confused and hurt and hopeful all at the same time. "You're talking as if you plan on being in my life for . . . for a long time." She had barely dared to hope.

He turned to face her, and his look was soft and somber. "Just wait on that. I can only tackle one problem at a time." He gave her a tight smile. "It's exhausting trying to deserve you, and I just can't do it. I'd rather just fade out of your life than live like that."

"Cathy said you don't think you're worthy of love."

"I guess. Cathy's pretty smart, but she doesn't know everything. It's ironic because I was first drawn to you because you didn't care about my money or my fame or my baseball career. I thought maybe you would like me for who I am, not for what I could do for you or give you."

Mary nodded eagerly. "That's right. I don't love you for any of those reasons. I love the real Clay Markham, not the one everyone sees on TV."

Clay sighed, folded his arms, and leaned back against the shelf. "You may not understand this, Mary, but you *also* love a version of me. You won't know the real Clay

Markham until you know everything, and it scares me that you don't *want* to know everything. Are you afraid you'll stop loving me if you know the truth?"

"I don't . . . know." Mary hesitated. Clay had obviously been thinking seriously about this. It warmed her to the bones that he cared so deeply and hurt her heart that he still didn't think he could count on her. "Now you've made me doubt myself."

His smile relaxed into something more natural. "Thank you for being honest about it."

She shook her head. "Leif McIntire revealed some very private, personal matters. What else can I say but that I still love you?"

"But do you love me because you're *supposed* to as a true Christian? I don't want you to love me or forgive me because you're *supposed* to." His lips twitched. "That makes you a saint, but not someone I want to date."

Clay probably wouldn't believe it, but as long as he hadn't murdered someone, Mary adored him no matter what he'd done. She laced her fingers together. "Tell me everything, and I promise not to forgive you. Would that make you feel better?"

He laughed. "Yes and no."

"Okay, then. I'm listening."

He glanced at her doubtfully, cleared his throat, and motioned for her to sit on a cardboard box on the floor next to the door. He pulled a box next to her and sat down. It cracked under his weight. She grinned as he grimaced, stood, and found a short metal stool that was too small but didn't look as if it would collapse under his weight.

He sat knee-to-knee with Mary and took both of her hands. He seemed to think better of it and stood up, kicking the stool to the side. "This has been eating at me for months. I think I'd better stand. First of all, the drinking. After I got called up to the Majors, I wanted people to like me, so I started drinking hard. You already know about my dad. I suppose I was chasing the approval I didn't feel like I ever got from him, but I need a lot more therapy to unpack that one. I handled the drinking real well for a while, but then the addiction just crept up on me. I couldn't go for more than a few hours without a drink, and when I went out, I couldn't seem to stop drinking. My sister Amy noticed at Thanksgiving two years ago and was pushy enough to sit me down and demand I get help. She called and tattled to my manager and my pitching coach. I resisted rehab for a few weeks, but then I woke up one morning in a strange apartment in a strange girl's bed with no memory of how I'd gotten there. Being out of control like that scared me enough to finally check myself into rehab."

"Thank the Lord you got help."

He frowned. "I guess, but I wasn't talking to God much at that point. I felt like he was punishing me for all the bad things I'd done. I was real mad at Him." He held up his hand as if to stop Mary from saying anything. "I know. I shouldn't talk about God that way."

Mary grinned. "He already knows, and He appreciates your honesty."

His eyebrows traveled up his forehead. "You didn't used to think so."

"*Ach, vell,* I've learned a few things from you."

He seemed to like that answer. "Good to know. Anyway, I hadn't had a drink for over a year that night I crashed into your barn, but like I said, I'd just lost the playoff game for my team, and I'd gotten bad news from the doctor about my arm." He cupped his hand over his elbow and rubbed it. "I haven't had a drink since, though I've been sorely tempted several times. You, Mary, as they say, are the kind of woman who can drive a man to drink."

Her lips curled involuntarily. "Don't

blame this on me."

He stepped back in mock surprise. "But you're usually willing to take the blame and forgive me for everything."

"I promised not to forgive you, remember?"

"Thank you. I really appreciate that." He cleared his throat. "Not a lot of people knew about the rehab, but Leif McIntire caught wind of it, and he was pretty brutal. He writes for a sports magazine, but he despises athletes, kind of like the clumsy kid in high school who wants to get revenge on all the jocks. Anyway, Leif was very interested when he heard about me crashing into your barn. I'm sure he was hoping I'd started drinking again. I'm sure he was ecstatic when he found out the Amish were involved. He said some horrible things about you, added a little innuendo, and sold a lot of magazines."

"The drinking doesn't matter, Clay. You've worked hard to put that behind you. I know it wasn't easy."

Amusement danced in his eyes. "That's nice of you to say, but you promised not to forgive me."

She raised her thumb and index finger to her mouth and pretended to button her lips together. "No forgiveness. Sorry."

His smile was reluctant and warm. "Okay, then. That was the lesser of two evils. Now let's talk about Paige Templeton."

Mary tried not to show any reaction to that name, though her stomach sank to her toes. Paige Templeton was the one who reportedly had a child with Clay.

"It's the same old story with me. I've been looking for someone to truly love me for over a decade, Mary. I don't know that I felt like I deserved love even after I made the Majors. I make indecent amounts of money for what? Throwing a little ball into a catcher's mitt."

"It's more than that. You're one of the most talented people in the world, and you make millions of people happy every time to step onto the mound."

He snorted. "Happy or miserable. It's a mixed bag."

Mary sighed. "I'm sorry. I'm trying very hard not to make you feel better."

"Thanks. I appreciate it."

Someone knocked on the door and opened it. A wall of voices came in from the other side, and Ron stuck his head into the room. "I hate to interrupt, but I need more cups and napkins."

"Are the reporters bothering you?" Clay asked. "Because I can tell them to go away."

Ron burst into a grin. "No such thing. There are twenty people in here who want coffee and donuts and a glimpse of Clay Markham. Thanks to you and Mary, I've never been so busy." He pulled a box of cups from one of the shelves and grabbed a pouch of napkins.

Clay glanced at Mary. "Do you need help?"

Ron shook his head. "No way am I going to stop whatever you've got going on in here. You two need about five years of couple's therapy. Haley and Cathy are helping me. We've got it covered." He backed out of the room and closed the door.

Clay cracked a smile. "I'm glad it's going well for him."

"Thanks to you."

He hung his head. "I'm not a saint, Mary."

Mary resisted the urge to roll her eyes. Clay was suddenly as touchy as a porcupine. "What were you saying about Paige Templeton?"

He tensed his shoulders. "Okay. Couple's therapy." He turned his back on her again. She noticed he didn't look at her when he had something hard to say. "I've had a lot of girlfriends, but I always felt that they wanted something from me, like fame or my money." He turned and peered at her with an almost sheepish look on his face. "Or arm candy."

"What does arm candy mean?"

"Okay, don't accuse me of being arrogant, but women think I'm good-looking. They want to be seen with me."

"That's not arrogance," Mary said, stifling a laugh. "That's just a fact."

"Anyway, Paige is a nice lady, an actress on a sitcom. I had a little more confidence in that relationship because Paige already had a good career, unlike Gwen, who really needed my fame to get on that game show. I hope she's happy opening suitcases for a living." He said it with just a tinge of acid in his voice. "Paige and I lasted almost a year, but we figured out we didn't really love each other and broke up. About a month later, she called to tell me she was pregnant."

Mary had read it in the magazine article, but hearing it from Clay felt like a punch in the throat. "That must have been a shock."

He exhaled a long breath. "I've had relations with five different women. I'm not proud of it. My mom taught me better than that."

Mary's face got warm. "You're an Englischer, Clay. I'd be surprised if you hadn't."

"Yeah, well, your opinion of Englischers doesn't make me feel better or absolve me of wrongdoing."

She gave him a mildly amused smirk. "If you want my forgiveness, you just have to ask."

A surprised laugh burst from his lips. "I really don't know if I want forgiveness or a rebuke."

Mary folded her arms. "Please let me know when you decide."

He laughed, crossed the room in one stride, and knelt next to her. "I love you to pieces, Mary Yoder."

"And I love you, but you really want to tell me this story, so please continue so I can withhold my forgiveness." She emphasized *withhold* and made him smile.

He sat cross-legged next to her. "I offered to marry Paige when I found out she was pregnant, but neither of us really wanted that. She made a great sacrifice to have the baby, then we both decided it would be better for the baby to give her up for adoption." Pain traveled across his face. "It was the hardest thing I've ever had to do, and I can't even begin to imagine how it was for Paige. I still wonder if it would have been better for me to raise the baby. What kind of father gives up his own child?" He cleared his throat. "That was when I really started drinking hard. I felt like dirt. I felt lower than dirt. I still do."

Mary slid off her box and knelt next to Clay on the floor. "Can I try to make you feel better?"

He sighed. "I hate it when you do that."

She curled her fingers around his arm. "The only person who matters in a situation like that is the child. We must always do what is best for the child, not what will make us feel better or be the most convenient."

"Believe me, I've heard the whole spiel, but I still feel like I failed my daughter. I still feel like dirt."

"You know in your heart that giving that baby to a loving family was the unselfish decision, no matter how hard it was for you."

He nodded. "That's what Esther said."

Mary frowned. "You told Esther about the baby?"

"No. We only talked about Winnie and her sister Ivy. She said Ivy loved Winnie enough to let Esther adopt her. Winnie is much better off because Ivy made the unselfish choice, and Esther doesn't think less of Ivy. Paige and I both wanted to do what was right. It was ultimately her decision, and she was amazing."

"I hope you never have a second thought about what you did. I don't wonder but that is exactly what God wanted you to do."

Clay didn't look convinced. "I guess so."

Mary lifted Clay's arm and tucked herself beneath it. His eyes lit up, and he pulled her closer to him. "Is there anything else you'd like to confess before I *don't* forgive you?"

"I once hit Dirk Johnson with a pitch on purpose because he was a jerk."

Mary laughed. "Let's skip past your baseball mistakes."

He rested his chin on the top of her head. "The last thing I want to say is that I'm not good enough for you, and sooner or later you're going to figure that out."

"I don't know what to say, Clay. I've already scolded you until I'm blue in the face." She lifted her head and pointed to her cheek. "See. I'm turning blue."

"You're beautiful."

She laced her fingers through his. "All right, then, tell me this. What do I have to do to deserve your love?"

He smirked as if he knew exactly what she was up to. "Nothing. You already have it."

"That's right. Either you love me for who I am, or you don't. Just like you don't have to do anything to deserve my love. I love you with all your flaws — and there aren't many. I hope you love me even with all my warts."

He cocked an eyebrow. "You have warts? Where are they? Are they big? Have you tried freezing them off? I might have to reconsider. Warts give me the creeps."

Mary giggled. "I'm not being noble when I say that I love you. I certainly don't want to be a martyr. You are the most wonderful person I have ever met, and I can't live without you. God wants us to be happy simply because He loves us. You and I deserve every good thing. Together."

He smoothed his thumb over her knuckles, sending a shiver of pleasure all the way up her arm. "Which brings us to the next problem, which I've been thinking about almost since the day I met you." He looked into her eyes, and the emotion she saw there was overwhelming. "I want to spend the rest of my life with you. Will you marry me?"

Mary's heart flew to the ceiling and crashed to the floor simultaneously. This was the question she had been hoping for and dreading. She had gone back and forth in her head for months, and now the decision was staring her in the face, forcing her to choose between the family she loved and the man she couldn't live without. A choice between staying safely comfortable in the life she'd always known and entering a strange and exciting world she knew nothing about and didn't fit into. Could she be happy in Clay's world? Could she live without her *schwesteren* and Dat and the goats?

She immediately knew the answer, even though she hadn't known what she was going to say until this very minute. "Yes, Clay, I'll marry you. There is nothing I want more."

He jumped to his feet and pulled her with him, laughing as if he was the happiest man in the whole world. Wrapping his arms around her, he kissed her until she couldn't remember her name. She kissed him back, though her happiness felt like mourning.

He kissed her on the lips, then the cheek, then the forehead. She was giddy with relief and yearning. "So you're okay if I get baptized?"

She caught her breath. "Baptized? What do you mean?"

He grimaced. "I haven't exactly been the best example of Christian devotion, but if you put in a good word for me, I'm hoping your bishop will approve." He studied her face and drew his brows together. "What?

Don't you think your bishop will give his permission?"

Mary felt a little dizzy. "Approve of . . . Clay, what are you talking about?"

Concern spread across his features. He slid his arm around her shoulders and led her to her cardboard box. "Are you okay? Did I say something wrong?" He knelt next to her and looked positively stricken. "I was afraid of this. You think the bishop will say no."

She grabbed onto his hand, her heart thudding against her chest like a giant bass drum. "Clay, are you saying you want to be baptized into the Amish faith?"

Puzzlement replaced his concern. "I . . . well . . . yes. Isn't that the only way we can get married?"

Mary held her breath for fear she was dreaming the entire conversation. "Well, no. I mean, yes. I mean, I've been baptized, so if I marry you, I'll be kicked out of the community. My family would have to shun me."

"I know."

She slid off her box and knelt beside him on the floor. "But it will be harder for you. You love baseball. You love your old truck. I can't ask you to give up your life and career to marry me."

Realization dawned on Clay's face.

"Mary." Her name was a caress on his lips. "Mary, were you considering leaving your family and faith for me?"

She nodded slowly. "It's the only way."

He closed his eyes and exhaled as if he'd been holding his breath for five months. "You don't know how much it means that you would do that for me."

"I love you, Clay," she said, her throat tight, her heart as big as the sky. "I would do anything for you."

His smile was subdued and stunning. "Like call a press conference and give me a heart attack."

"*Jah.* Like that."

He took her hand. "Mary. My dear Mary, no one has ever offered me anything half as precious as what you just have, but if we marry outside of the church, you would have to give up your whole world for me."

"I want to. I love you."

He squeezed her hand like a lifeline. "I will not allow you to do that. I am the one who is going to make the sacrifice this time. I'm getting baptized — if the bishop will allow it — and then I'm going to marry you and live happily ever after."

"But you'll have to give up cell phones and TV and your old, run-down truck."

His lips twitched upward. "I love that

truck, but not nearly as much as I love you."

She pinned him with an intense gaze. "Clay, you'd have to give up baseball. I can't ask you to do that. You love baseball. Baseball has been your whole life."

He didn't seem concerned. "*Was* my whole life until I met you. I can live without pitching in the Majors. I *cannot* live without you."

Mary would have fallen to her knees had she not already been sitting on the ground. The yearning and dread that had been pressing on her chest for months dissipated, and she took her first deep breath since the day she'd met Clay. She burst into tears. "I thought I'd have to choose between you and my family."

He scooted closer and gathered her in his arms. "I would never ask you to make that choice. You've already given me so much, and I have given you nothing."

"That's not true."

He laughed. "I'm not going to argue about why I'm right and you're wrong."

She rolled her eyes.

He laughed harder. "I'm just happy I can finally offer you a gift you'll accept. It will help even things up between us."

"I'm not keeping score," Mary scolded.

"I am, and I'm still way behind. I can't

even buy you a wedding ring."

"The Amish don't wear wedding rings."

He eyed her with mock annoyance. "Yeah, I know. I would have bought you a rock so huge, you wouldn't have been able to lift your left hand above your shoulder."

"Very impractical."

"Oh, I know," he said. "You Amish are nothing but practical. You set your own dislocated shoulders, you buy sensible shoes, and you don't stand for purple fence posts."

Mary giggled. "Are you sure you want to marry into that?"

He gave her a swift kiss on the lips. "I've never been more sure of anything in my life. Are you sure you want to marry an Englischer who doesn't know the rules and will mess up about a thousand times a day?"

She smiled with her whole body. "If you kiss me every day, I'll do my best to overlook your transgressions."

"Good, because I will definitely be the worst Amish man in the history of Amish men."

"As long as you're *my* Amish man, I don't care."

She snaked her arms around his neck and gave him a longer, more eager kiss. He didn't seem to mind at all. She had never,

never, been so deliriously happy.

They both jumped when the storage room door opened and Cathy stuck her head in. "Look, I know you need some private time and Ron is trying to be noble, but we could really use your help out here. Ron is frying a batch of donuts while also filling coffee orders, Haley is arguing with one of the reporters, and I can't figure out how to use the cash register."

"Let's go," Clay said, beaming like a hundred-watt lightbulb. "I know how to use a cash register, and I make a mean double espresso."

Mary giggled, her heart too full to speak. Cathy was as grumpy as ever, Ron's coffee shop was full of people, and Clay loved her wildly and without reservation. All was right with the world.

Chapter 17

Mary tapped the magazine against her thigh, opened the screen door, and stepped out onto the wide wraparound porch where she had a perfect view of the baseball field, the growing alfalfa, and Dat's house and farm just beyond the purple fence posts. It was hot outside, but even hotter in the kitchen where she'd just taken a pan of cinnamon rolls out of the oven.

Mary sat down on the porch swing, unwrapped her mango-flavored popsicle, and opened *Pro Day* to the article about her and Clay written by the new reporter on staff, Haley Thorpe. Mary smiled to herself. Haley had done Mary a huge favor by organizing that press conference, and Gotte had blessed Haley with a new, more important career. Leif McIntire hadn't been fired from his job at *Pro Day,* but because he'd exposed the magazine to a possible lawsuit, he was now covering badminton, racquetball, and poker.

Haley's article featured a photo of Clay's back while he was in the act of pitching a ball to one of the players from the local high school. In the picture, Clay wore a straw hat, a cream-colored shirt, suspenders, black trousers, and black, sensible Amish shoes. The article was titled "Clay Markham Finds His Rhythm."

Three days after the terrifying press conference, Clay announced his retirement from baseball and started baptism classes. The retirement announcement had shocked every Peaks fan in the country, and the baptism classes had shocked every Amish person in the San Luis Valley.

Baptism classes had taken four months, and Clay had claimed that having to wait so long would kill him, so he found some little projects to keep himself busy until the wedding. First, he sold his house in Denver and gave his old, beloved truck to Esther's brother-in-law who was in Rumspringa and could drive his family around until he got baptized. After giving away his truck, Clay paid too much money for two hundred acres of land right next to Dat's farm and then had a house built on the property with solar panels, a barn, and three goat milking machines. After that, he'd drafted some of his old Englisch friends and some of his new Amish friends, and they'd graded and smoothed ground thirty yards behind the new house and built a regulation-size baseball diamond with a regulation-size pitcher's mound.

Clay, with all those projects to divert his attention, managed to survive until the wedding, which was held in early October in the barn. Joanna had hung three fire extinguishers on the wall in Clay's honor, and each cake was tied with a yellow ribbon. Every guest got a tiny baseball keychain as a favor, and Dat even agreed to fireworks, though he said fireworks would draw too much attention and would probably keep the whole family out of heaven. Dozens of Clay's Englisch friends attended the wedding, most of them looking bewildered and a little unsure about an Amish wedding, but they were all glad for Clay. His teammate Ricardo Guzman said he'd never seen Clay so happy, not even when the Peaks had made it to the World Series four years ago.

Clay's entire family had flown in for the wedding, and Mary had gotten to know Clay's dad better. The time they'd all spent together had truly been a gift from Gotte. Clay's dad was a stern man who seemed dissatisfied with everything and anything, but he was also a *gute* man with deeply held beliefs, a solid work ethic, and a fierce love for his children, even though he didn't know how to show it. He hadn't been happy when Clay had told him he was giving up baseball, but when the family had come for the wedding, he had expressed his approval that Clay was planning to "settle down" and become a farmer. Clay's dad was a farmer, and he'd told Clay and Mary it was an honor that one of his sons was following in his footsteps.

Clay had been so touched, he'd given his dad a hug. His dad hadn't known what to do with so much affection, but it was a lovely moment between them, all the same.

Clay, as well as Mary, had finally been able to forgive his dad for all his mistakes. Who didn't make mistakes? Who didn't need forgiveness every day for a thousand different things?

Clay enjoyed farming, but he also had the heart of a coach and mentor. With the bishop's permission, he coached the men's baseball team at the college in Alamosa, and this summer, he was holding a series of pitching clinics for aspiring Major League pitchers across the country. Boys would sign up for the clinics through a website that Cathy's grandson set up and then travel to

Colorado, stay at a hotel in Alamosa, and attend Clay's pitching clinic for five days. Cathy would pick the boys up each day from the hotel and bring them to Mary and Clay's farm where Clay would teach them the basics of baseball pitching and Mary would feed them lunch and tend to any bruises, scrapes, and sprains they got during the week.

Clay still signed autographs when an occasional fan wandered onto their farm — purple fence posts notwithstanding. He was still good-natured and still cheerful about it, though the sight of a reporter made him just a little bit testy.

Mary finished reading the article and ate the last of her popsicle, then stared at Clay, who was standing on the pitcher's mound giving instructions to five very attentive players gathered around him. She grinned. She had always dreamed of a husband and home, but she had never dreamed she'd have a full-size baseball diamond in her backyard. It was really quite the spectacle.

Clay must have felt her gaze on him because he glanced in her direction and dazzled her with one of his brilliant smiles. His beard was thick and sandy and he grew more handsome every day. Clay said something to the boys, then jogged off the field and up the porch steps to Mary.

Her heart beat as fast as the first day she'd met him. "You don't have to interrupt your lessons just to say hi."

"Yes, I do. I really can't breathe properly without being near you every few minutes," he said. He looked behind him, then bent down and planted a quick kiss on her lips. She trembled with happiness. "That should do me for another hour or so."

Mary watched Clay jog back to the baseball diamond, her cup overflowing with love. She set down the magazine and ran her hand down the dark pink and white quilt draped over the back of the porch swing. In celebration of her marriage, Esther and Cathy had made Mary a Drunkard's Path quilt with a tiny silver car in flames embroidered in one corner. Mary would never question Cathy's opinion again.

Thank Derr Herr, a drunkard's path had brought true love to her door.

ABOUT THE AUTHOR

Jennifer Beckstrand is the RITA-nominated and award-winning author of *The Amish Quiltmaker's Baby, the Matchmakers of Huckleberry Hill,* The Honeybee Sisters series, The Petersheim Brothers series, as well as a number of other novels and novellas. Novels in her Matchmakers of Huckleberry Hill series have been RITA® Award and RT Book Reviews Reviewer's Choice Award finalists. *Huckleberry Hill* won the 2014 LIME Award for inspirational fiction and *Huckleberry Hearts* was named a Booklist Top 10 Inspirational Fiction Book of the Year. Jennifer has always been drawn to the strong faith and the enduring family ties of the Plain people. She and her husband have been married for thirty-six years, and she has four daughters, two sons, and seven adorable grandchildren, whom she spoils rotten. Please visit her online at JenniferBeckstrand.com.

The employees of Thorndike Press hope you have enjoyed this Large Print book. All our Thorndike Large Print titles are designed for easy reading, and all our books are made to last. Other Thorndike Press Large Print books are available at your library, through selected bookstores, or directly from us.

For information about titles, please call:
(800) 223-1244

or visit our website at:
gale.com/thorndike